# THE LAST CARRIAGE

Alex J. Milan

Publisher's Note: This is a work of fiction. Names, characters, businesses, places, events, locales, and incidents are either the products of the author's imagination or used in a fictitious manner. Any resemblance to actual persons, living or dead, or actual events is completely coincidental.

Cover ©: Zoonar/wolfgang rieg/ZOONAR GMBH LBRF/age fotostock
Formatting by Polgarus Studio

The line from L. P. Hartley's novel, The Go-Between, has been reproduced by kind permission of New York Review Books.

ISBN 978-84-09-18661-7 (print)
ISBN 978-84-09-19801-6 (ebook)

Writing is a solitary job, but producing a book is a team effort. In particular, I would like to thank Jessica Espejo Hernández for her work in producing the cover and Polgarus Studio for preparing the text for publication.

My thanks also go to my family and friends who have supported and encouraged me throughout this process.

*Nel mezzo del cammin di nostra vita*
*mi ritrovai per una selva oscura,*
*ché la diritta via era smarrita*


*In the midst of the journey of our life*
*I found myself within a dark wood,*
*Where the way was lost*

*Dante Alighieri, Inferno*

# The Past

# Rome, Friday 10th July 1992

*'Getting to the truth is like picking at a scab. You know it's not a good idea, but once you start you can't stop, and then you start to bleed.'*

Jenny had first heard her mother's words at an impressionable time in her life and had taken them to heart. Throughout her life since that time, her instinctive reaction to trouble had always been to retreat; to keep her head down and wait for the storm to pass, but that option had now become impossible. She had become so consumed by her need to know the truth that she had forgotten to consider what the consequences of discovering it might be; to contemplate what she would do with it once it had been uncovered. She had laid it out, examined it, and then wished she could pack it away, wrapped so tightly that it would never be able to escape to hurt anybody again.

*　　*　　*

That night, a soft breeze murmured through the leaves of the plane trees lining the banks of the River Tiber and skimmed across the water's surface. It wound through the squares and cobbled lanes, bringing temporary relief to the crowds now out on streets, which only hours earlier had been deserted by all but the hardiest and most determined of tourists during the intense heat of mid-afternoon. The most popular music of the day blared out from bars and clubs although it sometimes seemed as though Snap's "Rhythm is a Dancer" was the only song which had been released that summer, such was its ubiquity.

On the balcony of their flat in Ripa, the twelfth rione of Rome, tucked away between the Tiber and the Circus Maximus, the breeze brushed across Jenny's face. She had thought about it for days now, each one more agonising than the last, and night had now fallen on yet another day of contemplation. Once again, as on every other day since she had found out, she was trying to work herself up to confront him. She considered how he would react; she feared his temper, but she hated what she perceived as her weakness with almost the same intensity. She took a deep breath, felt it catch in her throat as she tensed, but still she tried to convince herself she was ready.

Her husband, Carlo, and their children, thirteen-year-old Teodora, or Teddy as she always insisted on being called, and seven-year-old Francesco, were inside. Francesco. The thought of him made her falter. It was him she worried about the most. Teddy was stronger, frustratingly strong-willed at times, but Francesco was more sensitive; a quiet, thoughtful boy. She feared what another confrontation might do to him.

From inside, she could hear the muffled voices of the presenter and contestants on one of the television game shows she had never been able to grow to like. Occasionally, she heard her children giggling, but even the sound of their happiness did not comfort her. On the contrary, their laughter made her feel worse.

If she had been asked which word best summed up life at that moment, she would have selected turmoil. Italy, her adopted homeland, had been stunned by the assassination of Giovanni Falcone that May and also by the Clean Hands investigation which seemed to result in more arrests and the uncovering of further scandals every month. Life appeared to carry on as before, but beneath the surface, there was anger, fear and confusion. As the old certainties had disappeared, it was as though there was now a collective holding of breath as everyone waited for the next blow to strike. In her own life too, she had discovered nothing was quite as she had thought it to be; the ground had somehow shifted beneath her feet when she had not been paying attention, and now she did not know if the damage could be repaired.

At forty-two, she had lived exactly half of her life in Italy. Her love affair with the country had been passionate and enduring, but just lately she had thought more about England, and even the possibility of returning, than at any time since she had left the country of her birth.

'Mamma?'

She turned to see Francesco looking at her. He was holding on to the glass door. It occurred to her that she would have to clean his fingerprints off the next day. He placed a foot on the threshold, thought better of it, stepped back and remained where he was.

'Yes? Come here,' she said and put an arm around his shoulders as he joined her.

He looked up at her. 'Why are you so sad?'

Jenny tried to think of an answer which would not hurt or confuse her young son but found nothing.

She sat down and drew him towards her. 'I'm not sad now you're here.'

As he snuggled in beside her, she looked down, and the need to protect him overwhelmed her. She realised this wasn't the country in which she wanted to raise him, and Carlo wasn't the man she wanted as a role model for her son. Teddy seemed lost to his influence already; she couldn't lose Francesco too.

Time passed, and she felt his breathing slow as he fell asleep. She looked up at the stars, wishing she could stop time at that moment of brief contentment. As the temperature started to drop, she reached for a blanket to pull over them, waking Francesco in the process. He pressed himself closer to her but was unable to settle again and started to fidget and rub his eyes.

'Time for bed,' she said, sitting him up and brushing his hair from his face.

Francesco started to protest, but the cooling night air persuaded him to go inside. Alone once more, she repeated to herself that she was ready, really ready, this time and resolved to speak to Carlo as soon as Francesco and Teddy were asleep.

# Manchester, Thursday 30th August 2018

'Do you have any news?' Francesco asked.

'Not yet, sir. That's not why we're here.' The two police officers exchanged glances. The older of the two nodded at the younger one, encouraging him to continue.

'The hotel contacted us about the unpaid bill. They don't know about the accident of course. They asked us to see it got passed on.' He shifted from one foot to another, his discomfort apparent and produced an envelope, which he offered to Francesco. 'They'd like you to settle the bill.'

'The hotel?'

'Yes, sir. The hotel your wife had intended to stay in that night.'

'Sorry?'

'Your wife. The reservation she had at this hotel. They want you to pay,' he said, nodding at the invoice in his hand.

Francesco looked at him and then at the envelope, waiting for comprehension to dawn, unable to say anything.

The older of the two officers studied him. 'You didn't know about this, sir?'

Francesco shook his head, words still eluding him.

The older one continued. 'Had you and your wife been having any problems, sir?'

Francesco looked at them, stunned by the question and the abrupt change of track. 'What? No. Why do you ask?'

'You don't seem to know about your wife's movements and the airport's not that far from here, so why would she need a hotel room there? It seems strange, that's all.'

'What?' Francesco repeated. In the last few days he had been presented with a tragedy of proportions he could barely grasp and now, on top of everything else, the state of his marriage was being questioned.

'I'm just asking, sir. I've never liked loose ends.' He seemed to linger over the last two words.

'I have no idea why Lauren would have booked a room in a hotel there. I don't understand.' He felt the vice-like grip of his headache ratchet up another notch.

'Would you agree it seems unusual?'

'Yes. I don't understand. We have,' he stopped, forced himself to make the correction and began again. 'We had an extremely happy marriage and we didn't have any secrets. And if she had booked a room for some reason, she would have told me.'

'But she did book a room, sir,' the younger officer reminded him gently 'and it seems she didn't tell you.' And, with that, the wound of doubt their previous questions had opened up was injected with the poison of suspicion.

'I don't know what to say. I don't know anything anymore.'

'Well, if anything occurs to you, be sure to get in touch.'

Francesco nodded slowly, staring at the floor, trying to make sense of what he had been told, but the headache which had been present ever since the accident was tightening its grip on him further, making the ability to think clearly ever more elusive.

The older officer looked at his colleague and nodded towards the door. 'I think we've taken enough of your time for now. Your family liaison officer will be in touch but feel free to contact us if anything occurs to you in the meantime. Goodbye, sir.'

He heard the click as the front door shut and then their footsteps receding down the corridor, measuring out the chasm Francesco felt opening up between him and the rest of the world. He felt himself sliding towards it. He searched for something to anchor him to the world. Lauren. She had loved him; their relationship had been real. He knew it. He willed himself to believe it. And Francesco returned to doing the only thing he had been able to do since the accident; he thought about Lauren.

*　　*　　*

Francesco had met her at a time when he had just about given up on dating anyone, much less starting a serious relationship. He had been immersed in his job and ongoing studies, and his social life had taken a back seat. One night, his colleague Dan had talked him into going to a salsa class. Despite his protestations of being a hopeless dancer, Dan had somehow talked him into it.

'No, it's not my thing,' he had insisted for the second time.

'Listen mate, you're coming. There are lots of pretty girls there and, let's face it, my Uncle Fred has seen action more recently than you — and he's seventy-four.'

'Dry spell,' Francesco had said, laughing, and trying to say what sounded appropriate although it sounded forced and awkward coming from him.

Dan had snorted. 'Dry spell, my backside. It's a bloody drought. I'll pick you up at seven on Friday.'

So that Friday, Francesco had agreed to go and had then proceeded to sit on the sidelines wondering how anyone remembered all those steps, and then how they managed to do them in time to the music when Lauren had appeared.

She had noticed him from the moment he walked in: dark hair, brown eyes and tanned skin. She thought he was very attractive, but more than that she sensed a gentleness about him which was very different from the laddish behaviour of so many of the men she encountered. She had hoped he might join in. As the instructor had taken them through the new steps, she had looked across at him several times, but he had shown no inclination to participate; in fact he had looked as if he wished he were anywhere else. Lauren was an extrovert, but felt strangely shy about the idea of approaching him. Yet she knew she would regret if she didn't speak to him so, during a break, she took a deep breath and went over.

'Hi,' she said, sounding much more confident than she felt.

'Hello.'

'Are you going to come and join in?'

'I don't think so.'

'Why not?'

'Two left feet,' he said, smiling ruefully.

'I wouldn't let that stop you. It doesn't stop anybody else,' she said, laughing.

'They all look like they know what they are doing to me.'

'Trust me, they don't. Come on.'

'I don't know,' but he was wavering. He had noticed her earlier, and now she was standing here right in front of him, he couldn't take his eyes off her. The idea of spending some time with her was definitely appealing, but the thought of making a complete idiot of himself was distinctly less attractive.

'Please?' she said with a big smile. She leaned in to whisper to him. 'If you don't, they'll put me with Ken again, and I don't think I could face that.'

'I suppose I could try,' Francesco said. 'But don't be surprised when I tread on your feet.'

'I can't imagine anyone I'd rather get trodden on by.' She blushed, and then with another huge smile, took him by the hand and led him back to the group. In those seconds, he took in numerous things about her: her long dark hair, the curve of her hips and the soft skin of her hand.

'So that's what you do first.'

Francesco had been so distracted he realised he hadn't taken in a word. 'Could you show me again?'

So she did, and Francesco made a concerted effort to pay attention and found she was a good teacher. After about half an hour, Francesco was, to his immense surprise, actually managing to put a few, very basic steps together.

At the end of the evening, the instructor called them all together for a few parting words, and then he and Lauren were left looking awkwardly at each other. He was working himself up to asking her out when Tom came bounding over to talk to them. There would be no opportunity to ask her now.

'Well, see you next time then,' said Francesco.

'I hope so,' she said with another one of those smiles. 'Bye.'

'Mate, you're punching there, aren't you?' Dan remarked as they walked back to the car.

'Hmm?'

'That woman you were dancing with. She's hot, yet she seems to like you. Just goes to show that the world is full of mysteries and women are the biggest of the lot.'

Francesco had laughed along with Dan, but he had thought about Lauren every day for the next week. On the night of the next class he had felt strangely nervous, but when he arrived and she came over to greet him, the nerves disappeared immediately.

Their relationship had developed quickly. They discovered mutual passions for long walks in the countryside, running and music. Francesco became a reasonably proficient dancer, thanks to Lauren's gentle coaching and, in return, he taught her Italian. They married a year to the day after their first meeting, overjoyed at the thought of building a life together and, as they exchanged their vows, Francesco felt he had finally left his troubled past behind him.

# Spring 2019

# CHAPTER ONE

The alarm rang. Shrill, insistent, unforgiving. Francesco half opened one eye and slapped his hand over the off button. He had never been good at getting up. Not even before. Before. He rolled onto his back and willed himself to open his eyes properly.

He stared at the ceiling, the fan turning endlessly above him and wondered if there would ever be a time when his first thought on waking would not be about before. *No. Stop. Shut it off. Get up.* The same, relentless internal dialogue every day. Not for the first time, he asked himself how he had reached this point. The exhaustion he felt would never be cured by a good night's sleep, not that there were many of those to be had. It was not so much tiredness as a weariness that had settled into his bones and brain and become his constant unwelcome companion. He supposed he had adjusted to its presence as he had adjusted to everything else that had come afterwards, but adjustment did not equal acceptance.

He turned over and sat on the edge of the bed. The

coolness of the tiles underfoot was welcome in the warmth of a late spring so hot that it suggested a furnace of a summer ahead. Elbows resting on his knees, he buried his face in his hands and massaged his forehead, trying to relieve the dull ache right at its centre just above the bridge of his nose. At least that night he had managed to sleep for a few hours. His nights, or his days, depending on his shifts, usually consisted of insomnia or a fall into a sleep severed by dreams so vivid and disturbing he would be forced to get up, knowing there would be no further chance of rest. He sat up straighter, stretched and found the strength to force himself to stand up and get ready for work.

On his way out, he paused at the mirror by the front door to pick up his identification badge and straighten his tie. He moved closer to the mirror and examined his face. The shadows under his eyes appeared more pronounced or maybe that was just his imagination. He was so tired, but he had to push through it, just as he had learned to do in the past. It had been an essential skill in the life he had led before. Before; that word again. He reminded himself the very fact that he had a job at all was a gift of sorts. He had to keep going. He could not do anything to jeopardise what precious little he had left.

*　　*　　*

Rome's Termini station was as noisy and chaotic as ever on a weekday, and Francesco welcomed the endless opportunities for distraction. On busy days, he liked watching the purposeful movements of those who knew where they were going and their occasional frustration as they had to weave between baffled tourists who would suddenly stop in the middle of the concourse to try to orientate themselves. Francesco had always been a great people watcher. In his previous life it had often proved to be useful. However, even during the relatively quiet times, he found it preferable to be at the station rather than be confronted by the bleak emptiness of his flat.

The heat of the day was continuing to build steadily. The sunlight angled its way into the station, dust drifting in its shafts, and sketched the tangled patterns of metal beams and guard rails on the floor. In the background, the constant hum of trains and endless announcements, punctuated by the occasional squeal of brakes, provided the soundtrack to the life of the station. People who had been unwise enough to bring extra layers of clothing paused to discard them while others stopped to check platform numbers, but Francesco knew exactly where he was going.

His new existence was mainly a solitary one, which suited the person he had become; a person who usually avoided human interaction. Until one day. The day he met the couple whose names he never learned.

*    *    *

They had been sitting in the last carriage, just the two of them, facing each other so that both had a seat by the window. He had checked their tickets, which they had silently handed over, and then settled down in one of the seats opposite them where he had a set of four seats completely to himself. It was as good a place as any to pass the time. He preferred the comfort and space afforded by the carriage to the cramped cab and occasional forced small talk with the driver although, when a train was full, he had no choice but to sit up front. He was diagonally opposite the woman. He looked across at them. He guessed they were in their mid-forties, around ten years older than him. They were casually dressed in jeans and T-shirts. Big suitcases; on holiday; definitely not Italian. American he thought, although, if pressed, he would have found it hard to define why.

'Well, we made it!' the woman said, leaning across and touching the man on the knee. Her wedding ring caught the sunlight.

Francesco heard the North American accent but was not familiar enough with the United States to guess where she came from. She might even have been Canadian, but he couldn't determine the difference between the accents. That would have made Lauren laugh. He could almost hear her telling him there was no way she sounded like an American. Lauren. He forced himself to stop before he went too far down that road and went back to his paperwork.

The man grunted and continued to stare out of the window, elbow resting on the sill, chin cupped in his hand. It was as though he had barely noticed she was there, much less that she had reached out to touch him, to communicate with him.

His wife sat back, biting on her lip. Francesco watched her rearrange her features into something resembling enthusiasm before trying again. 'I'm really looking forward to this vacation. Shall we just run through our itinerary?'

'What for? You know where we're going.'

'I just thought it would be fun to talk about all the places we're going to see. Maybe plan a few extra things." He heard her aim for levity but her voice was taut and there was a nervous break in it as if she was anticipating what was to come.

He waved his hand at the luggage piled up beside them. 'All the paperwork's in there. You can get it out and look at it if you want.' The emphasis fell heavily on the first 'you'. He couldn't have made his lack of interest any clearer.

'Maybe later then,' she said neutrally.

He slammed the tickets down on the seat beside him, and Francesco saw her flinch. 'I thought you wanted to look at the information,' he snapped with a degree of anger that shocked Francesco.

'I wanted us to look at it together.' She tried to sound calm, but her voice trembled.

'Either you want to look at it or you don't.'

'I just thought it would be nice to look over what's coming up. Please don't get angry.'

'What makes me angry is you not being able to make your mind up. First you want the damn paperwork then you don't.' He was sounding closer to losing control by the moment, and Francesco started to feel afraid for the woman.

He had been trying not to look, but now he chanced another glance in their direction. The man seemed to be shaking with fury and barely holding himself back while the woman had tears sliding silently down her face. Suddenly, she noticed Francesco looking at her. She turned away, quickly ran her hand over face, brushing the tears aside, and he saw try to fix a composed look on her face.

'Could we just start again?' she said, the brightness in her tone even more brittle now and so very close to shattering.

'Start what again? Are you crying? Well, this is a great start to our vacation. Well done. You've ruined it before it's even started.'

'I …'

'Don't. Don't say anything. You've already screwed everything up, the way you screw everything up. I can't say anything without being in the wrong. I've had enough.' His rage was now almost a tangible, living creature. He shifted his weight, pulled his phone out of his pocket, flipped open the cover and quickly immersed himself in whatever was on the screen.

The woman looked across at Francesco who realised he was now staring at them. The flood of her despair washed over him, promising for a moment to obliterate his own. He saw the tension in her face; the pain of loneliness; the torment of indecision. He wondered why she didn't defend herself. He longed to ask her, to find the courage to speak up, to challenge the man, but nothing came out. His throat felt locked and dry. Eventually she broke his gaze and turned away again to look out of the window.

Time passed in a silence so painful even Francesco felt tense, and then she got up and left the carriage. Her husband appeared not to notice but, even so, Francesco waited for a few minutes before getting up and following her. He found her standing between the carriages with the windows open on both sides, her eyes closed, caught in the cross hairs of an impossible situation, trapped between anger and anguish.

Now that he was there with her, having wanted to speak to her, he had no idea what to say. He stood there weighing what to do or whether just to retreat. She opened her eyes. 'Oh, I'm sorry,' she said, moving to let him pass.

'I imagine you have to say that a lot,' Francesco said before he could stop himself.

'Excuse me?'

'You know I heard everything he said. That I saw the way he treated you.'

She seemed to diminish physically as though ashamed. Gradually she looked up to meet Francesco's eyes.

'Why do you let him speak to you like that?' Francesco asked.

She cast around for a response, as though her surroundings might present her with an answer. No help was to be found, and she made several false starts in the process of trying to reply. Eventually, with a hint of defensiveness, she settled on, 'He's not always like that.'

'What I saw didn't seem like a one-off.'

'Why do you say that?' There was an attempt at defiance, but it was not a convincing one.

'The way you reacted. It's not the first time, is it?' he insisted. He was unsure why it mattered so much but it did.

'You don't understand. You couldn't …' Tears appeared again and she furiously blinked them away.

'Try me.'

'I … I …. it's me. I deserve it; always going on at him. I'm sure I must be hell to live with. I'm lucky he puts up with me. Nobody else would, that's for sure. If he left me, I'd never find anyone else.' She paused, struggling to find the words. 'But sometimes … it's like he sucks the joy out of everything and I feel as though I can't breathe.' She looked at him and seemed stunned by the feelings she had just articulated.

'Why shouldn't you be happy about a holiday? And that's all I saw – someone excited about the start of a trip.'

'I always mess things up. I should just be quiet. Leave him be.'

'Why? Why should you have to be quiet? Why shouldn't you be able to speak to your husband without fearing how he will react? Husbands and wives should be able to tell each other everything.' He suddenly realised his voice was rising and his own experience, his before, was threatening to break through and rupture the affable image he worked so hard to present to the world.

She looked startled. Any rapport they might have been starting to build seemed to crumble. 'Look, I'm sure you mean well, but I have to get back.'

Francesco gently caught her hand as she turned to leave. 'I'm sorry. I didn't mean to frighten you. I just hated the way he treated you.'

'That's kind of you.' Her smile was weak but genuine. 'But you don't need to worry about me.' A shrug. 'I'm used to it. Tonight or tomorrow, he'll apologise. Or he won't.

Either way, I'll be expected to forget about it and move on. Then things will be fine for a while. Until the next time anyways.'

Francesco let her go and watched her take her seat opposite her husband who, apparently, didn't see her return. After some time had passed, he returned to the seat opposite them. The woman looked over at her husband who was still studiously ignoring her and then chanced a look at Francesco. She smiled at him, the sad, resigned smile of someone who believes there are no more options, and her fate is sealed.

After what seemed an interminable time to Francesco with the strained silence in the carriage, the train reached its destination. In all of that time, he never spoke to his wife again.

Francesco had gone home that night still thinking about them. He had wondered what it would be like to live with someone who laced every interaction with the same anger and manipulation he had witnessed. To have to live like that, just waiting for the next outburst triggered by the most innocuous of remarks; to have to wait for the calm after the storm and then for the pattern to repeat again and again until you were so worn down you truly thought you were worthless. To believe that you deserved it; that you were unlovable and should be grateful for what you had. He wondered how anyone could survive that.

Physical abuse he knew about from his previous job; shouting and screaming were not strangers either, but psychological abuse was something he knew less about. He pulled his laptop out and started doing some research, ashamed of how little he had known and shocked by how tragic the stories were. People so cowed and confused by their experiences they had no idea how to fight back and reclaim themselves.

He read late into the night, and only when he stopped did he realise that while he had been immersed in those stories, while he had been thinking about what had happened earlier, while he had been listening to her, he had not constantly been thinking about before. He had found some relief in listening to someone else talk about their life. Even though her sadness hung over him, he had, temporarily at least, not been consumed by his own chaos. His mistake had been to stop listening and start talking.

As the months had passed, he had discovered – or remembered – that people wanted to talk, to unburden themselves and to do so to a stranger in transient surroundings, proved to be the perfect place to do that. He became something of a counsellor, much as he had been before. It was a strange twilight world, one in which he lost himself in other people's worlds and inhabited them briefly, for better or worse, to save him from inhabiting his own.

As he went to board the train on that hot day in late May, he thought of the couple again. Was she still with him? Judging by her comments, he supposed that she probably was. If so, how was he treating her? Presumably she was still trapped in the endless cycle she had spoken of. He would never know, and in some ways he was glad because he preferred to imagine she had somehow moved on. The reality that she had not been able to do so would only have been as depressing and frustrating as, he reflected, reality usually turned out to be.

# CHAPTER TWO

As the train pulled out of Termini, Francesco started the process of checking tickets and helping people with their questions and problems. Many of the passengers spoke no Italian and were pleased to find his command of English was perfect.

About halfway down the train, he paused and took a seat in the deserted bicycle carriage: nobody usually sat in there unless they were the only seats available. He looked out of the window. May was one of the most beautiful months in Italy. The countryside was still lush and green despite the fact it had been such a dry spring, and flowers were in bloom everywhere, especially the poppies. He started to drift off. Being on a moving train or bus was about the only time he could guarantee that he would get some sleep.

He started to dream about Teddy; he was a child again, and they were running through those glorious Tuscan fields brimming with poppies as they had done so often before. Teddy wanted to play hide and seek so he had to count to ten. He dutifully did so and then went to find her, but she had gone and no matter how long and hard he searched or how often he called her name and told her it wasn't funny anymore, she didn't come back. His seven-year-old self started to panic and he awoke with a start. He wondered what was worse. The endless nights when he could not sleep? Or the times when he did sleep, but was awoken by images which left him so unsettled? He rubbed his face, stood up, straightened his jacket and resumed his progress down the train.

As he entered the next carriage, the first thing Francesco noticed was a shock of thick, pure white hair, perfectly cut and combed. As he approached the passenger, he saw he was smartly dressed in a jacket and tie and that an intricately carved wooden box was cradled in his mottled hands. The man traced a finger over the pattern with a delicacy which seemed completely at odds with his thickened fingers.

Francesco cleared his throat to announce his presence and asked for the man's ticket.

The man looked up at him. His face also suggested great age, the skin as mottled as his hands and deeply wrinkled, but his eyes, although now a faded shade of blue, sparkled with warmth and intelligence. Francesco guessed he had to be well into his eighties at least.

He set the box down on the table with great care, produced two tickets from his shirt pocket and spoke for the first time. 'Do you speak English?' His diction was perfect: he sounded almost as though he had stepped from a 1950s newsreel although age had tempered its strength to some extent.

'Yes, I do.'

'Oh, good. I have two tickets here, you see. This is mine and this is for my grandson, Adam. He's gone to the restaurant car. I expect he'll be back presently.'

'That's fine, sir.' Francesco checked them and was about to continue on his way when he said, 'Make sure you don't leave that box behind. It looks quite valuable.'

'This thing? No, not really although I suppose the contents might be worth something but whether they are or not is neither here nor there. I'd never sell them. They mean a lot to me.'

Francesco waited. He sensed the man wanted to say more and he remembered what he had learned: talk less, listen more. After a few moments, he was duly rewarded. 'You're probably busy, but if you've got a minute, I'll show you.'

Francesco took the seat opposite him and watched as the man opened the box and turned it around for him to see the contents. Francesco looked at a row of immaculately kept medals resting on a cushion of blue velvet. He raised his head and met the man's gaze.

'World War Two medals. Terrible times; there's no real glory in war, you know. This one was for the Battle of Monte Cassino, not so far from here.'

'That was later in the war, wasn't it?' Francesco asked, feeling suddenly conscious in the presence of this man that his knowledge of historical facts was shaky.

'Yes, 1944. It started in the January and finally came to an end in the May.'

'Would you mind telling me more about it?' he asked,

hesitantly. He almost didn't like to pursue it, but the feeling persisted that this was someone who needed to talk as much as he needed to listen.

'I'm not sure you want to hear my old war stories.'

'I'm ashamed to say my knowledge of World War Two, particularly in Italy, isn't very good. I feel I should know more about it, and I would much rather learn from you, from someone who actually experienced it, rather than a history book.'

'Well then, I suppose I should introduce myself first. My name is Henry.' He reached over and they shook hands as Francesco also introduced himself.

'So it's Monte Cassini you want to know about, is it?'

'If you are willing to talk about it.'

'I was called up in 1943 when I turned eighteen. We had conscription then. By 1944, the war was turning in our favour. By 'our', I mean the Allies of course. The Germans had lost North Africa, the Americans had got involved and we'd captured Sicily so it was decided that we had to keep pressing on up through Italy to get to Rome. It wasn't just the British. There were many other nationalities fighting alongside us. I remember the Indians and the Ghurkhas particularly. The Italians had surrendered by then, but the Germans had occupied the country. Churchill called it the "soft underbelly" of Europe. In my opinion, he was wrong. The Germans had created something called the Gustav Line. It ran right across the country from the west coast to the east. Have you heard of that?'

Francesco shook his head, looking as embarrassed as he felt.

'I'm not surprised. The fighting in Italy was some of the most brutal of the whole war, which is saying something. It's been compared to the bloodiness of some of the battles from the First World War, yet not many people really know much about it.'

'Why?'

'All in good time. Cassino and the monastery on the hill, Monte Cassino, were on the main road to Rome so of course that's where our lot decided to focus the efforts to break through the Gustav Line. The site was being defended by German paratroopers. They were an elite unit so not to be underestimated.

'Anyway, in the January, there was an assault on Monte Cassino but we couldn't make any progress. It didn't help that the Germans had the advantage that they were defending high ground. By February, we had to retreat. There had been so many deaths, and we had to try to regroup; find a new strategy.

'That strategy was to bomb the town and the abbey. That was later in the February. By the end of it, the town was just rubble with the odd piece of wall looming up out of the smoke, set against a background of complete devastation. The trouble was that in some ways, the bombing made things worse. The Germans found lots of places to hide out in all those ruins, and they took up defensive positions in what was left of the monastery.

'Then the winter really set in, and the rain came. We thought that rain would never end. The whole area flooded. Knee deep in mud we were, but at least there was a break in the fighting. It all started up again in the March.' Henry sighed wearily. 'To cut a long story short, the Polish Second Corps joined us for the fourth assault. On the eve of what was to be the final battle, Feliks Konarski wrote "The Red Poppies on Monte Cassino". It was May, this time of year, so by then so the whole of the countryside was covered in poppies.'

Henry paused and looked out of the window at the poppy-strewn countryside. 'Just like now. I can't remember exactly how it goes, but there was a part about how the poppies would be redder because of the Polish blood spilt there. I've never forgotten that.'

He sighed again. 'I met so many fine men of all the different nationalities I fought alongside, and I saw so many of them die. For years afterwards, I tried to avoid being on my own or anywhere too quiet because if I was, all I could hear was the fire of machine guns and the screams of men begging for death because they were in so much agony. I held more than one chap's hand as he passed. Nobody can imagine the horror of it all unless they were there, and I'm glad for them that they can't. It was inhuman.'

He slipped into his own thoughts and just when Francesco thought he would say no more, he continued. 'Finally, and after far too much death and suffering and two more offensives, Monte Cassino fell to us on the eighteenth of May. The Allies captured Rome on the fourth of June. They estimate fifty thousand casualties all round. Of everything I saw and somehow survived, nothing from the war haunts me like those days. Can you imagine it? Fifty thousand lives destroyed.'

They both fell silent as they contemplated that. Finally Francesco asked, 'Why isn't it better known, compared to other events in the war?'

'D-Day. The Normandy Landings took place on the sixth of June, two days after the Allies moved into Rome. Honestly, a lot of the soldiers who fought in Italy felt we had been forgotten. It wasn't that we wanted special treatment but being forgotten was hard.'

There was a further lull in the conversation. It was not an awkward silence, but Francesco did not want to finish their conversation on that note. Casting around for something to say, he broke Henry's reverie by asking, 'You mentioned your grandson. You're on holiday with him?'

'It's a holiday of sorts, I suppose. It's half-term for him so I'm taking him to see the war graves at Monte Cassini. I think it will be my last chance and, more importantly, he's got this daft idea into his head that he wants to join up. I've tried to talk him out of it and so has his mother, but he's having none of it. I thought that if I could only make him see the reality of war, the scale of loss, the sheer tragedy of it all, it might have some effect. Perhaps if I had done that with John, everything would have been different.'

'John?'

'John was my son. He enlisted when he was eighteen too. I never tried to talk him out of it.' Henry paused. 'And that will always be the biggest regret of my life.' Another pause and Francesco sensed that Henry was trying to summon the courage to say the words without showing any loss of composure. 'He died in Iraq in 2008. Operation Telic. He was forty-five. His son, that's Adam, was only six.'

The brevity of the declaration had more of an impact on Francesco than any longwinded explanation could have done, and he sensed that even that simple statement of facts had cost Henry a great deal to articulate.

'I'm very sorry for your loss.' Francesco hated the triteness of the words he had had to say far too often in the life he had lived before. 'I wish I knew what to say,' he admitted finally.

'There's nothing you can say, son. Death never gets any easier however often you have to face it and it never gets any easier to find the right thing to say to someone else.'

Francesco realised the truth of those words only too well, but said nothing for fear of being drawn into talking about himself. For reasons he did not care to examine, he never talked about his own life.

Henry moved around in his seat, as if bracing himself for what he wanted to say next and faced Francesco straight on. 'Back in World War Two, I had total belief in what we were doing and I still believe in what we fought for. Or maybe I just recall the absolute conviction of youth. In the wars that have come and gone since, I've often wondered what it's all about. I can imagine my old sergeant major. He'd have given me hell for questioning anything, but I can't help wondering. Don't get me wrong, I'm a staunch supporter of our armed forces, but it's not them I have an issue with.

'More and more I think we're just pawns in games and we have no idea what the bigger picture is. I'm not sure how much of it is real or worthwhile and I think I'd be saying the same thing even if we hadn't lost John. There's just so much loss and sadness on all sides – people seem to forget the other side is made up of humans too – and what's it all for? Back then, when we defeated Hitler, well, that made sense but now …'

He stared out of the window and Francesco thought of their earlier conversation and of the horrors he must be recalling.

'You know, I remember everything about the day they flew him home but my Evelyn, my wife that is, she always said she couldn't remember anything, that she was too numb. They flew him to RAF Lyneham and then there was a procession through Wootton Bassett for him and some of his comrades. I don't suppose you know what or where I'm talking about.'

'No, I do know. I lived in England for a long time. I saw reports about those processions on the news a number of times.'

'That accounts for your English then. Well, you'll know Wootton Bassett always turned out to honour those who were flown home. My wife and I were there in the street to see our boy come home. We saw the undertaker first. He was walking ahead of the cars. It was so quiet you could hear his footsteps, a sharp clip against the road. Then we saw the cars. There was a fine drizzle and the headlights were blurred but the reflections off the tarmac were sharp and clear. Why would I even have noticed that, much less remember it now? The undertaker stopped regularly so people could pay their respects and put flowers on the cars.' He stopped, fished a cotton handkerchief out of his pocket and briskly wiped his eyes.

'Evelyn had brought flowers. I remember her stepping forward to place them on the roof of the car. I was amazed by her strength. I was rooted to the spot, couldn't move. I'd fought my way through World War Two and I couldn't walk a few steps to a car, the car carrying our boy. I watched her as she put them down, so gently, and then, instead of stepping back, as I'd expected, she stroked the roof of the car. It reminded me of the way she had stroked his hair when he was little and had needed comforting. That almost broke me.' There was a long pause. Henry was lost in his own thoughts. He took a deep breath. 'We stayed until the end. We wanted to honour all of the boys they brought home that day. It was so cold, so damn cold. That damp cold that worms its way so far inside you that you feel like you'll never be warm again.'

'And Adam and his mum?' Francesco said, genuinely wanting to know. He was no longer on a train winding its way through the green Italian countryside on a warm sunny day but there in cold, misty Wootton Bassett with Henry and Evelyn.

'His mum, Karen, our daughter-in-law, was in labour. She was giving birth as her husband was brought home. Bringing life into the world while death was being brought into ours. We thought Adam was too young to be there with us. I still don't know if that was the right decision. Maybe if he'd seen his dad come home like that … it's all maybes and what ifs. You see if I had just tried to talk John out of joining up, he might have listened and then he'd still be here with us, and Adam wouldn't have taken it into his head to try to be just like the father he idolises, but can barely remember.'

'You can't blame yourself for what happened to your son.'

'No, but those blasted politicians aren't happy unless they're stirring things up. There's always going to be another war sooner or later. It's just a question of how many innocent people on all sides have to lose their lives before there's a truce. Then, after a while, the whole circus starts up again.

'The trouble is that my generation weren't brought up to talk about feelings or our experiences of war. It was all stiff upper lip and get on with it so I didn't talk about it. I was one of the lucky ones. I returned in one piece physically and, mentally, I learned to accept things. No, that's not quite right. I learned to accept how the war had changed me. That's not quite the same. I don't want Adam to experience any of the things I did, and I don't want to lose him. Of course, it's different now. People are more open. They're encouraged to talk about things and that's good except it's all gone too far the other way. Emotional incontinence at every turn especially all over that wretched social media the youngsters use these days. Never a happy medium with people, that's the problem, but I digress. If I hadn't been like that, perhaps things would be different, and I wouldn't be here with Adam now.'

'Speaking of whom…' said Francesco, getting up as he saw a young man heading towards them. He was wearing ripped, faded jeans and a T-shirt that looked as though it might have been slept in.

'Are you OK, grandad?' He turned to Francesco and attempted to say buongiorno. What he lacked in pronunciation, he more than made up for with an engaging, happy-go-lucky smile.

'Adam, where have you been? Those drinks must be cold by now.'

'Not at all. It's all under control, don't you worry. I met this really nice girl and we got chatting and swapped phone numbers. I got the drinks after that. I reckon she'll like me even more once I'm in uniform.' He winked, manoeuvered himself into the seat which Francesco had vacated, and put the drinks down. Francesco caught Henry's troubled gaze.

'Adam …'

'No, see.' He peeled the plastic lid off of the first cup. 'They're still hot. Not sure whether it's tea or coffee, though. Looks a bit dodgy to me. I had no idea what the bloke was saying to me. Oh, and I got some biscuits. Here you go.' A crumpled packet landed on the table.

Henry started to say something but as he did, Adam's phone started ringing. 'Sorry grandad, just a sec.'

Francesco made to leave, pausing to place a hand on Henry's shoulder, searching for words of comfort or support. 'Thank you, lad,' Henry said looking up at him. 'No need to say anything.'

*     *     *

Bright flashes of red in the tall grass; images of Teddy running through the fields; poppies dancing in the periphery of his vision. It was always fields of poppies he associated with those carefree days. His mum was there too, laughing as she watched them play and unpacking a picnic. She always seemed happier when his dad was not there.

The images merged with ones of battle and bloodshed, and then an altogether different association with poppies, in remembrance of soldiers who had given everything and others who had survived, but had had to bear the injuries and memories of appalling events. Then his mum and dad were shouting at each other again. Teddy was sitting on the edge of his bed, comforting him. He always got so frightened when he heard them arguing. "Shh," she soothed. 'Sono qui. I'm here. Don't be scared.' And after a while, as his parents' voices receded, he drifted back to sleep.

Images of Teddy merged with the battle Henry had described, and he saw her struggling to get through the mud. He could see her so why couldn't he get to her? Then Lauren was there too, and she stood up, seemingly unaware of the danger to which she was exposing herself. He knew what was going to happen, but he couldn't save her. He could never save her. It made no sense. She wasn't supposed to be there. He called out to her and reached out to try to pull her to relative safety. As she was almost within reach, the image shattered into a million pieces, like bright shards from a kaleidoscope spiralling out of control.

He sat up in bed, shaking, sweat pouring off him. Of the dreams which plagued him and at times made his frequent insomnia seem like a gift, this had been one of the worst. He found the clock; it was just after 5am. He was not due at work for hours, but he could not stay in bed any longer.

He got up and, as he made coffee, he thought about Henry. He carried his pain with dignity and had managed to overcome so much. Meanwhile, here he was trapped in a cycle of grief and unanswered questions, leaving him unable to move on. The comparison between them made him feel even worse. He took his coffee and went out to sit on the balcony. He could not shake the dream off; it clung to him, clawed at him and tried to draw him back into its world.

He put down his coffee and walked to the railings. The stone pines stood still and watchful in the remnants of the warm night. How easy it would be to fall into their embrace, to let go and never have to feel anything again. Shocked by where his thoughts were taking him, he tried to focus on the activity in the street below. As always, thinking about others' lives helped him to forget his own.

The city, never entirely at rest, was starting to prepare for a new day. Lights were on and there were already a few people out and about. The real world started to pull Francesco towards it and as it did, he slowly retreated from the edge of the balcony.

# CHAPTER THREE

Francesco made his way down the train, checking tickets and, as always, helping passengers with various issues switching easily between Italian and English.

Near the end of the train, he noticed a woman studying a photograph intently. As he approached her, she looked up, and as she went to find her ticket, the photograph fluttered to the floor.

'Oh bother,' she exclaimed in English.

Francesco retrieved it for her but couldn't stop himself from looking at it before handing it back to her. It had clearly been taken many years ago, the once brilliant colours faded and the white border slightly yellowed. The clothes worn by the young woman suggested the late 1960s or early 1970s although fashion was not a subject Francesco knew much about.

She was undoubtedly beautiful despite the less than flattering clothes. The fact that she was standing in front of the Colosseum caught his attention too but, more than anything, he noticed her smile. More vibrant than any colours could have been even on the day it was taken, it transcended the years and he could almost imagine her standing in front of him at that moment.

'Pretty girl,' he said, using English as she had done, and smiling to cover his feeling of awkwardness for having studied the photograph so carefully. How long had he been looking at it, he wondered. One minute? Longer?

If she had found his behaviour strange, she showed no signs of it. 'Thank you, dear.' She paused.

'That's me, you know. Or it was me. I'm not her anymore.' She looked at him. 'That probably doesn't make much sense to a young man like you.'

'Not so young,' Francesco replied.

'Oh you are, from my point of view.' She smiled and the years slipped away. Despite the weight of the years which had come and gone in the intervening time, the same smile he had been captivated by in the photograph was right in front of him.

He perched on the edge of the seat opposite her, not wanting to appear too settled. 'I see you've been to Rome before,' he said in English which carried no trace of an Italian accent, but with a gesture of his chin towards the picture which was unmistakably Italian.

'Yes, but that was so long ago. A lifetime ago. Almost another lifetime really.' She rested her head against the seat back and closed her eyes. He thought she had gone to sleep for a moment, but then she opened her eyes again. 'I first came to Italy when I was 18. I'd visited a few other countries by then but when I came here, I felt this sense of belonging, of coming home. I'd never felt like that before. Never have since either, come to that. I never wanted to leave. I had to of course or, at least, I thought I had to. It's funny the things you think you have to do when you're young, and then you realise you really didn't have to do them after all. Anyway, it upset me dreadfully. Leaving, that is. I can still remember my father on one of the rare occasions I phoned him from here. "Stop gallivanting Dorothy and get back home. It's time you settled down." '

Is this your first visit since then?'

'Oh no, I've come back a few times. Not as often as I'd have liked to, though. Of course the Italy I remember has changed but then again so has everywhere else.'

'True enough.' Francesco thought about the Italy he remembered from his childhood and the changes which had surprised and in some cases shocked him since he had returned to the country of his birth.

'Everything about Italy captivated me, you know. I suppose part of it was the intensity of the passion you can only feel for something when you're young but … it was more than that. I loved everything, the language, the landscapes and the cities, the food and the people. The people most of all. I wanted to stay so much.' He heard a longing in her voice which was almost painful.

Francesco waited. If he said anything now she might not continue, but she seemed to have finished anyway. He ventured, 'Why couldn't you stay?'

'Because I was brought up in a world which was very different to the one we live in now. People talk about the swinging sixties, but they swung right past me and a lot of other women too. Just to compound it, my parents were very traditional. I was taught, programmed, I think now, to do the right thing. And the right thing was to get a job, find a "nice man", settle down and have two children – and maybe a dog.' She laughed; it was a full, hearty laugh with no bitterness but a trace of regret. 'You have to remember life wasn't the way it is now. Do you know we women couldn't even get a mortgage at one time without a male guarantor? We didn't get equal pay; we couldn't get loans or credit cards; we could even be refused service in pubs. Young woman today would find it incredible if they really knew what life was like back then. There's a quote "The past is a foreign country; they do things differently there." Do you know it?'

'I've heard it, but I don't know where it's from.'

'It's the first sentence of The Go-Between by L.P. Hartley. It's an excellent book. I recommend it. Anyway, it sums up what I'm trying to say perfectly. It'll happen to you one day as well. You'll wake up and realise you come from the past too, and the present has moved on without you.'

She caught Francesco's expression. 'Oh, not for a long time, and it's not as bad as I make it sound. Now, where was I? Oh yes, I was restless. I didn't want all that conventional nonsense. I wanted to have adventures. This photograph was taken on my first day in Rome and, just for a fleeting moment in high summer, my world seemed infinite. All the rules and expectations that had been suffocating me vanished, or I thought they had. I imagined I could do anything and yet … you don't realise how much your upbringing conditions you. When I had my chances, I didn't take them. I don't know why really. Part of it was certainly the way I had been brought up, but I can't blame my parents for everything. I just didn't have confidence in myself. I was always too short, too fat, too plain, too stupid, too, well, anything and everything, as long as it was negative. Yet when I look at this photo, I see that really wasn't the case at all. I was perfectly fine. Not ravishing, but I certainly wasn't all those "toos" I thought I was.'

'So what happened?' Francesco asked quietly.

'I stayed for one magical summer. Well, Italy was magical, but I didn't make the most of it because of all my wretched "toos". I visited some other cities but for me, when I came to Rome, I knew this was the place I'd always dreamed of. Everywhere seemed exotic, and the names were so evocative even when the actual places weren't quite as beautiful. I loved everything and everywhere.' She reeled off a list of places in Rome and Francesco noted that her pronunciation was excellent. 'Even the imperfections of Rome made me love it more. I suppose that's what love is.'

She reflected on that for a moment. 'I met some gorgeous men. I could have got to know them better,' she paused and gave Francesco a meaningful look mixed with a playful twinkle, 'but my lack of confidence held me back. I wanted that glorious, passionate, reckless, summer romance so badly.' She sighed. 'I'm sorry if I've shocked you, my dear. One of the few benefits of getting older is that you feel you can say almost anything you please. Well, it's a benefit for me, but possibly not for those around me.' He heard that throaty chuckle once more.

'Really, there was only one special man – Rafaello – he was so beautiful. It's not a word we use for men, is it? But it's the best one to describe him. He was interested in me as well, which I couldn't quite believe. He even took me to meet his family. If only I'd had the courage, but I was sure I would be a disappointment to him and I couldn't have borne that you see. It seemed easier to walk away than see the disillusionment in his eyes when I failed to live up to his expectations. I couldn't believe that he would care for me enough to like me once he really got to know me. I still think of him regularly. Sometimes, it's just with a sense of nostalgia and then at other times, it's like a true sensation of loss. Even now.'

'Are you going to try to find him while you're here?'

'Goodness me, no. Apart from anything else, I would have no idea how to go about finding him. Don't forget, I went to his house once, over half a century ago. Even if he still lived there, I wouldn't have a clue how to get there. But that's not all. I'd prefer him to remember me, if he ever does, as a young woman and I think it's better that I remember him as he was too. There are some things you have to learn to let go, however hard it is.'

'I suppose so,' Francesco said and wondered if he would ever learn to do that.

'Do you know what I do on the days when I really miss him?' She leaned towards Francesco and gave him a conspiratorial look.

'What?'

'I imagine him in a string vest with a pot belly, moaning about the state of the world and making some poor woman's life a misery.' She laughed, but it wasn't quite convincing. 'It's a coping mechanism, my dear. In my most rational moments, of which I still have a few, I don't imagine he turned out like that for one moment. But one does what one has to in order to get by, to keep going.'

They lapsed into silence while Francesco thought about what she had said. Then Dorothy said, 'I never answered your question, did I? At the end of the summer, I went home because it was the "right thing" to do. I got a job in an office, in a typing pool, and I hated that. I don't think they even have them these days. Do you have any idea what a typing pool is?'

'No,' Francesco confessed.

'A room full of women – and it was always women – typing men's – and it was always men's – letters all day. It was ghastly and hot and noisy with all those typewriters clattering away, and it was stressful. We were assessed on how many words we could type per minute and heaven forbid you fell behind.'

'It sounds awful.'

'Oh, it was. Endless typing and shuffling pieces of paper around all day. It was soul destroying. With every letter typed and envelope addressed, I felt like I was dying inside just a little more. I'd wanted to be an actress. Not a film star, none of that glamorous stuff or fame interested me. I wanted to work in the theatre. Shakespeare, Chekhov, Ibsen, all the classics. But I didn't have the courage to try. Too lacking in self-confidence. Then I got married, and I didn't like that much either. Oh, I sound dreadful, don't I? I don't think he was very happy either, but as a person, I mean. He wasn't a happy person. Perhaps the problem was that we both settled for safe. We settled for a life of, how can I describe it? Quiet acceptance. Yes, that's it. I believe it's actually better to be alone than to live like that.'

They sat in comfortable silence for a while and then suddenly Dorothy said, 'It was the miscarriage, I think. That's when everything really went downhill. Women tend to cope better because we're not expected to be strong and silent and bottle things up, but men are, aren't they? I think they suffer terribly for that.'

The comment resonated with Francesco more than Dorothy could have imagined. He was relieved that she carried on speaking, sparing him the need to try to maintain the conversation.

'But we had two beautiful daughters so I can't complain. I'm not sure I was a good mother, though. I loved them with all my heart, still do, of course but is that enough? I was never very good at giving advice and guidance, probably because I hadn't had the courage to do what I wanted with my life. Not everyone is cut out for parenthood, you know. A lot of people just blunder into it because that's what everyone does, but they don't think about what it really means.'

'I have a feeling you probably did pretty well,' said Francesco, recovering himself and smiling at her.

'Well, if nothing else, I hope the one thing I did do right was to tell them they could do anything they wanted to do. There is no set path in life. You make your own. You must. Following the path you feel is expected of you is all wrong.' There was absolute conviction in her voice. She fixed her gaze on Francesco. 'Never do something simply because you think it is expected of you, because it's what everybody else does and never settle.'

Francesco thought about that for a while. 'Where are they now?'

'Sorry?' She had become lost in her own thoughts and it took a moment for his question to pull her back to the present.

'Your husband and your daughters. Where are they?'

'My husband passed away a few years ago. It's a strange thing. I said we settled, but I still missed him. More than I expected. Not in the sense of a romantic longing for him to be with me again, but just in the way you miss someone you're used to having around. That sounds terrible as well, doesn't it? Honesty often does, though. Most of us say all the right things because that's what we're expected to do and it oils the wheels, but I spent so much of my life doing and saying what was expected of me that I've had enough of it.'

'And your daughters?'

'Jess is an artist. Goodness only knows where she gets her talent from. Not from me or her father, that's for sure.' She chuckled. 'Abigail is somewhere in South America. She's backpacking and doing volunteer work here and there. She disappeared for a few months. It turned out she was working in a remote community in the Amazon with no Internet or whatnot. I did get quite cross about that, but I'm so pleased she's doing what she wants to do. They both are and that gives me so much pleasure.'

'And you?'

'Am I doing what I want to do, you mean?'

'Yes, exactly.'

'In a way I am. Over the years I've learned Italian at evening classes. I'm not very good. My teacher told me that she was very pleased with my pronunciation but that my grammar was all over the place.' She laughed again, that earthy, infectious laugh. 'Speaking of languages, your English is perfect. In fact, are you English?'

Francesco felt his insides start to turn and twist, the way they always did if he was ever asked anything about himself. He sometimes wondered why he worked so hard to avoid talking about himself. Was it too awkward? Too painful? Was it the reactions of other people? Reactions which left him feeling he had to take care of them and make them feel better about what he had told them? That was something nobody ever mentioned about bereavement; the having to take care of other people's feelings. Or was it simply that he felt there was so little of himself left to give? In any case, he preferred listening, preferred asking questions, not answering them. Even in what he thought of as his previous life, in the life before everything had been destroyed, he hadn't much liked talking about himself; other people were far more interesting

'English mother, Italian father,' he offered blandly,

sidestepping the need to make any reference to the past or present. He wouldn't have known which one to use for his father in any case, and he had no wish to get drawn into a conversation about his own life. 'Anyway, what's your plan now you're here?'

'I've rented out my house in England so here I am. It was something Jess said which finally made me do it. Isn't it funny how the most innocuous of comments can hit you hard?'

Francesco nodded. If only she knew.

'One day she said to me, "Mum, if you want to do it, just do it. Don't leave it until you're too old." And then all my "toos" came flooding back. All the things I hadn't done because of too this or too that. All the insecurities and worries which had held me back. And I decided I wasn't going to add "too old" to that list. So now I can be here where I feel I belong even though I've left it a bit late to have romantic adventures.'

Francesco started to protest but she continued. 'Oh no, my dear. I know you mean well, but it's just the way life is. You know, when I was younger, I could immediately tell when a man was interested in me. His eyes would widen just a fraction, and I would know. Then he would start to flirt, and although I was flattered, I'd secretly be terrified. You know, because of my famous "toos". At some point, men's eyes stopped widening, and that frightened me as well because I knew my time had passed.'

She stopped, as if she was trying to remember when that shift had occurred. 'I don't really know when that happened.

Someone once said that women die twice. I've no idea who it was but, goodness me, they were right. One becomes invisible, in terms of being considered an attractive human being anyway. Then people refer to us as old bats because we have to be assertive just to get served in a restaurant or shop.

'It's ironic really. When I had youth on my side, I didn't have the confidence. Now, I have the confidence but … so, no, I'm under no illusions about that. No "adventures" for me, well, not that of that kind anyway,' she paused and her eyes sparkled again with that mischievousness the years and regrets had been unable to extinguish, 'but I can spend as much time as I want here now and I am more than happy with that.'

'Not settling anymore?'

Dorothy gave him that astonishing, decade-defying smile once more. 'No more than old age necessitates, my dear.'

*     *     *

Francesco went home that night thinking about Dorothy as he always thought about the people who had shared something of their lives with him.

He considered what she had said about not settling and also about knowing when to let go. He admired her spirit and determination to live at least a part of her life purely on her terms. He felt he had settled although in a completely different sense. He had settled for not knowing what had happened to Lauren, to Teddy, to his father. Perhaps he hadn't tried hard enough. No, that wasn't true. He reminded himself he had tried to find his family when he had first returned to Rome.

And Lauren? He looked across at the photo of the two of them together. He was standing behind her, his arms wrapped around her with their entwined hands protecting their unborn child.

He reached over to pick it up and examined it more closely. He saw the look on his face; contentedness radiated from him, an emotion now lost in time. What had Lauren been thinking when that picture had been taken? Revisiting the photo now, her smile seemed more strained, less sincere. Was it just his imagination playing with him after what he had learned following the accident? He would never know. There were no paths left to follow to find out why his wife had acted as she had. He wondered if he would ever make peace with that fact and learn to let go; to accept that the past guarded its secrets well.

And then he reflected on Dorothy's observation that men felt they had to keep their emotions to themselves and that they paid a heavy price for that. Perhaps there was no shame in needing to express pain in some way, particularly when it sometimes seemed that the world asked too much. He felt his heart cracking under the weight of the burden he carried every day and for the first time since the accident, he allowed himself to cry.

# Summer 2019

# CHAPTER FOUR

Francesco opened the door to his apartment. It was as dark and silent as ever. He quickly turned on the lights and the television. He wasn't interested in watching it, but anything that broke the oppressive silence was welcome. He went to the fridge, found a can of beer, slumped on the sofa and opened the drink.

That day had been one of those when the numbness had set in afresh and he had had no desire for any human contact. The need to avoid any real engagement with other people had been as intense as the need he had on other days for some type of interaction and the chance to lose himself in another person's life in order to forget his own.

He played back the events of the day: the petty dispute over a seat reservation which had escalated and culminated in him being called a brain dead idiot who was a ticket inspector because he wasn't intelligent enough to get a proper job; the teenage girls who had giggled every time he walked past and managed to make him feel uncomfortable; the middle-aged married couple. He had noticed, not for the first time, how so many older couples seemed to have nothing to say to each other and, particularly, the look of disengagement on the man's face as if wondering how he had ever reached this stage in his life.

From there, his thoughts inevitably strayed to Lauren. They had only been married for a year. Would they have ended up like that? He would never know now, but he didn't think so. They had been so happy and Lauren had always been full of life, ideas and enthusiasm for just about everything. When she had come into his life, it was as though a light had come on. His difficult childhood had receded and he had regained a sense that life was truly worth living and relishing. Their happiness had only been added to when Lauren had found out she was pregnant.

He remembered the day she had told him and how they had reacted; laughing, crying and hugging each other, imagining all the things they would do as a family. Francesco had also privately been a little afraid. Would he be a good father? He didn't want to let either Lauren or their child down. He vowed to himself that their child would have a better childhood than his own had been.

And then … Lauren's car had spun off the road and the light she had brought into his life had been extinguished. He sometimes thought he might have coped better, not well, but better, if it had not been for the circumstances. The visit from the police questioning the state of their marriage and asking him why she had checked into a hotel near the airport on the day of her death had haunted him ever since.

The same questions ate away at him constantly. Why had

she checked into that hotel? Having done that, why did she leave again? Why hadn't she had any cases with her? What did that mean? Had she been seeing somebody else? Had she been planning to leave him? He couldn't believe that. He had never met anyone as open, honest and utterly loyal. If she had met someone else, she would have told him, but he couldn't quite believe that was what had happened. But still the little voice at the back of his mind taunted him with "what if". What if he hadn't known her as well as he had thought he did? What if their whole life had been a sham and would have come crashing down around him sooner or later anyway? And on the worst of days, that voice wheedled away at him and asked what if it hadn't even been his baby? And doubting her made him feel guilty. He was caught in a tangle of doubts, regret and guilt which wrapped around him and sometimes made life seem almost intolerable.

'Lauren,' he said to the darkness, 'what happened?'

His mind wandered to the weeks leading up to her death. She had been acting strangely; he had asked her if something was worrying her and she had insisted she was fine, laughed and said if she seemed off it was probably her hormones. And Francesco had believed her because he had wanted to, because it was the easiest thing to do, because it was plausible. But now there were so many things that would forever be unknowable. Sometimes all those unanswered and unanswerable questions seemed almost more overwhelming than the grief of losing her.

And now as he sat there alone in this flat in Rome, he remembered the day she had been brought into the hospital's accident and emergency department where he had been on duty.

Frantically, he had tried to work on her until his colleagues had realised that he was her husband. He remembered being pulled away from her, screaming for them to let go of him, trying to push them away because he had to save her. Only he could save her and save their child.

Much of the time in the immediate aftermath was a blank space in his memory which he suspected was just as well. The hospital trust had been supportive and had given him compassionate leave. When he had tried to go back to work, he had been unable to even make it through the door before the flashbacks had started. He had returned to his car and sat there trembling and sweating holding on tight to the steering wheel willing the panic to pass. And, at that moment, Francesco had realised he would never be able to go back. Ashamed and unable to tell anybody what he was going through, he had resigned on the grounds he wished to pursue new opportunities elsewhere.

His friends, who had drifted away to some extent as girlfriends, wives and children had come along, had called in to keep an eye on him from time to time. They had expressed surprise and concern about the fact that he had given up on medicine which had always been his vocation, but he had insisted he was fine and it was simply time for a change, to take stock of things and get off the A&E merry-go-round.

He was so convincing that his friends gradually gravitated back to their own families and worries as Francesco retreated into the shadows. The isolation of grief claimed him and built an invisible and impenetrable barrier around him. Alone and lonely, Francesco tried to convince himself over and over again that men didn't wallow, they coped, but however many times he had repeated that mantra, it did nothing to help him, and he felt himself crumbling inside.

One day bled into the next; days and weeks passed in a hollow existence and then one morning, Francesco had driven out into the Peak District and gone walking in the hills as he had done so often with Lauren. It was late December with a fine dusting of snow on the higher ground. The grey sky pressed down on him like an unbearable weight which threatened to crush him. He felt claustrophobic and could barely breathe. He had to escape and in that moment he remembered his early childhood in Italy: green, sunlit fields scattered with poppies; the vibrancy of Rome; brilliant blue skies; warmth. All such a contrast to the bleak landscape stretching before him. Perhaps he would even be able to find Teddy. And the decision was made. Within one month, he had sold, donated or packed what little he had owned, packed a couple of cases and handed the keys of their flat back to the landlord.

A reckless abandon had taken hold of him while he was following through on his plan. It was only when he had landed in Italy that the fact he had no idea what he would do or where he would go, really dawned on him. The euphoria evaporated as he stood in the terminal of Rome's Fiumicino airport on a cold January morning feeling more lost than he had imagined possible. He wondered what he had done. He was half tempted to buy another ticket and fly straight back. But back to what? The harsh truth was nothing. There was absolutely nothing to go back to or for.

The idea that he might track down Teddy and his father was the final factor which stopped him leaving. Perhaps they would have forgiven him by now. So eventually he had taken a train to Termini station. As he walked out onto the concourse, he found it totally transformed from the place he remembered. He glanced up and saw heavily armed soldiers on the first floor walkway watching over the station. He was sure they had never been there when he was a child. He realised he had imagined Italy would not have changed in the long years he had been away, but it seemed that was not the case.

He had trudged around for a dispiriting half an hour and had some lunch he didn't really want. Finally he had booked into a cheap hotel nearby. It was on the fifth floor of a building with no lift, paper-thin walls and a middle-aged man at reception who clearly wished he didn't have to be there. Its only redeeming features were that it was clean and cheap.

A few days had passed during which he went through the motions of existence but nothing more. He did not speak to anyone beyond Arturo, the man at reception who seemed to consider a grunt a meaningful conversation, and he barely ventured far beyond the street in which the hotel was located. On the fourth day, however, he had woken up with a sense of resolve and decided it was time to go and visit his old family home. Was it possible that his father and Teddy would still be there? And if they were, how would they react when they saw him? Would they welcome him or reject him? At the thought of further heartache, he sat back down on the bed. Could he cope with it? He wasn't sure he could, but if he wasn't here to find them, what was the point?

Arturo had given him a map when he had first arrived. He reached across, retrieved it from the bedside table and spread it out on the bed. It felt strange to realise he needed a map to find his way around the city of his birth. It had been his home until that night when he was seven and his life had changed for the first time and he had ended up in England, torn away from everything that had been familiar to him.

Having plotted a route, he stopped at the breakfast room for a cappuccino. He received the customary grunt, a raised eyebrow and a vague nod from Arturo, which was more than most of the other guests, and then he made his way down the five dimly lit flights of stairs and out into bright sunshine.

His walk took him past the Basilica of Santa Maria Maggiore. He remembered it as being huge and, although it was certainly imposing, it did not look as big as it had done through the eyes of a seven year old. He decided to go inside, but when he approached the entrance, he was shocked to discover that to get inside, it was necessary to go through a security check. The same feeling he had experienced at Termini washed over him again and, after a brief visit, he found he couldn't wait to get back outside into the sunlight.

He continued past the Colosseum and down Via di San

Gregorio, lined with mature stone pines on both sides of the road. He walked past the Palatine Hill, and then he saw the Circus Maximus and had to catch his breath as a sense of déjà vu rushed over him. The present fell away, and he was there with his mother, peering through the railings. He suddenly remembered her saying that whenever she arrived there, she knew she was almost home. He paused, not to look at the site so much as to collect himself, as memories from his childhood pressed in around him. He looked over at the Palatine Hill rising above the site, looking down at the remains of the Circus Maximus; the broken and abandoned dreams of another age.

He crossed the Via del Circo Massimo and continued on into the heart of the rione of Ripa. The atmosphere was just as he remembered. Here, the constant drone of traffic which pervaded most of the city was absent and people greeted their neighbours in the street as they passed by. It had the atmosphere of a small town rather than a big city. He made a couple of wrong turns, but then suddenly his caramel-coloured childhood home with the balcony and its green and white striped awning was there in front of him.

Memories of his childhood rushed back again and he remembered with frightening clarity that night in the summer of 1992 when he had been forced to leave. He remembered everyone had been crying except his father and everyone except him had been shouting. He remembered the fear; the sadness; the confusion; wondering what he had done wrong and if it was possible for him to put it right so that they would all just stop shouting. His heart was pounding and his palms felt sweaty. He had to walk around the block twice before he could bring himself to approach the front door. His finger hovered over the buzzer corresponding to their apartment. Finally, he took a deep breath and pressed it.

There was a pause and then a woman's voice said, 'Si?'

'I'm sorry to disturb you signora, but I'm looking for Carlo De Luca.'

'I've never heard of him.'

'Or Teodora De Luca?'

'No.' The woman cut the connection.

Francesco turned to leave and then stopped. Supposing that woman was Teddy? Or perhaps, even if she wasn't, would she have a forwarding address for them? He had to know for sure.

He rang the bell again.

'Si?' She sounded more impatient this time.

'Signora, please may I speak to you?'

'Why? Who are you?'

'My name is Francesco De Luca. I'm trying to find my father and sister and they – we - used to live here."

'You don't know where your family is?' Impatience gave way to confusion, but her voice had softened.

'No, signora, I do not and if you can give me any information, it would mean a great deal to me.'

There was another pause and then he heard the door catch release.

He arrived at the front door to find it ajar but with the safety chain in place. A woman peered round the door, looking at him cautiously.

'Thank you for letting me in.' He made no attempt to move too close to the front door.

'What is it that you want to know?'

'My family are from Rome and, as I said, we used to live here. It's a long story but I lost contact with my father and sister and I'm trying to find them.'

'We've lived here for eight years. We bought it from a couple who were returning to the north.' She uttered the words as if she could hardly believe anyone would voluntarily do such a thing.

'A couple?' He supposed his father could have met someone else by then. 'But was the man's name Carlo? Carlo De Luca?'

'No. What was his name? Russo, I think, but if your father was from Rome it couldn't have been him. They definitely said they were moving back to the north. I thought it seemed strange so that's why I remember it.'

'I see.'

'I'm sorry that I can't help you.' Concern had struggled with suspicion for supremacy and won.

Francesco shrugged. 'It's OK. Thank you for your time.' He turned to leave.

'I hope you find them,' she said and with that she closed the door.

He had walked for the rest of the day, too restless to keep still and hoping that he would exhaust himself enough to get some sleep that night.

Guilt, fear and everyday life had stopped him trying to contact them before and now it was finally too late. He thought of all the years that had passed and realised it would have been too late even if they had been there. Why had he entertained the idea they would have welcomed him with open arms after so many years?

When he had finally returned to the hotel, Arturo was pacing up and down shouting at someone on the phone.

'Porca miseria,' he said with intense feeling and jabbed at the end call button.

'Buonasera,' said Francesco, fighting the impulse to slink away as quickly as possible.

'Ah, but it's not a good evening, is it?'

'Well…'

'No, exactly.' A glint appeared in his eye. 'But you can help me.'

'Help you with what?' Francesco said warily.

'Beds.'

'Beds?'

'Yes, beds. Those things people sleep on.' He extended his index finger, pointed it at his temple and twisted it back and forth, clearly demonstrating he thought he was dealing with someone who had difficulty grasping the simplest of concepts.

'I know what they are, but what do you want me to do with them?' Francesco said. He was not quite English enough to remember to at least appear to be patient, but not quite Italian enough to lose his patience relatively quickly.

'I have new beds coming tomorrow and you can help me get them up here.'

'What? With five floors and no lift? Besides, I'm a paying guest.'

'Si, si. We will start after breakfast tomorrow. Be ready at 9.30.' Francesco was about to protest, but Arturo added, 'As for paying, three nights' free accommodation - if you help me and stay for more than a week. It's not as if you usually do anything all day.'

Francesco returned to his room. Not having to pay for three nights wouldn't be a bad thing as he had no job and he actually didn't mind the idea of helping Arturo despite his permanently gruff manner.

The next day, after hours of moving old beds out and new ones in, they were both exhausted. Arturo motioned for him to sit down and brought them coffee. Francesco almost choked on the first sip.

'Ristretto,' Arturo said and almost smiled for the first time since Francesco had met him. 'Are you Italian or not?'

Francesco ignored that. 'Strong stuff.'

They sat in silence surveying all the discarded packing materials still scattered around the breakfast room. Doing something together seemed to have led to some kind of camaraderie between them.

'How long are you going to stay here?' Arturo asked him after a while.

'Here,' Francesco said, looking around him. 'Or in Rome?'

Arturo shrugged.

'I don't know. I have to … organise things.'

'Like?'

'Just things,' Francesco stalled, aware there were no things to be sorted out.

'If you're going to stay, here or in Rome, you need a job.

It's not healthy sitting around all day.'

'A job? That would make things more – permanent.'

'Yes, so you're going to stay?'

'I have nowhere to go back to so I suppose I might as well.' Francesco realised he didn't really care anymore where he was.

'I used to be a train driver. Good job and good pay. I liked it because it was solitary and I was always on the move.'

'I wouldn't mind a job like that. Trouble is I can't drive a train.'

'There are other jobs you could do. You could be a ticket inspector.'

'Maybe.'

'There are worse things. If you're interested, I can put you in touch with someone who can help you. Contacts, they're the only way you ever get anything done here. Think about it and while you're doing that, you can help me clear this lot up.' His conversational tone vanished abruptly. He stubbed his cigarette out in the remains of his coffee and it was clear it was time to get back to work.

After they had finally finished, Francesco returned to his room and thought about his conversation with Arturo. He couldn't get to sleep despite the exertions of the day. He realised that everything he knew about leading an adult life was based on his experience in England. Here, in Italy, he had no idea how things worked or what paperwork he needed. He felt like a child in an adult's body.

Eventually, tired of waiting for sleep, he had got up and, leaving a note telling Arturo he would be back the next day or the day after, he had walked to Termini and bought a ticket. It didn't matter to him where he went. It was the idea of movement that appealed to him, and it worked. That night he slept better than he had done at any time since Lauren's accident. As the weeks passed, it became a regular habit. Arturo became used to him disappearing and reappearing, and if he thought it was strange, he said nothing. Francesco went, not to go anywhere, but simply to go. The movement soothed him and lulled him to sleep. It was as though, if he could only keep moving, he would be safe, outrunning the demons snapping at his heels. Movement was safe; staying still was not.

On one of those journeys, it occurred to him that perhaps he should take Arturo up on his offer. He had arrived in Italy with enough money to keep him going for a while, but it would not last forever. So he had been introduced to various contacts of Arturo's who had helped him to survive the horrors of Italian bureaucracy and before too long had found himself with all his paperwork and standing in Termini station about to start his new job as a ticket inspector.

He had found he enjoyed the work: the constant moving about suited his restlessness; the fact that he didn't see the same people every day suited his desire for solitude and, finally, nobody's life was in his hands. Later his chances to talk to people had come, to learn about their lives, their triumphs and failures.

For a while he had continued to live at the hotel. He had developed a rapport with Arturo by then and liked the fact that there was a familiar, if not always friendly, face around.

Arturo never asked him personal questions, and he sensed Arturo would not welcome them from him either. There was a type of unspoken understanding between them that they were two damaged characters who would not enjoy much scrutiny of their pasts. He also found comfort in the fact that there were other people coming and going. People he could nod and say good morning to over breakfast, but people he would never be obliged to get to know and exchange more than pleasantries with.

At last, though, as the first signs of spring arrived, he realised a more permanent and, more pressingly, a cheaper, solution would have to be found and he managed to rent an apartment close to the Via Appia Nuova just outside the Aurelian walls. Arturo had gruffly accepted he would be moving on and said nothing more on the subject until Francesco reached the door with his cases. Without a word, he took one of the cases and carried it downstairs. 'There's always ristretto available here,' he said, his offhand tone at odds with the meaning his words conveyed.

'Just as well. I've developed a taste for it now.' It wasn't true, but he had come to welcome Arturo's company if not his coffee.

They had patted each other awkwardly on the back, and then Francesco had flagged down a taxi. When he had turned around to say goodbye to Arturo, he found he had already disappeared.

Arriving at the apartment, he had tried to keep himself busy, going out, buying the household items he needed, cleaning the flat and unpacking what little he had brought with him. On one of the trips back from the shops, while juggling bags and keys, he had dropped the little aluminium coffee pot he had bought. It had crashed on the marble floor, and the noise had reverberated around the hallway. He had flinched at the sound and the memory of the signs posted by the entrance to the building forbidding noise.

For a moment, he had thought he had got away with it, but then he had heard a bolt shoot back, and a woman had appeared and told him off, reminding him about the importance of peace and quiet. He had heard the expression "bella figura" used, which he remembered was something to do with behaving appropriately and creating a good impression, but he had been too dispirited to protest that it had merely been an accident and simply apologised. Back in the flat, he had kept finding things to do. The thought of stopping, of night and quietness falling, creeping in around him had been unbearable.

He had turned the television on and flicked through the channels. His unfamiliarity with the programmes and people who were obviously so well-known, reinforced his sense of being out of place. A feeling of homesickness overwhelmed him, but he could not identify where it was he wanted to be. Everywhere felt wrong. Manchester had been wrong and now Rome was wrong.

He had thrown the remote control on the sofa as he got up. Why had he given up the career he loved? He knew the answer of course; he hadn't trusted himself to practise anymore. Why had he come back here? To run away from losing Lauren or to chase the dream of finding a family who had moved on without a look back? And then he had caught a glimpse of himself in the mirror; a shell of a human being, standing among the debris of his life, surveying the destruction.

Finally, he had collapsed onto the bed that night and, for the first time since Lauren's death, the enormity of everything had seemed to hit him even harder than ever. Losing her, the unanswered questions surrounding her death, the self-inflicted loss of his career and moving out of the home they had shared. The hotel had been different, temporary. This was permanent, and its permanence carried enormous implications with it. He had arrived with nothing more than a wild dream to reconnect with his family and to make a fresh start but he felt utterly alone, alienated from everything and everyone. Maybe he didn't belong here either. Maybe he was past belonging anywhere. A weight pressed down on his chest. It was almost unendurable, but he told himself he had to carry on.

And somehow he had done just that and here he was, in June, on the anniversary of the date she had told him that she was pregnant. One year on from that wonderful day; ten months on from the day of her accident; ten months on from his before. Surviving rather than living, appearing to function perfectly well, but sometimes feeling he was barely managing to do so. A life only made tolerable by a job which allowed him to be on the move all the time; which had no requirement to build relationships with colleagues or any other people and that aspect was, on the days the darkness descended, a blessing.

Yet he also been given the privilege of listening to the stories of other people's lives and seeing the world through the prism of their experiences which, on the days he yearned for some human contact, provided temporary respite from the images and questions which plagued him. Lauren's preoccupied state before the accident. Why hadn't he forced the issue? Lauren checking into a hotel near the airport, only a few miles from their home. Why had she done that? Lauren's accident in clear, dry weather. How could it have happened? How would he ever move on from losing her, from the unanswered questions? Had she loved him? Had she been planning to leave him? Why had she been at that hotel? Why had she left again?

He was sick of all the questions, sick of the fact that he would never have any answers and sick of analysing everything over and over again. He feared the past would never let him go. The more he struggled to free himself from it, the more tightly it bound itself to him. He got up and tossed the beer can in the bin. Then he opened the vodka he had, against his better judgement, bought on the way home. What did it matter? He wasn't working the next day. One shot became two, became three, four. Francesco drank himself into oblivion and fell into a deep, apparently dreamless sleep.

# CHAPTER FIVE

Francesco had spent his day off suffering a hangover sufficient to put him off alcohol, or vodka at least, for the foreseeable future. Now, the following day, while he still felt far from recovered, the headache and nausea had subsided.

He had been fortunate in that it had been an easy day with no difficult passengers or delays. All he had left to do was a run down to Naples and back to Rome and he would be finished for the day.

As he approached her, the woman reached into the bag on the seat beside her and retrieved her ticket. She handed it over, and Francesco noticed the slight tremor of her hand as she did so. He looked at her, but she kept her eyes fixed on the ticket.

Francesco checked her ticket, and as he did so, the train jolted so sharply that it was sufficient to send the woman's bag and its contents sprawling across the floor.

After a moment in which they both recovered, Francesco asked, 'Are you OK?'

'Yes, but look at this mess.' She gazed at her possessions

which were now strewn around the carriage and suddenly appeared helpless.

'I can help you pick everything up.'

'No, no, I can do it,' she said, suddenly sounding defensive.

'It's really not a problem.'

'I said I can do it.' She was raising her voice now. He saw her make a determined effort to calm down. 'I'm sorry. I'm fine. I can manage. I expect you should go and see what happened.'

'Perhaps I should,' Francesco said reluctantly. He got up and walked towards the door. As he was about to leave, he glanced round. He saw her get up very slowly and carefully as if every movement was costing her a great deal. He was torn. Should he do his official duty or what he felt was his moral duty to help the woman? The woman had made it very clear that she didn't want help so, reluctantly, he chose his official duty.

Making his way back up the train, it seemed the only casualty was one caused by a suitcase, which had rolled across the carriage and caught a woman's ankle. She was rubbing it and looking aggrieved while the owner apologised to her profusely.

Once in the cab, he asked what had happened.

Some sort of problem up ahead,' the driver said. 'I got instructions to enter the station slowly.'

'Well, you'll certainly be able to do that.'

The driver grunted and shrugged, and Francesco was more than happy to leave him alone. He closed the cab door behind him, and his thoughts turned back to the woman.

He decided to go back down the train and see how she was; something about her demeanour had worried him.

When he walked into the carriage, she was back in her seat, the bag stowed beside her again.

'What happened?' she asked him.

'Nothing serious. Did you find everything?'

'Yes, I think so.'

'Oh, wait a moment.' Something underneath the seat next to her had caught Francesco's eye. He knelt down and retrieved a box of tablets.

'Levodopa,' he said, passing it back to her, and for the first time she made eye contact.

'Oh, yes. Just painkillers.' She hoped he would accept it, but she could see he knew.

'How long has it been?

'How long has what been?'

'Since you were diagnosed with Parkinson's.'

'How do you know?'

Francesco could have told her about how the tremor in her hand and the stiffness of her movements had already betrayed her, and that the Levodopa was the final piece of the puzzle. But then he would probably have had to explain why he recognised the signs, and that was a conversation he wasn't prepared to have.

'My friend's father,' he said, hating the lie. 'I remember he had those tablets.'

'Well, I suppose there's no point pretending then, is there?'

'Why should you have to pretend?'

She laughed. 'Pretending has become such a habit that it's hard not to do it anymore. When I found out, I didn't believe it. I went into total denial. I was only forty-six and I had a healthy lifestyle. I had a very demanding job. Maybe the stress of the job had something to do with it. Who knows? I'd just been promoted as well. I didn't have time to get a cold, never mind something so…' she searched for a word, 'something that would turn my life upside down.'

'Does anyone else in your family have it?'

'My father died thirty years ago. My mother doesn't have it, but she's … it's hard to explain.'

Francesco looked at her and waited.

'When she retired she moved up to Queensland. My life is, well, it was, in Melbourne, and then when I got a promotion, I was transferred to Sydney. I didn't see her as often as I should have done; I was so wrapped up in my own life. I regret that now, but maybe it was for the best.'

'Why?'

'Because if she'd seen me, she'd have known. Even when the symptoms were hardly visible she'd have known. That's just the way mothers are. As it was, we only kept in touch by phone so it was easy to pretend I was fine. Then she started to develop dementia so I couldn't confide in her anyway, and that's when I really started to wish I could have done.'

'You never told her?'

'No and not anyone else either. The only people who know are my doctors.' She paused. 'It was easy really. I was always so damn busy at work that I didn't have many friends and the people I worked with were equally preoccupied. I could have walked in with a flashing sign on my head announcing I had Parkinson's, and I doubt anyone would have noticed. People don't really see each other or make time for each other these days.'

'No, they don't, do they?' He knew from personal experience that that was exactly how it often went.

'No, and then people excuse it by saying they're busy leading their own lives. I did it often enough myself so I can hardly take the moral high ground, but since … since everything I've thought about that a lot and, really, what are our lives made up of if not our connections to other people?'

Francesco considered what she had said. There was truth in her words, but where did that leave people who were totally alone? People like him. That was something he did not care to examine too carefully so he said, 'I think it's a reflection of the world we live in now. We're supposedly more connected than ever before and yet, at the same time, we're not.'

'That's the truth, but it worked to my advantage because nobody noticed anything and I could continue to pretend – even to myself – that everything was fine and the doctors were talking out of their behinds. But then the symptoms I already had started to get worse and I got other ones too. One day, my hand was shaking so much I couldn't put my lipstick on. And then I cried for the first time. Not because of the lipstick, but because I knew what it meant; the game was up. It was real.'

'What happened then?'

'I went back to my doctor. I got put on the Levodopa and I learned everything I could about Parkinson's. None of it was pretty. I went through a few months of anguish and then I decided what I wanted to do. I felt better once I'd decided. I jacked in the job. My colleagues were stunned that I would give up such a good position. While I was working my notice, I watched the jostling for my position start. I felt so removed from the whole thing. It all suddenly seemed so insignificant that I found it funny to watch them scrap over it. Then, when I finally told them I was going travelling, several of them confided in me that they were envious and wished they were me. How ironic is that? Meanwhile, my doctors were horrified, but I'd decided. I was going to do it while I still could.'

'Why did you choose Italy?'

'Italy is actually my second trip. One good thing about being a workaholic was that I'd saved a lot of money. I went to places I'd always dreamed of, but that I'd never seemed to have time to visit before. Thailand, Cambodia, India … the funny thing is, I'd probably have been scared to go to a lot of those places alone before. My diagnosis gave me a strange kind of freedom. Hell, I was going to die anyway so it didn't matter what I did.'

'Many people with Parkinson's live a long life.'

'Yeah, but how much of it is really living and how much of it is existing? That's a real question, by the way. I don't know the answer. My doctors don't know. Anyway, after Asia, I went back to Australia to check in with my doctors. They made me feel worse; doctors have always made me feel worse. I think I've got an allergy to them. Then, I decided to come here. My father's family were from Italy originally, but his parents moved to Australia. I can remember my nonna, my Italian grandmother, telling me lots of stories about the old country when I was a kid so I decided I wanted to come and see the place for myself. It's strange, but I have this need to know where I come from before it's too late.'

'Where are you heading?'

'First, to a small town in Calabria nobody's ever heard of as that's where they were from. I don't know if anyone I'm related to is still there and I don't plan to try to find out. I just want to see the place. After that, I'm going to work my way north. See as much as I can while I can.'

There was a finality to the way she said that which unsettled Francesco. "But what are you going to do after that? And shouldn't you be seeing a doctor from time to time?"

'I've had enough of doctors. And I know what my prognosis is; I can't be cured. I'm only going to get worse, and I don't want to be around for that. You might think I'm a coward, but I'll go to Switzerland when the time is right.'

Francesco was momentarily lost, and he scrambled to catch up with what she was leading up to

'You know,' she said, 'there's that clinic where you can go and kill yourself. I've got it all sorted out.'

The bluntness of the statement shocked him and she interpreted his expression as one of disapproval.

'You think that's wrong?'

Francesco felt himself edging towards an abyss. If he got

into a discussion on medical ethics, he would inevitably give away too much about himself. Besides, there were some issues he had struggled with himself in a professional capacity. There were no easy answers, and he had seen both sides so many times – the fight to hold on and the fight to let go – and even though it had not been his fight, it had never failed to move him or make him feel utterly powerless.

'I think it's a very personal decision, and it's not for me or anybody else to judge.'

'I reckon that's a cop out.'

'No …'

'I saw the way you reacted. I'm going to guess you're one of those people who think you should soldier on whatever happens. That there's something noble about suffering.'

The words sliced through Francesco. Is that what he had been doing? Suffering, albeit in a very different way, and considering himself to be noble? Why hadn't he just decided to end everything? What made him hold on day after day? Something from his previous life kicked in and replaced the pain and anger her words had inflicted upon him.

'I was taken aback by the totally matter-of-fact way you said it, not what you said. And, believe me, I am well aware there's nothing noble about suffering.'

'I'm sorry. I get so tetchy these days. You're being really nice to me, and I'm biting your head off.'

'No worries.' He paused. 'That's what you Aussies say, isn't it?' he asked, deciding to risk it to lighten the mood.

'Yeah, we do.' She had the grace to take it in the manner in which it was intended and laugh. Growing more serious again, she said, 'If I had a family, or even really close friends, perhaps I'd make a different decision, but it wouldn't be the right one. I'd be trying to carry on for them, not for me. The way it's worked out isn't exactly great, but at least I don't have to worry about leaving people behind. I can go out on my own terms. Does that make sense?'

'Yes, it does, but will you let me say one thing?'

'Go on.'

'There are treatments that you may not have explored. Perhaps you should just look into them a bit more before you …'

'I understand what you're saying and my doctors told me about the various options I had, but I'm not interested. And do you know why?'

Francesco shook his head.

'Well, for a start there's my allergy to doctors. And there's something else too. Apart from the days when the symptoms seem worse, in a weird way, I'm actually having the time of my life.

'I'm not saying I'm happy about it but … this is so hard to explain … look, before my diagnosis I was on a treadmill. It was just work, work and more work. I never really stopped to question why I was doing it or appreciate anything around me. I'd probably have gone on like that until I retired and then dropped dead of a heart attack – or boredom. Now though, I appreciate everything. Colours seem more vivid, landscapes more breathtaking, every minute is precious and special because I know how limited my time is. There's an irony for you – the more I feel myself fading away, the more vibrant the world around me seems.'

Neither of them said anything for a while, and then she continued. 'If I went back to Australia, it would all be about doctors and hospitals and being prodded about. There would be no pleasure left in life and what for? There's no cure; there are only ways to alleviate the symptoms. And, another thing, euthanasia is illegal in Australia so I'd be stuck. This way, I get to really live for the first time. On my terms, and I choose when to say enough is enough. I'm not afraid, you know. I was but I've gone through that phase. Now, I feel … liberated. Pissed off sometimes but liberated.'

'I honestly don't know what to say, but I can promise you I'm not judging you. I think you're quite remarkable.' Francesco paused. 'Can I ask you something?'

'Sure.' She shrugged and smiled. I've already bared my soul to you.'

'Would you let me give you my phone number? I mean, just in case you need something.' He felt slightly light-headed as he made the offer. What was he doing?

'That is so kind of you.' She looked genuinely appreciative of the offer. 'OK, but don't worry, I'm not going to bug you every time I can't understand what someone's saying to me.'

They both laughed at that and he wrote down his number and handed it to her. 'What's your name?' she asked him.

'Francesco.'

'Francesco,' she said. 'I'm Paula, by the way. Don't take this the wrong way, but I'm not going to give you my number. You might ring me up and try to talk me out of my decision.'

'That's fine. I just want you to know you have someone here you can turn to.' Then he added hastily, 'If you need to, that is.'

'You really are one of the good guys, you know that.' She glanced down at his hand and noticed he wasn't wearing a ring. 'I hope someone comes along and snaps you up and realises how lucky she is.'

Francesco felt the pain of her words cutting through him again, but he was not angry with her. She could not possibly have known how much those words hurt him, but they were drawing into the station and he knew he could keep a smile fixed on his face just long enough to help her off the train and see her on her way.

They said goodbye and he started to walk towards the public toilets at the far end of the platform. He couldn't face anyone and it was the most likely place for him to find a place where other people were not; they were almost always deserted because they were so far from the main thoroughfare.

As he walked along the platform, he saw her. Her long dark hair was pushed back over her shoulders and she was wheeling a suitcase. It was like a million other cases but at that moment, to him, it was exactly the same as Lauren's case had been. He called after her, but she did not respond and instead stepped on to the train. He started to run, but the doors closed before he could make it. He caught sight of her through the window as the train started to move; a face that would be considered beautiful by almost anyone's standards but not the one he had so desperately wanted to see. One that shattered his irrational moment of hope and left him utterly bereft.

He went into the toilets and shut himself in a cubicle. He knew he was having a panic attack, and he could feel himself falling through the gaps in his life. Breathe, he kept telling himself, just breathe. He slowly started to calm down a little. He rested his forehead against the side of the cubicle, its laminated surface cool against his clammy skin.

Nobody in Paula's life had known what was really happening to her. They hadn't truly known her or seen her. Had Lauren been keeping something from him? Had he perhaps not known her as well as he had thought? Or had he not really seen who she was? Why hadn't he paid more attention when he had known something was different about her? The same damn questions over and over again.

The raw emotions uncovered by the conversation he had just had with Paula pulled him down further. He could never fix things. Why could he never fix things? And then the impact of the incident on the platform set in, and he punched the partition wall so hard that the whole cubicle shook on its already fragile frame.

# CHAPTER SIX

Francesco had started his day, as had become his habit when he worked a daytime shift, with a visit to his local bar, Caffè Lazio. A power cut in his block had led him there and the quality of the coffee and croissants had kept him returning so that he had started to become a familiar face. Now he only had to appear for Matteo, the barman who was about the same age as him, to produce a cappuccino and cornetto con marmellata di albicocca, a warm, fresh croissant filled with apricot jam.

Feeling slightly better, Francesco had continued on his way to Termini and got ready for the day ahead. He had just finished checking tickets when he was stopped by a family travelling from Ireland and he had got tied up explaining all the different ticketing options available to them for their trip around the country.

Having completed that task, he looked around for somewhere to sit and sort out his papers. The only free seats were one row down from the family opposite the single seat at the end of the carriage where there was a young man with multiple tattoos who, for reasons Francesco found hard to rationalise, had made him feel slightly uncomfortable. The fact that he thought he might be coming face to face with his own prejudice against tattoos made him feel even more uncomfortable as prejudice of any kind was not something he liked to encounter in himself or anyone else. For a moment he debated moving back to the previous carriage and then told himself he was being ridiculous and settled down, opposite the man.

As he finished his paperwork, he heard the passenger opposite address him. 'Hey man.'

He looked up, for some reason expecting a confrontation.

'You wanna beer?' The man was holding a can out to him.

'I think there's a rule somewhere about not drinking alcohol on duty,' said Francesco.

'Hang on.' He rummaged around in the cool bag at his feet. 'Soda?'

Francesco hesitated.

'Dude, I know there's supposed to be air-conditioning in here, but it's no match for this weather, and you look like you're about to expire all trussed up in that tie and hat.'

Francesco relented and accepted the drink with a smile. 'Thanks.'

'No problem.' A pause, then, 'You like your job?'

'Most of the time, yes.'

'That's good. Nobody should have to do a job they hate. Plenty do, of course.'

'What do you do?' Francesco asked, steering the conversation away from himself.

'Well, now I'm a musician, but I've been a lot of other things.'

Francesco's curiosity was aroused by the final remark, but he decided to settle for, 'What instrument do you play?'

'Drums. Trouble is they're not exactly portable. I always envy the guys with the guitars. They can take them just about anywhere.'

'Are you in a band?'

'Yeah, we're on tour right now. It's high season for the music festivals in Europe. We've got a few days off so I'm going to visit my sister and then I've got to head back to Milan and meet up with the rest of the band again. Next gig is Saturday.'

'What sort of music do you play?'

The man gestured at himself. 'Take a guess,' he said good-naturedly.

Francesco, who rarely paid much attention to the details of people's appearance, took in the Boston Red Sox converse, the black jeans and the Motörhead t-shirt, and then the tattoos and the man's shoulder length hair.

'Rock?'

'Yeah, well, it's a mixture - hard rock, alternative metal, a bunch of different stuff. I don't much like labels.'

'Do you play covers or your own music?'

'Our own stuff, but we often play one or two covers during a concert. They normally go down well and they're fun to play. You wanna hear some of our music?'

'OK.'

He selected something on his phone and handed it and

the large headphones he had been wearing around his neck to Francesco.

The music exploded around Francesco and it took him a moment to adjust to what he was listening to. Then he started to appreciate the lyrics, the vocals and the musicianship of the band. It wasn't anything like he had expected. He listened to a couple of songs and then, reluctantly, switched the music off and removed the headphones. 'That's really good. Do you write the music?'

'I contribute, but most of it is written by our singer. I write some of the lyrics, though.'

'You said you're touring. Do you enjoy it?'

'I enjoy the concerts, but the touring itself sucks big time.'

'Why?'

'It's not the glamorous life people think it is. Not unless you're in the real big league and you get fancy tour buses and luxury hotels. The reality of it for us is hiring a van, taking it in turns to drive and usually sleeping in the damn thing too or hotels that are so bad that they make the van look good.

'That doesn't sound like much fun.'

'Yeah and then we start to get pissed at each other. I mean, they're like my brothers and all, but you can't be cooped up together and uncomfortable like that for weeks on end without starting to annoy each other. Then there are the lows after the concerts. On the other hand, we're making a name for ourselves so I guess it's worth it.'

'So you might make the big time and get all the perks?'

'I don't like to tempt fate, but it's starting to look that way. We'll see what happens when we get back to Boston.'

Wanting to keep the conversation going, but feeling he wasn't going to be drawn on the potential developments in his music career, Francesco said, 'Where does your sister live?'

'Salerno. You know it?'

'Not really. I've only been through it.'

'It's not a bad place.'

'It must be nice to have brothers and sisters.' Francesco heard his words as if they were coming from someone else; He had his own sister although he would never see her again.

'Now we're grown up it's cool, but I was the youngest of four and the other three are all girls. Three older sisters. Man,' he shook his head. 'You an only child then?'

'Yes.' It was a lie and yet not a lie.

'That's too bad. Rosa, the middle sister, is the one I'm going to visit now. She married a guy from the old country and moved back here about three years ago. The other two still live in Boston.'

'So your family is from Italy originally?'

'Yeah, both my parents' families emigrated to the States and my parents met in Boston. It's weird, you know. Back in Boston everyone seems to think of me as Italian even though I was born there. Maybe it's because I come from the North End, which is Little Italy, and I have an Italian name. Then I come here and everyone sees me as American. Rosa's husband's grandmother still sometimes calls me "the American". It's like I belong to both cultures, but neither one at the same time.'

'I can relate to that.'

'How's that?'

Francesco was already kicking himself. 'English mother, Italian father.' His standard reply which he always delivered in a tone intended to make the facts sound as dull as possible.

'I bet you feel at your most Italian when you're in England and at your most English when you're here. Am I right?'

'You are,' Francesco said, realising this stranger had articulated something he had felt acutely since he had returned to Italy.

'Yeah, it's strange, isn't it?'

'It certainly is.' He had to move the conversation on. For want of something else to say, he surprised himself by coming out with, 'Those are pretty impressive tattoos.' In spite of his prejudice against tattoos, he could see that these had been done by somebody with talent.

'Yeah, people often ask me really dumb questions like "Did getting them done hurt?" or say "You'll regret those when you're older." Like everyone without tattoos is gonna look so good when they're in their seventies or eighties or whatever.'

Francesco laughed; it was a valid point. 'OK, so can I ask you my stupid question?'

'Go for it,' he said amiably.

'What made you choose the tattoos you have?'

'See, in my opinion, that's not a dumb question. Some people get so pissy when they're asked anything about their tattoos, but I don't mind. A few I just like and they don't mean anything. The big ones, though I could sum up as reminders of significant events or life lessons. Oh and I've got my name tattooed here,' he pulled down the neck of his T-shirt to reveal the name Alessandro in italic script snaking from one shoulder to the other just below his collar bone, 'that's probably not my best one, but it could be useful if I ever get so hammered that I can't remember my name.'

Francesco smiled. 'What about the significant ones? If I can ask.'

'Sure you can.' He rolled up the left arm of his T-shirt to expose the top of a full sleeve of tattoos in black, white and shades of grey, with the principle piece being a woman looking into a hand mirror while a snake coiled around her other forearm and then down around Alessandro's wrist. She represented a classical figure that looked vaguely familiar to Francesco.

'This piece is Prudentia. She's the personification of the virtue of prudence. That's the virtue of being able to discipline yourself by using reason.' Rolling up the other arm of his T-shirt, he said, 'This one is Justicia, Justice.'

Francesco took in the robes which seemed to flow around her. The customary blindfold was tied around her eyes, but the part of her face which could be seen appeared uncompromising. In one hand, she held the scales and in the other, the sword. The amount of detail was extraordinary.

'They are incredibly well done.' Francesco surprised himself by realising he actually meant it and was not just being polite. 'How long did they take?'

'Each arm was about 10 sessions, about 5 hours per

session. 10 months for each arm, more or less; it was a bit stop-start as I was busy with the band. And they weren't cheap.'

'So I'm going to ask the dumb question. It hurts but how much?'

'You can't imagine,' he said laughing. 'The fleshy parts aren't so bad, but when they go over the bony parts like round the elbow ...well, that's not great.'

'You said they are significant. In what way?' Francesco was so involved in the conversation now he hadn't stopped to consider whether that might be a question too far.

Alessandro went quiet for a moment. He looked across at the family Francesco had been talking to earlier. 'When are the family getting off?'

'The next station.'

'If nobody else gets on, I'll tell you. But not with anybody else around, particularly not kids.'

Francesco had found Alessandro so disarming that he had completely forgotten his earlier apprehension. Now his unease returned, but he knew his curiosity would override that.

'OK.' With that they lapsed into silence and finished off their drinks.

At the following station, the family got off and Francesco got up to work his way through the train again to check the new passengers' tickets. He wondered what to expect when he returned to the last carriage. He half hoped Alessandro would be alone, and half hoped he wouldn't.

As he entered the carriage, he saw Alessandro and nodded

to him. The only other passengers now were down at the other end of the carriage, out of earshot of anything Alessandro might say. It seemed he was to hear the story. After checking their tickets, he took his place opposite Alessandro.

'You sure you're ready for this?

'Only one way to find out.'

'You already know I have three sisters and I'm the kid brother. I said it was hard having three older sisters, but really I was joking for the most part. My mom was, is, a sweetheart too, but my father - he was a real tool. Used us all as punch bags when things weren't going his way and it seemed like they didn't go his way a hell of a lot of the time. I was the only other guy in the house and I felt like I should be protecting everyone else but I really was the skinny runt of the litter.' He paused. 'You sure you're cool with this?'

'If you are.'

'OK. Anyways this went on for years and then … I don't know what happened. I was fifteen, and it was like I went to bed as that runt and woke up about six feet tall. I mean, I didn't, obviously, but I definitely had a growth spurt. I started going to the gym, worked out and learned how to fight. And I waited.'

An attendant appeared offering coffee and snacks which they both declined. Alessandro waited until he had returned to the previous carriage and the carriage door had closed behind him.

'The next time he had a bad day, he started on my mom. Sometimes it was one of us kids, whoever was unlucky enough to be around.' He took a deep breath. 'I punched him so hard that I floored him. Then I kicked the crap out of him. Every kick was payback for what he'd done to us over the years. Mom didn't do anything at first; I think she was too shocked to react. Then she pleaded with me to stop. I couldn't understand why. He deserved all of it and more. I only found out why later. She was terrified I'd go too far and end up getting arrested for murder.'

Alessandro looked at Francesco. It was a look Francesco had seen so often; waiting for criticism, hoping for validation. By now, Francesco had perfected a neutral expression which gave nothing away, but somehow made the other person need to continue.

'He survived it which I realise now was just as well. Mom made us all help with nursing him. I hated that we had to do that, but I knew by then she was doing it to save me. As soon as he was on his feet, he packed up and left. We never saw him again, but we heard he died some years later.'

'How?'

'He was working in construction. There was an accident on the site. I felt guilty for so long afterwards. Not about what happened to him in the end as that had nothing to do with me, or even about hitting him. I'd never been an aggressive kid and I've never hit anyone since, well not outside of a boxing ring. No, I felt guilty because it was like I'd deprived mom of her husband, not that he was much of one, but it wasn't my decision to make.'

'How did your mum cope?'

'As I said, she's a sweetheart, but she's strong too. She'd

stayed home when we were kids. She was very traditional, wanted to be there when we came back from school and make sure we ate huge amounts of food. How Italian is that? After he left, she went straight out and got a job. Never complained, just got on with it. She supported us all, financially and in just about every other way too.

'I guess I decided not to go for my college degree because I wanted to get out there and work to help her out. I did so many horrible jobs and the worst of it is, when you do crappy jobs, often times you get treated like you are crap. I had a job as a cleaner in a school once and, on my break, I was reading a book. One of the teachers came by and asked me what I was reading. When I showed him Ernest Hemingway's "A Farewell to Arms", he looked shocked. Right, so because I'm a cleaner, I'm incapable of reading and appreciating a good book.' He shook his head in disgust.

'People make a lot of assumptions,' said Francesco with feeling and as he did, he realised he had made his own about Alessandro, yet he was complaining about other people. Hypocrisy was another trait he was not pleased to find within himself.

'Way too many. Anyways, it was music that saved me. I ran into an old school friend one day and he invited me over to his folks' place. We must've been about eighteen. I was talking about going to the gym and boxing. He said he couldn't see the attraction of that and said if I wanted to thrash the crap out of something I should try the drums. From the minute I picked up those sticks I was hooked. Something just clicked and made sense. His whole family was cool about it. They let me go and practise just about every day. Meanwhile, I saved liked crazy until I could afford my own kit. Then I started to meet other people involved in music and now, here I am – twenty-four and we could be on the verge of something great. If it all comes good, I'll be able to help my mom out too. Everyone needs to be passionate about something. You need to have a goal otherwise you just drift through life.'

'I think I understand the tattoos now.'

'Oh yeah, I'd forgotten how we got on to this. Justice and the ability to control yourself. Bet you wish you hadn't asked after all that.'

'Not at all and I appreciate you telling me.' There was a silence in which Francesco sensed they could both do with moving on to a lighter topic. 'How did you get your band known? It can't be easy.'

'You'd have to talk to Scott. He's the lead singer, main writer, marketing guru, incredible networker and social media expert all rolled into one.'

'I haven't got a clue when it comes to all that stuff. I haven't got a single social media account,' Francesco admitted feeling as though he were almost confessing to a crime.

'Me neither now. I used to buy into it and I had accounts for all of them and it all made me so damn depressed.'

'I don't get it. I looked at someone's page once and it was all full of pictures of what people were about to eat and boring comments about what they had done or who they had seen that day.'

'I don't know what's worse,' Alessandro said. 'That stuff or the people who make out their life is so great when likely it's really not. When I was into all that stuff, I got duped into believing everyone's life was better than mine and I was a total loser and then I realised it was all BS. I got rid of all of it and it was like I could think clearly again. All the noise stopped, you know what I mean? I also realised how much time I'd been wasting on it. Now I don't go near any of it.'

'I thought I was the only one.'

'No, there are a few of us left.' Alessandro shifted gears. 'Why don't you come along and catch a show?'

'I think I'm too old for all that.'

'You kidding me? What are you? Thirty? Thirty-five? That's not old, but it doesn't matter what age you are. People of all ages go to concerts and festivals. Good music is ageless. And we play very good music.' He grinned and pulled a flyer out of his pocket. 'This is where we're playing.' He turned the flyer over and asked for Francesco's pen. He scribbled his phone number and name on it. 'Phone me and I'll see what I can do about getting you a backstage pass.'

'I'll think about it.' The train slowed, and Francesco saw that they had reached the outskirts of Naples. 'This is your stop,' he said to Alessandro. 'You'll have to change here.'

'Good to meet you man.' He extended his hand to shake Francesco's. 'By the way, you never told me your name.

'Francesco,' he said shaking Alessandro's hand.

'Come see us sometime. Next time you can tell me your life story.' He grinned, turned, picked up a case from the luggage rack and got off the train.

Francesco played his conversation with Alessandro back on the return journey to Rome. He was impressed and depressed in equal measure that someone a decade younger than him seemed to have his life together so much more than he did and it wasn't as if he hadn't had to face any adversity.

He thought about his comment about having a goal. He looked down at his torso; he wasn't fat, but he had definitely let himself go a bit. He remembered how much better he had felt in the days when he had been a regular runner. Maybe he should try to get fit again. That would be a goal, and the idea of taking out all his frustration on a punch bag suddenly sounded appealing. He didn't know where to find a decent gym, though. He decided to look in on Arturo on the way home. He hadn't seen him for a few weeks and felt sure he could put him in touch with one of his many contacts.

Arturo released the door catch, and Francesco puffed his way up the familiar five flights of stairs. The door to the hotel was open, and he found Arturo sitting in the kitchen with his usual cigarette and ristretto, wearing a shirt which was too small so it pulled tight across his midriff straining the buttons to a precarious degree.

'Do you want one?' Arturo said, indicating his cup.

'Too late in the day for me.'

'Suit yourself. There's some water in the fridge.'

Francesco grabbed a bottle and sat down at the table with Arturo. As was so often the case, they said very little to each other, but it was comfortable and Francesco sensed that Arturo was actually quite pleased to see him in his own way.

'How's the job going?' Arturo asked eventually.

'Good, good.'

'And the flat?'

Francesco shrugged, and Arturo grunted in response.

'You?' Francesco asked.

'Much the same.'

'Can you give me any information about gyms?' Francesco asked.

'Do I look like Mr. Universe to you?'

'I was thinking about trying to get a bit fitter. Coming up here half killed me. I'm still getting my breath back.'

'What do you want to know?'

'I want to go to one where normal guys go. Guys like me.'

'You need to speak to Gianni,' Arturo said, in a way which suggested everyone knew who he was. He got up and came back from reception with a scrap of paper with a phone number scribbled on it. 'Tell him you're a fr…, tell him you know Arturo.'

'Thanks. I knew you'd have a contact.'

They sat for a while longer and talked of inconsequential things such as the latest antics of Arturo's guests, all of whom seemed to try what little patience he had, and which routes Francesco had been travelling.

Francesco had no wish to go back to his flat, but he knew he should not put it off any longer as he had an early start the next day and he had to attempt to get some sleep.

'Next time, you come when you can drink ristretto,' was Arturo's parting shot. Francesco smiled to himself at

Arturo's way of extending an invitation.

He was in reasonable spirits as he walked back towards his flat. He liked the idea of having a goal. It had been a blisteringly hot day but there was a slight breeze now, and it was quite pleasant as long as he stayed in the shade. As he approached his flat, he felt his mood change. Despite the fact he had intended to try to get an early night, he wasn't ready for the silence which awaited him. He stopped off at Caffè Lazio and found Matteo polishing glasses.

'Ciao Francesco.'

'Ciao.'

'What can I get you?'

'What do you recommend?'

Matteo checked his watch. 'It's Aperol Spritz time.'

'Is it? I've never tried it.'

Matteo raised an eyebrow, which suggested this was an oversight which might be difficult to forget, put some ice in a glass, mixed the Aperol, Prosecco and soda, added a slice of orange and slid it across the bar.

'Thanks.' Francesco took it outside and settled himself at a table. He watched as the sun sank lower sending long slanting shadows of gold across the piazza. The drink was an orange as deep and intense as the heart of a fire. He sipped it and felt it fizz across his tongue, the taste turning from sweet to bitter, but with flavours he could not identify. As the sun dipped below the buildings, he drained his glass, took it back in and paid Matteo.

He continued on his way feeling momentarily cheered by the diversion from his daily routine. However, the moment he turned the key and opened the door his mood fell again. The silence and emptiness closed in around him once more and he dreaded the long night stretching ahead of him. He had a shower and went to bed but sleep eluded him, and he watched the clock as one hour ticked round to the next.

He tried reading, but it didn't help. He got up and made the herbal tea he had picked up a few days before which was supposed to aid sleep in the hope it might work; it didn't, it just tasted unpleasant. He put it down and then, finally, went out and sat on his balcony as he had done so often that summer. According to the television and newspaper reports and people he had spoken to, this heat was not normal.

He sat out there grateful at least for the fact that it was marginally cooler than inside. Across the road, a light came on; a small sign of life in the depths of night. He wondered about the people who lived in that flat. What were their lives like? At some point he must have drifted off, and he was only awoken by the sound of shutters being rolled up on the shop fronts in the street below. With a start he looked at his watch and swore; he had overslept and would only just make it to work in time to start his shift.

# CHAPTER SEVEN

Francesco sucked the ristretto back through his teeth. It never got any less potent, but as it was always the drink on offer whatever time of day he went to visit Arturo, he was resigned to getting through at least one cup per visit. He had come from a session at the gym and decided that lifting weights followed by half an hour on the treadmill was less challenging than consuming ristretto.

Across the table, Arturo observed him. It had been six months since the cold day in January when he had turned up looking for a room. Francesco had struck him from the outset as a mass of contradictions.

Arturo enjoyed playing a little game of guessing people's nationalities and had become good at it. Sometimes he felt like representatives of half the world had crossed his doorway. He had assumed Francesco was Italian immediately he had set eyes on him until he had spoken, and then he had been unable to decide. His accent was pure Roman, yet he had seemed to struggle to find some of the words he needed. His name was Italian, yet something indefinable about him made him seem like a foreigner. He was an enigma of sorts. Arturo was an expert at playing the unobservant dullard, but could recognise a fellow lost soul when he saw one. He supposed that was why he had taken him under his wing.

In all of their months of acquaintance, he had learned very little about Francesco. He was not one to ask questions and not much had been volunteered. Equally, he had never said much about himself, and he liked the fact that Francesco never pried into his business. Yet, somehow, this had become a friendship of sorts, or the closest Arturo had come to it in a long time.

'Another one?' Arturo asked, nodding at the coffee cup.

'Yes,' said Francesco although he meant no.

Another one duly appeared and Francesco sighed inwardly.

'You can stay for dinner if you want.'

'OK, thanks.'

Arturo got up and went into the kitchen. Francesco could hear him banging about and swearing occasionally which was nothing new.

'Need any help?' asked Francesco.

'No.'

Arturo's endeavours in the kitchen were brought to a halt by the arrival of one of his guests. A slight, young woman knocked on the frame of the open dining room door and Francesco beckoned for her to come in.

'Do you speak English?'

'Yes,' Francesco replied. 'How can I help you?'

'There's a problem with the hair dryer in my room.'

'Hold on.' Francesco went into the kitchen and told Arturo.

'Keep an eye on this,' Arturo said and went to attend to his guest.

'What is the problem?' Arturo said in English. Francesco had never heard him speak English before. Somehow, he sounded even more irascible than when he spoke Italian.

'The hair dryer's not working.'

'Va bene. I'll look at it,' said Arturo reluctantly.

He returned in about ten minutes and resumed his preparations in the kitchen.

'Did you fix it?' Francesco asked.

'It was working,' said Arturo, waving an arm in the direction of the woman's room. 'There was just a flashing red light on the side of the unit. She thought it was a warning light and that meant she couldn't use it.'

'Wasn't it a warning light?'

He shrugged. 'It's either working or it's not working. Anyway, I disconnected the light so now there is no red light and she has nothing to complain about. Guests. Pass me the garlic salt.'

Francesco was about to point out that the problem hadn't actually been fixed when he realised how British that would sound. He wondered if he would ever learn to think like an Italian.

Francesco helped Arturo dish up and take the plates and glasses through to the dining room. They worked their way through fettuccine drenched in a rich cheese sauce and Arturo's version of saltimbocca made with chicken instead of veal. Not much was said during the meal, but Francesco complimented Arturo on his cooking, while privately being amazed that Arturo even had the inclination, much less the ability, to cook so well.

'We all have to eat,' said Arturo dismissing the compliment, 'and if you can't cook, you can't eat.'

'True enough,' he said and made a mental note that he had to start learning to be more pragmatic.

'I'm thinking of entering for the fun run in August,' Francesco remarked as the meal drew to a close.

Arturo raised his eyebrows. 'I didn't know you were a runner.'

'I used to be. I stopped for a while, but I've started again.'

'Can't see the appeal myself. Bad for the joints if you ask me. But good luck anyway.'

'Thanks.'

They cleared the table and Arturo produced a bottle of a dark green liquid which had no label on it and two small shots glasses.

'What's that?' Francesco asked, eyeing it cautiously.

'Centerba, or my father's version of it. I make it according to his recipe. It settles the stomach after a meal. It's not good to finish a meal without a digestive.'

The thought of Arturo having a father, or any family, struck Francesco as strange. He seemed to exist in isolation.

'Where's your father now?'

'Dead,' said Arturo flatly, but Francesco sensed emotion hidden far beneath the harshness of his response.

Francesco watched as Arturo filled both glasses almost to

the rim with the thick potion. He had a feeling this was going to put his experiences with ristretto in the shade. Arturo handed him one of the glasses, took the other and then drank about half of his glass in one go. Francesco cautiously put his mouth to the glass and took a sip. An intense burning sensation hit his throat, his oesophagus and then his stomach in rapid succession. He tried not to cough.

'Knock it back. Don't sip it.'

Francesco wondered whether refusing to drink it would be seen as impolite and came to the reluctant conclusion that it would. He had no wish to offend Arturo so took a deep breath, steeled himself for what was to come and took a large gulp.

After he had recovered and his eyes had stopped watering, he glanced over at Arturo who had apparently not noticed anything amiss. Arturo finished his glass and looked at Francesco, waiting. Francesco realised half the glass was left, braced himself once more and finished it. He set it on the table, waited for the burning to subside and felt relieved that he seemed to have survived the experience.

'Excellent,' said Arturo and refilled their glasses.

The tone for the rest of the evening had been set and as the second glass was emptied and the third poured, the conversation began to flow.

'I inherited this flat from my parents. It's been in my family for generations. I was the one who turned it into a guesthouse, though.'

'Was it difficult to get planning permission?'

Arturo sighed and leant across the table. 'If you're going

to survive here, you must learn to think like an Italian. There's the correct, legal, way to do something, which only leads to never-ending bureaucratic hell, and then there's the right way to achieve something, anything.'

Francesco let that sink in. 'Do you like running this place? Sometimes I think … people annoy you.' The drink had loosened Francesco's inhibitions; he would never have said that if he had been sober.

Fortunately, it also seemed to have mellowed Arturo slightly. 'The problem with people is they talk too much and think too little.' He looked at Francesco. 'Why did you come back?' he asked.

'What?'

'To Rome, I mean.'

'This is where I was born,' Francesco said, aware it was not an answer.

'That's not an answer.'

Francesco shrugged. 'I spent years in England, but I chose to come back.'

Arturo snorted. 'That's not an answer either. Do you regret it?'

Francesco realised that the process of simply keeping going, of getting out of bed and going to work while getting very little sleep was so all-consuming that he had never really considered whether he regretted it or why he was doing it. 'I couldn't stay in England. I needed to come back, or I thought I did, but it isn't how I thought it would be.' He rubbed his forehead. 'Actually, I don't know how I thought it would be. I didn't really think at all. I just … arrived.'

'And?'

'And Rome is beautiful. Most of the people I've encountered are very kind, although dealing with the bureaucracy would have been intolerable without your contacts, the job is fine and the flat, well, it's somewhere to live.' He swallowed some more of Arturo's potion and, emboldened, said, 'I hate the traffic here. Red lights aren't even guidelines and you're not even safe on the pavement. I was minding my own business the other day and a moped came up behind me and started nudging me out of the way. And what's with the rubbish and graffiti all over the place?' he added indignantly.

Arturo nodded in that way Italians did when faced with unfortunate facts they knew they could do nothing about.

'Sorry,' Francesco continued. 'It's not my place to criticise.'

'Why not?'

'I'm not really Italian, am I? Not now anyway.'

'Aren't you? Well, whether you are or not, it makes no difference. Facts are facts. They don't change according to the nationality of the person stating them.'

They both took another gulp of centerba.

'I still don't understand why you came back,' said Arturo 'but it's your business not mine.'

'Everything changed for me in England after …' He felt his jaw muscles tightening and he struggled to get his emotions under control. Finally, he simply said, 'My wife passed away and I couldn't continue with my job.'

Arturo's eyes narrowed, he pressed his lips together and

nodded then pushed the bottle towards Francesco. Somehow that simple series of gestures conveyed more sympathy than most people managed with words.

Francesco poured another glass. 'So I came to find my family.'

Arturo was listening intently, but didn't say a word. Francesco realised that Arturo was doing exactly what he did when he met someone with a story to tell on the train.

'I couldn't find them. They've moved on.' He finished the shot. 'I never completely felt I belonged in England despite all the years I lived there and now I'm not sure I fit in here either.'

'What's so important about belonging somewhere?'

The alcohol had dulled Francesco's thought processes and he struggled to answer. 'Everybody belongs somewhere, don't they?'

'No. I don't.'

'But you do. You're Italian, Roman, through and through.'

'You think because I was born here and I've always lived here, that because I don't sometimes struggle to find the words I need, that I automatically fit in?'

Francesco was momentarily distracted. 'My Italian is much better now,' he said defensively.

'I'll give you that,' Arturo conceded.

'But getting back to belonging. You have a home, a business, a list of contacts as long as your arm.'

'None of that makes a person fit in. Belonging somewhere is a state of mind. Even though you said you didn't belong in England, I don't suppose that was uppermost in your thoughts when your wife was alive.'

The words were not spoken unkindly, but they hurt nonetheless. Even so, Francesco recognised the truth in them. Lauren had been his anchor, his home and he was lost and rootless without her. If he could only have found Teddy and his father, it might have helped a little. Then again, they might have rejected him as his mother had always suggested they would, and that would have been too much to bear on top of losing Lauren and their child. He pondered that while Arturo went to find another bottle and another round of shots followed in silence.

'She jumped.'

'What?' Francesco asked, utterly confused.

'That's why I had to stop driving the trains. She jumped right in front of me.'

'Bloody hell,' he said reverting to English, suddenly unable to find the words he wanted in Italian.

'I couldn't go back after that. I tried but ... I hated her. I hated her for years. Everyone felt so sorry for her, but she took away the one thing I loved doing.'

Francesco could not think of a single suitable response.

'So I ended up with this place and I suffer idiots who complain because their pillow is lumpy or their towel isn't soft enough or the hair dryer is on the blink. See what I saw that day and then tell me any of that's worth complaining about.' Arturo's tone expressed a pain that had never healed.

'I can't even imagine.' Francesco shook his head and then realised that had been an unwise move. It exacerbated the effects of the centerba.

'I always used to say that we Romans live among the ruins of other people' lives … and their deaths. In the shadows of their memories. That it shapes our character. I thought that was quite clever.' He laughed bitterly. 'I had no idea how true that would become for me.'

Under any other circumstances, Francesco thought that he might have commented on the poetic nature of his words. He had learned more about Arturo that evening than in all of the months they had known each other, but he decided to keep his thoughts to himself and they finished their drinks without another word.

'I think I've had enough,' said Arturo abruptly. 'You can stay here tonight if you want. Your old room is free.'

Francesco gratefully accepted the offer. He stood up slowly, and the room spun around him. Making it back to the flat and the emptiness that awaited him there would have been too much that night. He took the key from Arturo, stumbled to the room and collapsed on the bed.

He tried to remember how he had felt when he had first spent a night in this room. So much had happened since then, yet he was no further forward. Would he ever find peace? Had Arturo? Or had he simply accepted his fate? Would he ever feel that sense of belonging he needed or would it always elude him or, as Arturo had suggested, was it simply not important? His alcohol-soaked brain could not think any of the questions through. He gave up trying to make sense of any of it and fell asleep, fully-clothed.

He woke the next morning with a monstrous hangover. As the morning sunshine slipped across the bed inching ever closer to his aching eyes, he slowly started to come round and remembered that he had told Arturo about Lauren and giving up his job. He had told him about trying to find his family as well. He had not gone into any details, but it had been the first time he had told anybody anything about his past. It had not been as bad as he had feared although the centerba might have had something to with that. But even so, he had done it and it seemed important to him for some reason he could not quite identify.

He made his way slowly into the dining room where Arturo was making ristretto.

'Coffee?'

'Yes,' Francesco replied weakly.

They sat and drank ristretto together. The atmosphere between them was companionable although very little was said, which was the way they preferred it. There was an understanding that confidences had been shared which would never be spoken of again, and both of them were perfectly content with that.

# CHAPTER EIGHT

Francesco checked his watch. He had enough time for another coffee before he started work so he took the exit from the underground at Termini which brought him out into the square rather than the station. In the short time it had taken to get from San Giovanni to Termini on the underground, the sun's strength seemed to have intensified even further. It was one of those days, of which there had been so many recently, when the sun seems to scald the skin and the glare reflecting off of buildings and cars made sunglasses indispensable.

On the underground, he had picked up a discarded newspaper and had been reading about the fires raging across the countryside. It seemed a summer without an end in sight, a summer which had become one to be endured rather than enjoyed. He drank an overpriced coffee and made a mental note to avoid eating and drinking in a place where so many tourists gathered as it meant the prices were far above what he normally paid. Then he walked across the square and through the doors of Termini and felt a slight respite from the heat which was boiling the tarmac outside. He reluctantly put on his jacket and cap. It was time to start work.

*     *     *

Francesco entered the carriage and requested tickets in both Italian and English. He had taken to doing that to save people from asking him if he spoke English. There were not many people: an older Italian couple arguing over their son's choice of wife; a business man dressed in clothes Francesco knew must have cost a small fortune and a young woman at the far end of the carriage, listening to music.

He managed to interrupt the argument and get the business man to look up from his laptop for long enough to check their tickets and then he stopped at the final passenger. Her eyes were closed so he tapped her gently on the shoulder. She jumped and opened her eyes, looking momentarily startled. Then she saw him and took her headphones off.

'I'm sorry. Just a moment,' she said in an attempt at Italian which was not bad, but betrayed the fact that English was her first language.

She started rummaging through her bag, getting ever more anxious as each piece of paper she pulled out failed to uncover her ticket. 'I know it's here,' she said, still using Italian. Paper was now flying all over the seats.

'May I help you?' asked Francesco, using English

'What? Oh no, I know it's here somewhere.' She had switched to English without even noticing and was getting visibly upset now. 'Where is it? It's got to be here. I had it earlier.'

'Here,' said Francesco, sitting down. 'Sometimes, you just need a fresh pair of eyes.'

He started picking up the papers and stacking then together. The woman did not resist, occupied with emptying what remained of the contents of her bag. Francesco started glancing through the papers, noticing a family tree which extended back through time on her mother's side, but was curiously truncated on her father's; copies of birth and marriage certificates and some old letters and photos before locating the ticket. Not the usual things tourists carried with them.

'Got it,' he said.

'Just as well. I don't have enough money to pay a big fine.'

'Well, you don't have to worry now.' He handed back all the papers. 'It looks like you're working on an interesting project there.' He shrugged. 'Sorry, I couldn't help but notice the family tree.'

'That's OK. Yes, I got into genealogy a while back. I thought it would be interesting and fun. It's certainly been interesting. Enlightening, even. I'm not so sure about the fun part.'

'I suppose you have to accept you never know what you'll find if you're going to do that. I've seen some of those TV programmes where well-known people trace their family tree and find out things they wish they'd never known.'

'Yeah, I can see where they're coming from. Even being a celebrity doesn't protect you from certain things.' She looked at him as if deciding whether to continue, a look

Francesco knew only too well. He waited and the train confessional worked its magic.

'When I was doing my research, I found that my mother and father had married after I was born. Not such a big deal but they had lied to me about it. Not just by admission either. I mean they actually lied. We all helped them celebrate their twenty-fourth wedding anniversary earlier this year but it wasn't, it was their twenty-third.'

'Maybe they thought you'd be upset, but it's not a big thing for a lot of people these days. Being born before your parents marry, I mean.'

'No, the fact they lied would have been a bit strange but not much more. Perhaps, as you say, they did it to save my feelings and I could – should - have left it at that, but you know when you get a gut feeling something's not right? You just sense that you haven't got the full story?'

Francesco was immediately transported back to the moment the police had told him about the hotel room that Lauren had booked. What the hell had she been doing there? He pushed it away and nodded. 'Yes, I know that feeling.'

'You have two choices, don't you? Try to bury it and hope you've buried it so deep that it doesn't come back to eat away at you, or face it, whatever the cost. I decided on the latter. I found some old photos and letters. You know back when people actually wrote to each other. They were love letters between my mother and another man. They were dated between 1994 and 1996. I was born in September 1996.'

She hesitated. 'Look.' She pulled two photos out of a

plastic wallet brimming with papers and gave them to him. 'What strikes you about those photos?'

Francesco saw it straight away but said nothing, unsure what would be appropriate.

'It's OK, you can say it.'

'He looks like you,' Francesco said.

'I think he's my father, my biological father, I mean.'

'And look at this one. This is me with my mum and "dad" and two younger sisters. What do you make of that?'

Francesco barely knew her, but realised how much she needed honesty and to deny what he saw would have been an obvious and outright lie.

'Your sisters look similar to each other and very much like a mix of your mum and dad.'

'And I look nothing like my sisters or my "dad" although I suppose we've all got my mum's eyes,' she said, examining the photo again and frowning.

'Didn't you ask your mother about this?'

'And say what? Mum, I know you've been lying to me about how long you've been married, and then I just got this feeling something was up so I started snooping through your personal things and found all these letters and photos and the upshot is I don't think the man I've been calling dad my whole life is really my dad.'

'I see what you mean.'

'I couldn't say anything to her, but I need to know. I thought if I could find him, I could try to get to the truth that way. I might be on a fool's errand, but I have to try. That's why I've been learning Italian.'

'But what would you do - even if you tracked him down - and he refused to talk about it?'

'I haven't got that far yet, but as I said, I have to try. I have to know I've tried, that I've faced up to this and not just pretended none of this exists.'

'And if he says you're his daughter, what happens then? What if …'

'What if he rejects me? Or doesn't? They both open up a whole new set of questions but, I think it's always better to know the truth. It's the not knowing that's worse, isn't it? Not knowing the truth; not knowing what to do. At least I've decided what to do. Whether or not I find out the truth is another thing.'

Francesco's thoughts drifted back to the enduring mystery at the heart of his loss. The constant wondering that made it even harder than it would otherwise have been to find a path back to anything resembling what he would consider to be a normal life.

He thought about his visit to the hotel shortly after the police had notified him that Lauren had booked into a room she had never had the chance to stay in. He had spoken to the receptionist who had checked her in. Yes, she had said, she remembered her. He had made it appear that he was there purely to settle the unpaid bill, which had softened her up considerably. He had turned as if to leave and then had said as casually as he could possibly manage, 'By the way, do you happen to remember what time she checked in?'

'I can't remember exactly. I was doing a split shift. I think it was the afternoon.' She paused, checking her memory.

'Yes, that's right. I hadn't long come from the pub down the road, you see. Not that I'd been drinking of course, but I remember that day because I'd had the chef's special, and I felt terrible when I got back. I was fine in the morning. I should have known better. How that lad Jamie ever got a job as a chef is beyond me. I haven't been able to face an onion since. Sorry, what was the question?'

'I was just wondering what time she had checked in.'

'Oh yes. I'd say it was early afternoon.'

'How did she seem?'

'I'm sorry, I don't follow.'

'I mean did she seem worried? Happy? Excited?'

'Well, I don't know.' She considered the question. 'Not worried exactly but preoccupied, I suppose. Yes, preoccupied.'

Francesco tried to prepare himself for the answer which might come next. 'Was she on her own when she arrived?'

'Oh, yes.'

'Did anybody come to meet her?'

'Not that I noticed, and we do have rules about visitors. For starters, they have to sign in. It's the fire regulations, you see. And no unregistered overnight guests. I do try to make sure that the rules are abided by, but that day ...' Her face clouded with doubt.

'Yes?' Francesco prompted her.

'I don't want to get into trouble.'

'I won't repeat anything you tell me.'

'It's like I said, I was so sick. I had to keep running to the bathroom so I suppose someone could have come in without me seeing them. I did see her leave, though. I was here when she came back into reception. She was on the phone.'

'Do you have any idea who she was talking to?'

'No, sorry.'

'What was she talking about?'

'I couldn't tell you.' She saw the look of confusion and frustration on Francesco's face. 'It was all in a foreign language.'

'Which language?'

'I've got no idea. I don't know my Albanian from my elbow, but …' she stopped, trying to remember. 'I did catch the word "si". The Spanish say that, don't they?'

'And the Italians.' Francesco said to himself, remembering how he had taught Lauren the language.

'I don't know about that, but I do know one thing. You asked me how she seemed. Well, after that phone call, she seemed anxious. She went dashing out, fast as you like. I never saw her again, and she never paid her bill.' She sniffed.

Francesco reminded himself he had not told her he was Lauren's husband or what had happened to her. 'Well, I've paid you now.'

'Yes, and much appreciated, but what's all this about anyway?'

'I really have no idea.'

As Francesco turned to go, the woman called him back. 'There is one other thing.'

'Yes?'

'She didn't have any luggage with her. I noticed that because we girls always need to cart so much stuff about with us. I didn't mention it of course. Not my place.'

The woman seemed keen to chat further, bored on a slow afternoon shift, but Francesco was in no mood to talk further. He had mumbled an excuse about a meeting he had to get to, thanked her and left. He still had no idea why Lauren had been there, only that she had been alone when she arrived, but where did that leave him? And what was the phone call about? He left with more questions than he had arrived with.

He had gone home and forced himself to start to go through Lauren's possessions; all the inconsequential clutter people collect throughout life and value so much. He had been convinced he would find something which would answer his questions, but there seemed to be nothing and the task was so painful that he had given up before he finished.

'Hello? Penny for them?'

He awoke from his recollections to see the woman smiling at him. 'You were miles away.'

'Sorry, I suppose I was. Where were we?'

'Discovering the truth.'

'Oh yes, that. The truth.' Francesco reflected that the truth seemed an elusive concept, determined to keep itself hidden. He made an effort to pull himself away from the past which so often tried to lure him back into its quicksand. 'What's the plan then?'

'I have an address, and I hope that he still lives there or at least that somebody there will know him. I heard that the Italians don't like to sell their houses; that they prefer to pass them down to others in their family so I'm holding on to that.'

Francesco remembered how his own search for family had worked out but decided against dashing her hopes.

'I truly hope it works out for you and that you find your answers.'

On the way home, Francesco thought again about his attempt to discover the truth about Lauren's last days. Had he tried hard enough? And what if he had been able to do more and he had uncovered something he would have preferred not to know? Would that have been better?

On autopilot, he stopped at the corner shop to buy a sandwich and the sad-looking specimens with curled up corners left on display at that time of the day were enough to make him leave empty-handed. That reminded him he had to try to improve his diet if he was going to run in the race the following month. He carried on walking and just before the turning for his block of flats, he stopped to look again at the display in the delicatessen. The name, Il Buongustaio, curved across the glass panels above the door in an elegant script and the food on offer spilled out onto the pavement. Francesco had stopped there to admire it a number of times, always struck by the painstaking effort that the owners must put into displaying everything in such an exquisite layout every day. It was a work of art.

They seemed to have every type of risotto, polenta and pasta; different types of salt; neatly packaged combinations of herbs; dried tomatoes and mushrooms and a variety of liqueurs. Peering inside, he saw meats and cheeses and packets and jars containing things he would have been unable to name.

He was no cook and had never taken much of an interest in food but, on the few occasions he had eaten at a restaurant since his return, he had started to appreciate the quality of Italian food and was impressed to find that even the simplest of ingredients could be converted into something delicious. He suspected there was some trick to that to which he was not privy. He was tired of bolting down toast or a sandwich on the run or heating up some unappetising pre-cooked meal in the microwave. Apart from wanting to finish the race the following month, he had been admonished at the gym for his poor diet. He looked inside again. It was an unknown world to him. What on earth would he buy and what would he do with it once he got it back to the flat?

He was about to move on when a man came out of the shop. 'Can I help you?'

'I was just admiring your display,' he said, for want of anything better to say.

'Perhaps you would like to buy something?'

'I'm not much of a cook.'

'No problem. Come in.'

Francesco followed him inside, wondering what he had got himself into.

'This is my wife, Anna. The best cook in Rome and the best teacher. She even taught me to cook.' The man put his fingers together, raised them to his mouth and kissed them in appreciation of her skills.

'I have no idea about cooking.'

Anna tutted in a motherly away and gave him an appraising look as if to decide what he might be capable of managing. She started bustling about the shop, picking up things here and there and putting them in a large paper carrier bag. 'Do you have olive oil and balsamic vinegar?'

'No,' he said sheepishly, feeling like an errant schoolboy as she gave him a disapproving look.

She added the oil and vinegar to the bag and, setting the bag to one side, found a paper and pencil and started writing down instructions. She handed the bag and the recipe to Francesco. 'That's your first cooking lesson. The food costs eighteen euros, the recipe is free.' Her eyes twinkled. 'Come back when you are ready for lesson two.'

'Thank you,' Francesco said genuinely touched. He handed over the money and went home. As always, he felt the emptiness closing in around him as he opened the door, but he had an objective that evening and he was determined the darkness would not claim him, not that night. In the kitchen, he unwrapped all the goods and painstakingly followed the recipe he had been given. After a few stressful episodes, he emerged from the kitchen with Anna's angel hair pasta with tomatoes and peppers.

He was about to put the television on and sit on the sofa with his dinner, but stopped himself and went to sit at the dining table, putting the radio on instead. He could not bring himself to sit in total silence, but he wanted to try to appreciate the food he had spent so much time preparing.

He tried a tentative mouthful and was surprised. It wasn't quite restaurant quality, but it was the by far best thing he had ever produced by himself. He ate the rest of it feeling absurdly pleased with himself. And then it struck him how greatly he had reduced his expectations in life. Cooking a meal; training to compete in a race; making it to work every day. These were his achievements now. How things had changed from the days when he had been a respected doctor with a wife he adored and a child on the way.

# CHAPTER NINE

Francesco surveyed the wreck which was his flat and reluctantly decided he should make an attempt to tidy the place up. He started sorting out the endless bits of paper he seemed to accumulate so effortlessly. As he went through the drawers in the hallway cabinet, he came across a crumpled piece of paper. Smoothing it out, he realised it was the flyer Alessandro had given him back in June with his contact number and the dates of his European concerts. Francesco went to throw it away and then hesitated. He realised he had forgotten all about getting in touch with him. It was probably too late now and, besides, people, always suggested getting in touch when they didn't really mean it. It was just the polite thing to say. But Alessandro had had no need to give him his contact details. Perhaps he should contact him.

He took the flyer and scanned the list noticing all the dates he had already missed. Most of the remaining concerts would probably be impractical for him to get to, but then one caught his eye; the Waldsee Metal Meet in Germany from Friday 23rd to Sunday 25th August. He had already booked the time off as he was running on the 23rd and he had planned to recover over the weekend.

He opened his laptop for the first time in weeks and looked at flights. He could fly early on the Saturday and return early on Monday, well in time for his afternoon shift. He looked at hotels and then made the call.

'Hi. Alessandro?'

'Yeah. Who's that?'

'It's Francesco. We met back in June on the train when you were on your way to see your sister in Salerno.'

'Sure I remember. How are you doing?'

Francesco followed convention and stuck with a bland 'Well. How about you?'

'Better at the moment. I just spent two nights in a hotel. Four showers and now all my clothes are clean.'

'Sounds good.'

'Yes, but now we're back in the van.'

'How's the tour going?

'Really well. Apart from the van. Are you coming to see us?'

'Yes, I was thinking of coming to the Waldsee Metal Meet.'

'Cool'

'I can't get there until Saturday morning, though.'

'We're playing on Saturday evening so it's perfect timing. You got a place to stay? If not, you can crash in the van.'

'Yes, no disrespect, but you haven't really sold me on that idea.'

Alessandro laughed. 'I don't blame you. Where are you going to stay?'

'There's a small guesthouse by the station. I'll book in there.'

'OK, call when you've checked in and I'll come pick you up.'

'Cheers, bye'

Francesco put the phone down and wondered what he had just done. He was pretty sure he'd be the oldest person there by at least a decade, but it was done now. He booked the flights and guesthouse and looked at how to get from the airport to Waldsee. By the time he looked up from the laptop, he realised it was time to get ready for work. He looked at the mess and dust around him and sighed. It would have to wait for another day.

*    *    *

Francesco opened the compartment door and managed to edge far enough in to lean over a pile of suitcases and several boxes to retrieve the woman's ticket.

'You've got a lot of cases there. Would you like me to put some of them up on the luggage rack for you?'

'No, I'd rather you didn't. I've booked this whole compartment so I can keep everything with me and I'd never be able to get any of those cases down again on my own. They're all extremely heavy.' Her words were polite, but her tone was sharp.

'You don't believe in travelling light then?' Francesco said with a smile, hoping to disarm her.

'I'm moving house. Well, coming home actually. At least I suppose it's home. It doesn't feel that way at the moment.'

Francesco felt his interest piqued. He thought of the other passengers whose tickets he should be checking and hovered in the doorway for a moment, torn between work and the desire to talk to this woman. There were only a few compartments left; he had been down nearly all of the train. He would probably still have time to check the rest of the tickets even if he stopped to talk to her. On the other hand, he had come across a few colleagues who had admitted to sleeping through a number of journeys and not checking any tickets at all so he wasn't even sure it would matter if he didn't make it to the end.

The woman had returned to her book and then, realising he was still standing there, looked up. 'Is there a problem with my cases?'

'No, not at all. You've booked the seats and you're entitled to use them although you might have difficulty explaining that to any passengers who are hunting for a seat. I was just wondering how you got all these cases on in the first place and, more to the point, how you're going to manage to get everything off at the other end. Wouldn't it have been easier to fly?'

'I flew as far as Geneva. I needed to stop off there to collect some more of my things which were in storage. Then I had this mad idea that travelling the rest of the way by train might be fun. Or maybe I was just trying to put off getting here for as long as possible. It wasn't too bad in Geneva. Changing trains in Milan was awful, but it was a bit late by then. At least my brother is meeting me on the platform in Rome.'

'I'll try to come by and give you a hand too.'

The woman's tone mellowed. 'That's kind of you.'

'Where are you moving from?'

'England. London.'

'So you speak English?' Francesco said reverting to that language.

'Yes,' she said looking surprised and pleased in equal measure. 'In fact sometimes I find it easier to speak English now. Not that I would ever tell my family that.'

'I had that problem when I first came back to Italy, but you'll be surprised how quickly it comes back. How long have you been away?'

'Twelve years. Twelve long, hard years.' She sighed. 'How about you?'

'A lot longer than that. I left when I was a child.' Francesco was, as ever, keen to steer the conversation away from himself and kept talking. 'Are you glad to have left?'

'I don't know. I worked so hard when I was there and I reaped the rewards. Well, the material ones anyway. I had all the trappings – a smart flat in London, a new car, a wardrobe full of designer clothes. If I wanted anything I could pretty much buy it.'

'It doesn't sound like a bad life.'

'No, it doesn't, does it? But what was it all for?' She suddenly changed track, throwing him for a moment. 'Why don't you sit down?'

Francesco managed to step across the mass of baggage and squeeze into the seat by the window opposite her, his legs angled to one side. It was uncomfortable, but better than standing in the doorway. The door had closed behind them, sealing them off from the rest of the train.

'I realise now I was a slave to my job. I thought, in as much as I thought at all, that I was incredibly successful, but all I was doing was making rich people richer and acquiring "stuff". That doesn't seem very rewarding in retrospect. I suppose it's only when you step away from something that you see a situation for what it really is.'

'A lot of people never get the chance to step away and examine their situation. Most stay on that treadmill their whole life. At least you've escaped.'

'Yes, but it cost me so much on the way. I lost the love of my life because I was hardly ever there and even when I was there physically, I wasn't mentally or emotionally. I was always planning the next big deal. I convinced myself I was doing it for us, for our future but I wasn't. I didn't realise that until the day he told me he was leaving. Even after that, I just kept going.' She pressed her lips together. 'I'm really sorry. I don't know why I'm telling you all this.'

'I don't mind. I've been told I'm a good listener.' Francesco smiled and shrugged diffidently. 'My name is Francesco.' He offered his hand.

The woman looked at it hesitantly and then offered her own. 'Ellie.' She leaned across and said, 'Actually it's Eleonora, but I could never stand that name. When I moved to England, I started using Ellie straight away.'

'I won't tell your brother if I meet him at the station,' Francesco assured her with a smile.

'Thanks. That'll be the first battle, I suppose; to get my

family to call me Ellie. You know, I'm relieved I got away from that job, but leaving England, coming back here, particularly coming back here, I don't know how I feel about that. It took me so long to feel anywhere close to settled in London and now I've got to start all over again in a small town. I guess I'm destined always to be the outsider. Then there's moving back in with my family. For the time being at least until I get myself sorted out. I left home at eighteen to go to London so that's going to be difficult. And I've no idea what I'm going to do. I mean, I've still got to earn money, right?'

'What made you finally decide to give it all up and come back then?'

'My dad got ill about a year ago. I kept promising to come over and see him, but I never made it. There was always just one more deal to do and one more meeting to attend. I never got to say goodbye to him. I'll never forgive myself for that. When I arrived for the funeral back in May, I finally realised how much I'd hurt everyone from my boyfriend to my family, and I decided then that I wanted to do better for my mum.'

'I'm sure she appreciates the fact that you're coming back.'

'Oh, yes, she's already said how happy she is that I'm coming home. She doesn't realise it's not home for me, not yet anyway. I couldn't tell her that, of course. It would upset her so much.'

'Where does she live?'

'A very small village near Sulmona. Well, it's more of a

couple of streets with one tiny shop and an even smaller bar clinging to a hillside. I think the most exciting thing that ever happens there is the occasional wild boar wandering into the village.' She managed a smile, but it was a half-hearted one.

'Sulmona is up in the mountains, isn't it?'

'Yes, a world away from London and at times it feels a world away from everywhere. It's the sort of place where everyone knows everyone and everyone's business.'

'I can imagine that could be difficult to adjust to after living in London.'

'I'm dreading it. Don't get me wrong. They're good people. Strong, warm and kind, but there's no privacy. Everyone has an opinion about everything you do, who you date, what you wear and they're not shy about sharing it. I felt like that even before I went away. In fact, that's part of the reason I left in the first place. I have a real love-hate relationship with the place. In some ways, it's a magical place encircled by mountains which seem to touch the sky and populated by wolves, eagles and bears. It can seem like it's a long way from the rest of the world, which can be a good or bad thing, depending on how you are feeling. In summer or on a sunny day in winter after a fresh snowfall, it can be stunningly beautiful, but when it's cold and wet, it's like the mountains and sky have merged into one and you feel like you're walled off from the rest of the world. It just makes me feel claustrophobic. And then there are the blizzards.' She shuddered.

'Perhaps you could live in Sulmona. You'd be close to

your mum, but you'd be in a place with more going on. You don't necessarily have to live with her, do you?'

'Perhaps, but I'll have to move in with her until I get myself sorted out.'

'It'll take time to readjust. When I first came back, I thought I'd never feel settled here.'

'But you do now?' She looked at him hopefully.

'Let's just say it's a work in progress.' He saw her forming a question and realised he was in danger of having to answer rather than ask one. Before she could say anything, he stood up. 'I had better get on, but I won't forget about helping you out in Rome.'

A look of disappointment flashed across her face, but it was gone so fast that Francesco thought afterwards that he might simply have imagined it. 'I'd appreciate that,' she said in a tone of voice that was unreadable.

When the train drew into Rome's Termini station, Francesco went back and started helping Ellie to unload all of her belongings. As they got to the last case, she said, 'I don't understand why Michele's not here. I'm so grateful I've got you to help me.' Her hand brushed against his and their eyes met.

Francesco felt like he was seeing her properly for the first time. She had put her shoulder-length auburn hair up in to a messy topknot while they were moving cases and it accentuated the shape of her face. Her eyes were a warm shade of blue and her skin was pale, clearly having been deprived of sun for a long time. She was not what he would have described as his type, but he suddenly realised how pretty she was.

Her phone rang and the moment vanished. She answered, and he heard her asking questions in Italian in rapid and increasingly frustrated succession. She ended the call, and looked at Francesco in disbelief. 'He got the dates mixed up. He's just realised, and he says won't be able to get here until tomorrow now.' She looked round helplessly at all her bags and cases.

He looked at all her possessions. 'Wait here.'

He returned with a luggage trolley and Ellie's eyes lit up. 'I've never seen one of those at an Italian railway station before.'

'And you probably won't see one again.'

Ellie looked at him, waiting for an explanation.

'I found it abandoned here one day and thought it might be useful so I found a place to store it. Just as well.'

They loaded the trolley up and Francesco considered calling Arturo to ask him if he had a room free, but the thought of trying to drag all of Ellie's possessions up five flights of stairs did not appeal. He fleetingly considered inviting her to stay with him but, remembering his earlier abandoned attempt at tidying and cleaning the flat, he quickly wrote that off as a bad idea. She would probably have felt uncomfortable with that anyway. He was no more than a random stranger to her.

He looked at Ellie and found her studying her phone, looking at a map of Rome. He studied her delicate profile, illuminated in the artificial glow coming from the screen. 'Look at this,' she said and he hoped she hadn't noticed that he had been staring. She passed the phone to him. 'This hotel is just round the corner.'

Before Francesco could reply, Ellie had tapped the screen and was phoning the hotel.

Ellie finished the call. 'OK, the room's booked. Could help me get over there? I wouldn't ask but with all this stuff…'

'No problem.'

As they left Termini, the heat of the Roman night wrapped itself tightly around them. 'I'd forgotten how good these warm summer nights feel,' said Ellie looking around in wonderment.

'Be grateful you weren't here a few weeks ago. The heat then was unreal. It's still too hot now.'

'Still, better than what passes for a British summer most of the time.'

'A happy medium would be nice,' Francesco remarked.

They stopped to rearrange the luggage on the trolley and noticed a crowd watching some sort of performance.

'What's going on?' Ellie asked, unable to see over the crowd.

'It's a couple dancing the tango. Of course. It's the Gran Ballo di Ferragosto," Francesco said, referring to Rome's huge city party which took place on the 15th of August. He had forgotten all about it until that moment.

'I've heard of that, but I've never been to it.'

'Neither have I.'

'Do you want to go?'

'Sorry?' Francesco said, taken by surprise.

'Do you want to go? I'm too het up to sleep now and,

frankly, I could do with having some fun.'

'OK. Why not?'

Ellie checked in and they managed to get all of her belongings up to her room, Francesco silently thankful that not only was there was a lift, but that it was a modern one which could accommodate more than one person and one case at a time.

'Thank you so much,' Ellie said, surveying the bags stacked up along the wall in the entrance to the room. She selected a case from the top of the pile, unzipped it, took out a dress and grabbed her handbag. 'I'll just go and change,' she said, heading for the bathroom.

And with that she was gone and the door clicked shut behind her, leaving Francesco to wonder what she had in mind. Was he just along for the ride or was he expected to entertain her? Chaperone her? Was she expecting more than that? He was not ready for a date with anyone, and he suddenly had an uneasy feeling that their expectations for the evening ahead might be different.

# CHAPTER TEN

Francesco took off his jacket, hat and tie, which he had been longing to do ever since he had got off the train. Only the fact he had had no wish to add them to the pile of things to carry had stopped him. He removed the lanyard from around his neck which was attached to his identification badge, placed it in top of his jacket and ran his hands through his hair, trying to make himself look vaguely presentable. He felt hot and sweaty and wished he could have a shower, but then realised that as soon as they stepped outside, he would feel just as hot and uncomfortable as he did at that moment. He switched on the air-conditioning, paced up and down for a while and then went to look out of the window.

Ellie looked at herself in the bathroom mirror. *What the hell are you doing?'* she demanded of the person staring back at her. She had confided things in a total stranger that she had not told, and would not tell, friends or family although perhaps it was sometimes easier to talk to a stranger; someone whose judgement, however harsh, would not be able to hurt you in the same way as those close to you could. But Francesco had not judged her at all, and that had touched her.

Then she had brought this stranger up to her room and suggested they go out together. *This is not you. This is not what you do,* she said to her reflection. Francesco was undoubtedly very attractive, but he also exuded kindness and warmth and those things had been in short supply in the cutthroat environment in which she had competed for so long. Beyond that, she felt a sadness and an emptiness in him, which had resonated with the emotions she recognised in herself as well. She had felt like that since, when was it? When Ian had walked out? When she had heard her dad her died? A long time in any case. *Pull yourself together. Put on your game face,* she told herself and remembered all those time she had had to chair meetings or give presentations and had had to appear far more confident than she felt.

Francesco was still observing the comings and goings in the wide sweep of the Piazza dei Cinquecento. It was really not much more than a glorified bus station, but good for people watching. Ellie emerged from the bathroom with her hair down and wearing a dark green off-the-shoulder dress. Francesco silently thought how pretty she was again and felt even more acutely aware of the fact that he had not had a chance to shower and change.

'Right, shall we go?' she said brightly while feeling disappointed that he had not said anything complimentary about her appearance. *Don't be ridiculous,* she said to herself. *What do you expect?*

'I suppose so, but I don't know where we're going.'

They returned the luggage trolley to its hiding place and then drifted through the city, carried along on a wave of crowds until they found themselves in Piazza della Madonna dei Monti. The square and the area around it was one Francesco had discovered some months earlier, and it had become one of his favourite parts of the city.

Rome was so often associated with frenetic activity, crazy traffic and hordes of tourists vying to tick off all the must-see attractions, but here, particularly early in the morning, in those winding cobbled lanes lined with houses in shades of coffee, cinnamon, gold and burnt red and in the small squares, the chaos seemed a long way away.

That night, though, the square was packed with people enjoying the carnival atmosphere of Ferragosto. The shutters of the windows throughout the old town had been flung open as if helping the city to breathe.

'Wait here and I'll get us some drinks,' Francesco said. 'What would you like?'

'A beer, please. As cold as possible.' Ellie wasn't much of a drinker, but tonight she felt different. She had thrown off the shackles of her old life and those of her new one had yet to be imposed. It was a brief and unexpected interlude of freedom and she intended to relish it.

Francesco manoeuvered through the crowds, moving more slowly on the way back once he had their drinks in his hands. They perched on the steps of the fountain and Ellie sipped her drink. At that moment, in that fragment of time, the weight of everything which had been bearing down on her – moving back in with her mother, caring for her, looking for a job, living in a small village - seemed so far away as to be almost unreal. It was an unexpected gift, and she wanted to cherish every brief moment. 'I think I'll just stay here forever,' she said dreamily.

Francesco looked at her again, and she smiled at him. The fairy lights garlanding the nearby café reflected in her eyes which seemed to shift from blue to green to an even deeper shade of blue.

'Let's join in,' she said, indicating a group of people dancing in the crowd.

They put their drinks down where they had been sitting, and she led the way. Francesco remembered another time when a woman had persuaded him to dance. Another life; the life before. He remembered the touch of Lauren's hand, how he had been unable to take his eyes off of her.

'Hey, are you OK?' Ellie asked, looking at him curiously.

'Yes, just a little tired I suppose.' Francesco made a monumental effort not to think about Lauren. And hated the fact he was trying not to think about her.

They alternated dancing with a couple more drinks, and Francesco started to find it easier to shut out the past. 'I haven't had this much fun in ages,' she shouted over the music as they stopped for another drink in their position on the steps of the fountain and watched the crowds.

'Me neither,' he admitted.

'Come on,' said Ellie, playfully taking his hand and attempting to drag him back to his feet. As he stood up, the music changed from pop to salsa. The physical contact and the rhythm of the salsa were too much for Francesco, and he was immediately transported back to his first meeting with Lauren. He was revolted by himself; having fun, dancing and drinking with another woman less than a year after Lauren's death.

'I can't,' he said pulling his hand away.

'Yes, you can,' she said misreading the situation. 'I'll show you the steps. They're easy.'

'I know they are, but I can't. Stop it.' He snapped at her, and his anger shocked him. He turned, walked back to the fountain, sat down and downed the rest of his drink.

Ellie stood where he had left her. She stared at him, catching glimpses of him through the ever-moving crowd, looking as shocked as he felt. Slowly, warily, she moved towards him.

The anger, which had been entirely directed at his own behaviour, subsided as he saw the effect he had had on her. He felt terrible. 'I'm sorry.'

I don't know what I did to upset you,' she said.

'I can't … it doesn't matter.'

'Perhaps we should go.'

'No, look, you were enjoying yourself. I don't want to spoil your evening. You carry on. Have some fun.'

'No, I think I'd like to go back to the hotel. It's been a long day, and it's starting to catch up with me.'

'I'll walk you back.'

'You really don't have to.'

'I'm going to walk you back. No arguments. Besides I've left half of my uniform in your room,' he said in a weak attempt to lighten the mood.

They walked back towards the hotel, occasionally jostled by over-enthusiastic revellers, but the party mood had deserted them, and they barely exchanged a word until they reached her room. Francesco followed her into the room and retrieved his jacket, tie, cap and ID. He put his jacket and tie over his arm, looped the lanyard around his neck and twisted the cap awkwardly in his hands. He took a few steps towards the door and then turned back. 'I'm sorry about earlier,' he said.

'Do you want to tell me what that was about?'

Francesco shook his head.

She tentatively closed some of the distance between them. 'You listened to all of my problems earlier. Perhaps I could return the favour.'

'I don't think so. I'm more of a listener than a talker.'

She moved closer and reached out to straighten the collar of his shirt; a small yet highly intimate gesture. He did not push her away so she moved her hand down the front of his shirt, slowing down as she reached each button as if it were a speed bump to be approached with caution. She reached his heart and her hand stopped. She looked up at him.

'We don't have to talk,' she said. Her meaning was clear and the tension which hung in the air following her unspoken suggestion was palpable.

Francesco struggled to think clearly, torn between past and present; loss and desire. Unbidden images of Lauren came to him; happy times and then her arrival in the hospital. 'No,' he said. 'It's not right. I'd be using you.'

'Maybe I'd be using you too,' she said and there were tears in her eyes. Francesco knew she was thinking of the man she had loved and lost, just as he was thinking of Lauren. It would be so easy to stay, but it would be wrong.

'You're beautiful, but I can't do this. I'm sorry,' he said again and started to open the door.

'I wish you would change your mind,' she said sadly. 'I feel so lonely, so …' she searched for a word, but could not find one in either English or Italian to describe what she was feeling.

'Damaged?' Francesco asked.

'Yes, damaged, that's it. I suppose we're all a bit damaged in one way or another, aren't we?'

'I suppose we are.' He didn't want to leave like that, but he had no words left. 'Good bye, Ellie.'

'Will you do something for me before you go?'

'What's that?' he said, wondering if his willpower would hold out.

'Say good night instead of goodbye.'

'Good night,' he said and stepped forward and kissed the top of her head.

He saw tears start to slide down her face and turned and walked hurriedly down the corridor, hating his cowardice but not trusting himself to stay any longer.

*　　*　　*

Francesco woke up and looked over at the alarm clock. 5.30. He had managed to sleep for about three hours which was quite good by his standards. He forced himself out of bed, made coffee and went to sit out on the balcony. It was still so hot that he was becoming convinced the oppressive heat of summer would never subside.

He thought back over the events of the previous night and the early hours of that morning and felt terrible about how things had turned out. Ellie had been so hurt by what she saw as his rejection of her, as though he had found her unattractive. Nothing could have been further from the truth. Most men would have gone for it he supposed, but in truth he didn't know. He had grown up without a father to act as a role model in his teenage years. His grandfather had been a good man, but he had already been in his seventies when he and his mother had gone to live with them and was not equipped to be the sort of father figure a young boy needed.

His mum had always done her best for him, but he felt acutely that not having had that male figure in his life meant he was sometimes unsure of how he was supposed to act. For some reason, Arturo crept into his thoughts, and he imagined him snorting and saying that there was no particular way that anybody was supposed to act. Even in his current mood, he was able to manage a wry smile at the thought of Arturo cast in the role of counsellor and philosopher.

He wondered if he should go back to the hotel and try to catch Ellie before she left and apologise, try to explain but he could barely explain it to himself and he very much doubted that he would be any more articulate when faced with Ellie. If he was completely honest with himself, he wasn't sure he wanted to go through a rerun of the previous night and he decided that it would be better to leave things alone whilst also realising he was taking the easy way out.

Needing to distract himself, he forced himself to think about the fun run. It was only ten days away now. He didn't feel in the mood, but he had to train if he was going to participate. He showered, dressed, took the underground from San Giovanni to Flaminio and walked to the Ponte Regina Margherita. He crossed the bridge and ran down the steps to the running and cycle track by the river. The Tiber was the colour of moss in the clear light of early morning. He warmed up, trying to ignore the graffiti scarred walls, and started his run to the Ponte Palatine, just past Tiber Island.

Occasionally when he ran, he cut through the old city but generally he preferred to stay close to the river. He needed the relative open space and clear stretch without traffic, and that day he wanted to avoid going anywhere near any of the streets or squares he had gone to with Ellie the previous night. The images, the guilt, were still too fresh in his mind.

He tried very hard to avoid thinking about Ellie, but the more he tried to stop thinking about her, the more she pushed her way to the forefront of his mind. He was angry; angry primarily with himself, but also angry with her; angry for making him feel guilty but, more than that, angry with her for making him realise he could feel attracted to another woman. And, as he pushed himself harder, he realised he was angry with Lauren too. The same old questions started to niggle away at him and then he started to feel angry with her for dying.

He pushed himself harder and harder, trying to exhaust the aggression eating away at him. As Tiber Island came in to view, he suddenly felt a wave of exhaustion and struggled to make it to Ponte Palatine. He made it and then slowed down, walked back to the Ponte Garibaldi, from where the prow of Tiber Island was visible, and sat down by the river watching it flow past. The ducks paddled past, serene and unruffled.

The anger drained out of him and he realised the only person he had truly been angry with was himself. It was not Ellie's fault that he had been attracted to her. It was not Lauren's fault that he had been incapable of finding out what had been happening in her life before she had died. He should have been more attentive. As the anger died, he became aware of his body's protestations at how hard he had pushed it. His lungs felt sore and his legs were aching although he had completed only half of his route. Wearily he got up and walked back to the bridge. He started jogging and gradually built up to a run and made it back to his starting point at the Ponte Regina Margherita.

He retraced his steps back across the bridge, noticing the small area to one side of the bridge which had been cordoned off; hopeful and happy lovers had affixed padlocks roughly engraved with names and initials to the railings encircling it. He wondered about that gesture as he continued down the street and crossed the Piazza del Popolo. He took the underground home, showered, changed into his uniform and set off for Termini.

He half hoped he might see Ellie, half hoped he would not. He did not, of course, and he realised he would probably never see her again. The lingering memories from the night before were only in his mind. She had probably gone by now, and his chance to speak to her and try to make things right had gone with her.

# CHAPTER ELEVEN

Another broken night left Francesco feeling groggy and unprepared for the day ahead. The night before he had considered a few drinks to knock him out, but lately, as he had regained his fitness, he had lost his taste for it. Besides, running with a hangover was not something he wished to entertain.

He made coffee and went to sit on the balcony, wishing yet again that he had been able to find a flat with air-conditioning. He had decided to forego Caffè Lazio and Matteo's excellent coffee for once, feeling unable to face anyone and disinclined to have to try to put on a sociable face. This morning of all mornings he needed to be alone with his thoughts.

The first anniversary of Lauren's death was only days away. A year was not a long time and yet already some of his memories of her were becoming blurred by the curtain of time and grief, which was imperceptibly being drawn across that part of his life. Would there come a day when he would not be able to hold on to those memories he had of her at all? Living with the anguish of bereavement, the constant wondering about her last days and trying to muddle through a life without her in it was hard enough; the prospect of trying to do that without her image and their shared experiences, vibrant and sharp in his mind, seemed unendurable.

He went inside and pulled out a photograph album, one of the few things he had brought with him from England. The images in the pictures were vivid even if his memories were less so. She smiled out at him from the past and the warmth of that smile; the way it transmitted her love of life and her sense of fun were almost too painful to look at. 'I'll run for both of us tonight,' he said as he closed the album and put it to one side.

Francesco had a free day ahead of him before the race. He ate a larger breakfast than usual and a light lunch, wanting to be as ready as possible for the race that night.

Eventually, sitting around in the flat, made him feel jittery and claustrophobic and by early evening, he had to get out. He took a bus and then walked along by the Tiber looking down from the street at the endless row of stands set up for Ferragosto, the scene of a seemingly non-stop party strung along the banks of the river. The last flares of a brilliant sunset disappeared and the street lights flickered to life.

He kept walking and found himself at the Ponte Sant'Angelo, at the far end of which stood the imposing floodlit facade of the Castel Sant'Angelo. He crossed the bridge, weaving between tourists and glancing at the various items on sale. It didn't pay to look too closely as being badgered to buy something would follow. In that short stretch, it would have been possible to buy paintings of views of Rome, bags, scarves and selfie sticks, which Francesco considered to be one of the most miserable inventions he had ever seen. Living in a city which attracted so many tourists, he had more than once nearly had his eye taken out by someone desperate for the perfect photo and totally oblivious to passers-by.

He looked up at the sculptures of angels which lined the bridge, soaring into the night sky. On the other side of the bridge, he saw a busker playing the blues and sat and listened to him for a while. He remembered there had been a time in his life when he had enjoyed music. When had that stopped? Why? He was glad he was going to the festival tomorrow. He thought he should try and get a music collection together again. He had had one once. Now it all seemed to be digital; his had been CDs. He found it within him to smile at how out of touch he was with the modern world.

Finally, as he walked towards the starting line for the run at the Ponte della Musica, he felt the sense of anticipation in the air. There was a party atmosphere with groups of friends congregating, chatting and taking photos. He felt acutely that familiar sense of being the outsider, the loner, looking in on other people's lives but never being a part of them.

He tried to focus on the training he had done and the improvements he had seen in his time and fitness. It had given him a goal, and that was something he had needed. Running also gave him a sense of freedom he rarely felt otherwise. Everything that crowded in around him on a daily basis usually lifted when he ran, apart from that day after Ellie. He still felt bad about that night and made a concerted effort to put that out of his mind as well. He didn't want to think about anything now apart from the race. He started warming up and felt the sweat trickling down his back. Even close to ten at night, it was still about twenty-five degrees.

The race started and Francesco allowed his body to take over, stopped thinking and just allowed himself to be. He enjoyed the pure physical sensation of what his body was capable of, the freedom, the air on his skin, the energy of his fellow competitors and seeing the city in a different way.

He crossed the line and clocked a time of thirty-six minutes and forty-two seconds. He saw other competitors congratulating their friends, and one or two of them came over and shook his hand even though they were complete strangers.

He permitted himself to feel proud of his achievement for a few minutes, and after the celebrations and jubilant hugging had subsided, he moved away from the crowds. He looked up at the night sky and dedicated the evening to Lauren, wishing more than anything else she could have been there with him. Why was he allowed to be there experiencing that adrenalin rush, being alive when Lauren was not? The injustice of it all threatened to crush him, and he returned to the finishing line where although he had nobody to talk to, there was at least activity going on to distract him.

As the crowd started to evaporate, Francesco wearily

made his way back home. The earlier high had gone, but so had the wave of grief. He was too tired now to feel anything, and he had to be up in a few hours to catch his flight. He sat down on the sofa and the next thing he knew, the alarm on his phone was ringing. He showered, threw a few things in an overnight bag and stopped off at Caffè Lazio before heading for the airport.

'Ciao Francesco,' said Matteo producing Francesco's habitual cornetto con marmellata.

'Ciao Matteo.' Francesco eyed the pastry and reflected that he had acquired such a taste for them now that it was just as well he had started running again.

Matteo noticed the rucksack. 'Where are you going?'

'Germany. I'm going to a festival called the Waldsee Metal Meet.'

Matteo raised an eyebrow. 'I didn't have you down as a fan of metal music.'

'Neither did I, but I know the drummer in one of the bands. They're called Antenor.' Francesco shrugged in response to Matteo's evident curiosity. 'It's a long story. They're good.'

'Antenor?' Matteo shook his head. 'I don't know them. I'll look them up on YouTube. You must have gone to Rock in Rome then?'

'No,' said Francesco, realising this was something else which had clearly completely passed him by.

'It was so good this year. You missed out. Next year.'

'Maybe,' said Francesco. He took a seat by the bar and winced slightly as he did so. He rubbed his thighs.

'You OK?'

'Yes, just aching from last night. I did the fun run.'

'Yes? I did it too.'

'I didn't know you were a runner.'

'I only started last year but my goal is to do a marathon eventually. What was your time?'

'Just under thirty-seven minutes.'

'That's good. I did it in thirty-nine. Maybe that's why I'm not suffering as much as you.' He chuckled. "There's another race in September. Are you going to run in that one as well?'

'I didn't know about it, but if I can get the time off I'd like to take part.'

'We can go together then,' said Matteo cheerfully, setting a cappuccino down in front of Francesco. 'We can train together too sometimes. It will be good for me to go with someone who runs faster than I do.'

*     *     *

Rome's Fiumicino airport was packed and, to add to the woes of the travelling public, the air conditioning had broken down. Various flights were showing up as delayed or cancelled and a mass of people, which could not even have loosely been described as a queue was forming around the customer service desk.

Discontent was brewing so Francesco found a seat as far away from the desk as possible and hoped he would not be forced to join the disgruntled crowd who were complaining ever more loudly.

Fortunately, his flight left on time and, as usual, the therapy of movement worked on him and he slept through the flight.

After landing, he made his way out of the terminal in Munich, which was an air-conditioned oasis of orderly calm, but found it was not much cooler outside than in Rome. He took the underground, a couple of trains and eventually found himself in the small town of Waldsee. He checked in to the guesthouse and decided to go for a walk before calling Alessandro.

The town itself consisted of no more than a few streets with a little square at the centre. Everything was so different; neat, quiet and efficient. The houses were all immaculately kept, some with frescoes on the walls, and the streets pristine. He stopped off at a baker's, bought a large warm pretzel and a drink and walked down to the lake. He found a bench and sat watching the water wash over the stony shore.

He remembered how he had loved travelling once, seeing the different character of the landscape and buildings, hearing a new language, trying new food, the excitement of arriving in a new, yet to be discovered, country. It struck him that, just as with music, it was something he had loved, but given up on somewhere along the way.

He returned to the guesthouse and phoned Alessandro; within twenty minutes, the infamous van had pulled up.

Alessandro jumped out. 'Hey man, good to see you. How are you doing?'

'Well and you?'

'Yeah, it's going great. Well, apart from the mess back there,' he said indicating the back of the van with his head. 'Come take a look if you're feeling brave enough.'

Francesco followed him round to the back of the van and as Alessandro unlocked the back door, he saw what he meant. There were three bunk beds on each side, each screened off with a curtain, some very basic cooking facilities and a battered sofa. It looked pretty much as he would have expected after four people had been living in it for weeks on end. 'At least there are only four of you.' said Francesco, trying to imagine how much worse it would have been for the six people it was supposed to accommodate.

'No, six.'

'Six?'

'Yeah, there are five of us in the band and our tour manager. Well, that's what he calls himself, but he's roadie, trouble-shooter, babysitter, agony aunt and wielder of big stick all rolled into one'

'It's a bit tight for six, isn't it?'

'Tell me about it. Bet you wished you'd taken up the offer to crash there, huh? You could have had the sofa.' said Alessandro with a grin.

'No comment,' said Francesco with a smile. 'And you've been living in this since June?'

'Pretty much and those bunk beds are hell. There have been a few hotels in between times, though. Like the one I mentioned.'

'When are you on?'

Alessandro glanced at his watch. 'In about six hours.

There are five bands on before us and one after. It's already kicked off for the day.'

'Close to the top of the bill then?'

'Well, it's not one of the big festivals. We're further down the list at those.'

They pulled up at the gates of the grounds with signs pointing in one direction to the palace and in the other to the fields to the side of the palace grounds. The road forked in two, with signs pointing this time to parking for the public and parking for bands and crew. Alessandro took the latter turn and arrived at a security checkpoint where his ID which was scanned. They drove in and parked near some other tour buses of varying sizes. As they got out of the van, Alessandro gave him a fluorescent green wristband. 'This gives you entry to the festival and also access to the backstage area. Whatever else you do, don't lose it.'

'Thanks. How much do I owe you?'

'Dude, you just came all the way from Rome to watch us play. I can stand you the entrance and as for the backstage pass, well, money can't buy one of those.' He chuckled.

'I really appreciate that.'

'You're welcome. C'mon, let's go. I'll introduce you to the others.'

Alessandro led him through another security checkpoint and to one of four huge marquees. Inside, at the far end, there was a bar and buffet. The whole area was busy with people wandering about, looking at checklists, making phone calls or just sitting around amongst boxes, guitars, drum kits, speakers and mountains of cables.

'This is Scott,' said Alessandro, introducing a man who looked just about as unlike a rock musician as Francesco could imagine. He seemed as though he would have been more at home behind a desk in an office. 'I think I told you about him; singer, songwriter and publicity guru.'

'Pleased to meet you,' said Scott, shaking his hand.

'Good to meet you too.'

'Over there is Gus.' He indicated a figure reclining on an air bed, his long hair splayed over a pillow. 'Gus only has two positions - horizontal or on stage. Lead guitarist and general layabout.'

Gus gave them a good-natured grin and lazily flicked his middle finger at Alessandro. He waved a greeting at Francesco, closed his eyes and started tapping out a rhythm on his thighs.

Alessandro worked his way through the tent introducing Francesco to Tom, the heavily-bearded rhythm guitarist; their harassed tour manager, Greg and Ryan their bass player who seemed glued to his phone.

'Girlfriend trouble,' said Alessandro as they left him to it and walked away. 'I've pretty much given up on having a girlfriend for now. I'm away too much, and when I get back I don't have enough left in me to make it work. Tom's the only one who's managing to keep a relationship going for any length of time. I don't know how.'

Francesco was listening, but also thinking about how different they all were, not only to each other, but also to how he had imagined they would be. He found it hard to imagine a more disparate group of people; the only thing they seemed to have in common was how quiet they all were whereas he had expected them to be loud and brash. This was not quite the wild rock and roll lifestyle of legend. Despite their differences though, Francesco sensed the bond between them, tested yet strengthened by the long weeks on the road.

After the introductions, they headed for the bar and got a couple of beers. Francesco was about to dig out some cash when he realised they were free of charge.

'Backstage perks. Cheers.'

'Cheers.'

'If I were you, I'd make the most of this area before the show. And I'd steer clear afterwards.'

'Why?'

'If we have a bad show, we'll all be really down. And if we have a good show, we'll all be really down.'

Alessandro caught Francesco's puzzled expression and shook his head.

'It's really hard to explain. In the run up to a show, there's this huge surge of adrenalin and then on stage … I can't even describe it. It's like the biggest high you could ever imagine, but then at the end, you come off stage and it all just stops and you feel so flat. It's like you've run into a brick wall, and then the physical exhaustion hits. I don't think we're much fun to be around after a show. In fact, in all seriousness, if you'd said you'd sleep in the van, I'd have talked you out of it for that reason alone. And because it's a pit. So I probably won't see you afterwards, but I'll catch up with you tomorrow.'

'I think I can imagine what you mean.'

'Also, festivals are always a tough call, way harder than normal gigs. People haven't always specifically come to see you so you have to win them over which is hard, but if you do, it's an incredible sensation.'

They wandered around the marquee and ended up by Alessandro's drum kit.

'You ever played?'

'Never.'

'I'll give you a quick demo, but I'll put the mute pads on first or someone will start complaining.'

Francesco watched as he set up and started to play. The sound was missing, but the speed with which he played was extraordinary. He noticed that both of his hands and feet were doing different thing at the same time. He couldn't imagine how that was even possible and admired the fact that anybody could do it.

Alessandro got up. 'You wanna have a go?'

'No, having watched you, I'm definitely going to leave it to people who know what they're doing.'

They went outside and had a look around the rest of the hospitality area. Alessandro started checking his watch more often, and when they headed back in to the marquee, the mood inside had changed. They all seemed more focused; more intense. Francesco decided it was time to make a move, wished them luck and left the backstage area so that he could watch the show. As he left and walked out into the crowd, he realised there were people of all ages, younger and far older than him. He found he didn't feel out of place after all. Everyone seemed to accept everybody else just as they were.

He managed to get close to the front while everyone else was still milling about, and he watched as the roadies started setting everything up, unravelling miles of cables and taping them down; setting up Alessandro's drum kit and the guitars and speakers. Greg appeared speaking urgently to one of the roadies, and then they all left the stage and the lights went down. It was already almost dark and there was a sense of anticipation. Francesco wondered how they must all be feeling backstage at that moment. Down where he was it was hot; he couldn't imagine what it was going to be like up there under the lights.

Strobe lights started to rake across the audience and then they stopped as abruptly as they had started and suddenly Antenor were there in front of the crowd. As they launched into their first song without any preamble, he could physically feel the power and passion of the music vibrating through him.

Francesco was stunned to see the transformation; to witness how five people who were totally unassuming off stage could flip a switch and completely command the stage and fire the audience up.

Francesco was no musician or singer so he had no idea what Scott's range was but it seemed capable of hitting just about any note and moving effortlessly from soft and tender to raw and hard.

He listened as Scott sang about anger, injustice, fear, shattered trust, finding a way and meaning in life, seeking courage. Then he remembered how good those songs Alessandro had played to him had been. He wondered why he hadn't listened to any more since that day.

The tempo started to slow down. Scott disappeared, and the others seemed to recede into the background. Gus came to the front of the stage and started to play a solo into which he poured an extraordinary amount of emotion, conveying longing, loss and pain. Francesco could barely reconcile the person on stage with the man he had met earlier.

Gus closed his eyes from time to time, utterly lost in the magic he was creating, and Francesco wondered if he was even still aware of the audience. He looked round and realised the crowd had grown still with everyone as captivated by what they were witnessing as he was.

Finally, Gus came out of his reverie and looked over at Alessandro to synch the ending. When it came, the roar of applause and shouts of appreciation, in which Francesco played a full part, sent tingles down his spine.

Scott came back on stage, applauding Gus and went on to introduce all of the band members to the audience. As Alessandro's turn came, he launched himself into a drum solo, twirling the sticks through his fingers and around his head; part martial arts expert, part magician, part juggler. His hands and feet were moving faster than Francesco would have thought humanly possible and if he had been impressed by what he had seen Alessandro do earlier, this surpassed that by miles. Francesco saw the look on his face – just as Gus had been earlier, he was in what Alessandro had called the zone. And then he was there as well, and there was nothing but a sensation of joy; a joy as pure and uncomplicated as the pleasure he got from running.

When they left the stage, the roar to get them to come back on blew him away. During their encore, the whole audience was singing with them, and Francesco wondered how that must feel, to have words you had written sung by hundreds of people you had never met and never would.

When their set finally finished, the five of them came together at the front of the stage, arms around each other's shoulders and Francesco understood what Alessandro had meant about labels. Nobody would have put the five people on stage together, and the music they played defied any one genre yet it all worked.

Scott waved at the crowd and pressed his hands to his chest. 'Thank you. We love you. See you next time. Good night.'

As they left the stage for the final time, Francesco thought about how Lauren would have loved it. He missed her exuberance, the joy she found in life and the sense of fun with which she had imbued everything. During his lonely journey through the last year, he had let everything he, or they, had enjoyed doing drop away. He had started running again, but his other passions – music, travelling, and medicine – had been discarded. He wondered if it was guilt at the thought of enjoying things which Lauren would never have the chance to experience that held him back, or if it was simply that he no longer felt inclined to do any of those things. Whatever it was, he had made the effort to go to the concert and, having done that, he had loved every moment of it.

He walked back to the guesthouse with a ringing in his ears so loud he wondered if it would ever subside, but a feeling he had not experienced in a long time; something that could be almost akin to happiness. He did not dare to examine it too closely, fearing it would slip away again all too soon.

# CHAPTER TWELVE

Francesco walked across the palace grounds, enjoying the cool morning air. The ringing in his ears which had continued into the early hours had finally gone away. It was definitely the morning after the night before; cool and almost unbelievably quiet, considering how many people were camped not far away.

The palace, which was, in reality, more like an overgrown country house, sat serenely at the top of a small rise, its white and yellow walls peering through the mist. It was locked up but, looking through the windows, he could see the ornately decorated interior. The sound of his phone ringing interrupted the silence.

'Hi.'

'Hi. Where are you?' Alessandro sounded sleepy.

'I'm up by the palace.'

'You're an early riser.'

'I don't sleep much. Anyway, I could say the same for you.'

'We've gotta start packing up in a few hours. I just

needed a bit of time out before the others get up.'

'Bad night?'

'No, a great one. Just the usual after-show thing I was talking about. And I think we're all just about ready to go home.'

'You haven't got long to go now,' said Francesco recalling the Waldsee festival was near the end of the list Alessandro had given him.

'Three more shows, seven days. Listen, how about I get some coffee and meet you up there?'

'Sure, thanks.'

'You haven't tried the coffee yet.' With that Alessandro was gone.

Francesco found a bench and settled himself down. He pulled his jacket tight around him and thought about the night before and going back to Rome. It struck him he had his own version of post-concert blues so he could only imagine what it must be like after being on stage, the high of performing, of people chanting your name, singing to songs you had written and then – nothing. Plus, he had seen what physical performers they were; that alone under those lights would have taken its toll.

He saw Alessandro coming towards the palace and waved him over. Alessandro handed him a paper cup with a plastic lid. 'All I can say is it's warm.'

Francesco peeled the lid off, sipped it, decided Alessandro was right, but then drank some more anyway. Any coffee was marginally better than no coffee.

'The concert was incredible.'

'Thanks. We felt it worked last night. It's like we were all totally in the zone.'

'And then you had the post-show crash?'

Alessandro grimaced. 'Yeah, but it goes with the territory. I think we've got to learn how to handle it better, though. Anyways, enough of that. What time's your flight?'

'Nine tomorrow morning.'

'Cool. You can catch tonight's show. There are some great bands playing.'

'Maybe, but I've got to leave at about five in the morning and I'm not sure I can take the pace these days. When are you leaving?'

'Supposed to be about twelve, but it's probably gonna be more like one or two. Greg will be tearing his hair out as usual, or he would be if he had any.'

'When's the next show?'

'Tomorrow in Austria.'

'You've covered a lot of ground over the last few months,' Francesco remarked remembering how long the list of tour dates had been.

'You can say that again. I told you earlier we all wanna go home now, but when we get home, it's hard in a different way. Nobody back there can understand what it's really like on tour, and you're expected to snap right back into normal life and talk about who's got kicked off some reality show or what to get at the supermarket. It's not easy to adjust.'

'Don't you ever think about packing it all in?'

'No, never. I know people who've had to, but I can't imagine any other life. I admit I have moments when I think it would be better to have a normal life and a regular job you can leave at the door when you go home – like you do, you know – but I know I couldn't.'

Something in Francesco's expression caught Alessandro's attention. 'Sorry man, I didn't mean any offence.'

'No, I know. It just made me think.'

'About?'

'Long story.'

'I remember you listening to my long story. Go for it.' He cradled the cup of coffee in his hands and drank some more.

Francesco felt that tight sensation he got when the prospect of having to talk about himself came up. 'I've only been doing this job for a matter of months.' He took a deep breath and said it. 'Before that I was a doctor.'

Alessandro whipped his head around, suddenly fully awake. 'No way. You're joking?'

'No.'

'That's definitely not the sort of job you can leave at the door.'

'No, it's not, but the one I have now certainly is.'

'Why?'

'Why what?'

'Why did you give it up? I mean that's a vocation and it takes a ton of commitment to qualify.'

'I was working in A&E.' He saw the look of confusion on Alessandro's face.

'What you call ER.'

'Oh, OK.'

'They brought my wife in.' Francesco stopped. The only other person he had told was Arturo, and they had both been very drunk at the time. Why was it so hard to tell anyone? Why was it so hard to get the words out? 'She'd been in an accident. I couldn't do anything to save her.'

'That's brutal.' Alessandro shook his head. 'No, I can't even imagine that. I've never lost anyone I love. And like that? I'm really sorry, man.'

Francesco nodded and managed to say, 'Thanks.' Telling someone felt strange, as though the ground beneath him had shifted, leaving him slightly dizzy. And then he realised that Alessandro's sympathy had been genuine, and he had not been judged for not saving Lauren or for giving up his profession.

They sat and stared out over the palace grounds for a while, watching the light mist slowly lift and evaporate.

Eventually Alessandro said, 'So this new job you have, are you gonna stick with it?'

'It gets me by.'

'Yeah, that's not exactly a ringing endorsement.'

'No, it isn't it, is it? I miss being a doctor. I think about going back, but I can't see it happening.'

'Maybe one day?'

'Maybe,' but Francesco was not convinced and did not sound convincing either.

'I don't know what to tell you. All any of us can do is keep going, keep plugging away and hope that someday it'll all come good. That's how it was for me … with my father, I mean.'

'When he was hurting you and your mum and sisters.'

'Yeah. Life really sucks sometimes.' Alessandro shifted position as if signalling he was about to change the subject, to make the change less unexpected. 'You ever been to the States?'

Francesco shook his head.

'You should come visit us. My mom would insist you stay with us and feed you until you burst, and my eldest sister would flirt with you like the sweet but crazy person she is but, apart from that, you'd have a good time.'

'I might take you up on that,' Francesco said and managed a smile.

'You should. Really. Keep in touch. I wanna hear the next part of the story.'

They got up. 'If there is one,' said Francesco.

'There will be. There's always a next part.'

They walked back through the grounds and down the lane, past the security checkpoint and into the backstage area. Francesco offered to help them pack away and the extra pair of hands was gratefully received. He found doing some manual work therapeutic; it helped to work out the tension he had felt building when talking about Lauren.

Once they had finished, he took the opportunity to walk out onto the stage. He looked out over the vast area in front of the stage, now deserted, which had been so packed the night before. What must it be like to stand there and have people scream at you, idolise you, even if just for an hour or so? Combined with his evident love of music and talent, he could see why Alessandro would never consider giving it up.

Alessandro spotted him and joined him on the stage. They watched a small group of people on the far side of the field, beyond the boundary fence. They had just scrambled out of their tents; a variety of ages, all laughing and joking. 'See that is what I love about music,' he said, nodding in their direction. 'It touches people and unites them in a way nothing else can. It transcends all the stuff that gets in the way: age, language, culture.'

Alessandro handed him one of the beers he had brought with him, and the others came to join them. They sat there for a while, occasionally trading banter, but generally preoccupied with their own thoughts. Greg appeared, looking as harried as ever. 'Let's get going. It's time to leave.'

Francesco saw them off and then idled around the festival grounds, ate food which Anna would have taken one look at and thrown in the bin, and then had a few more beers.

Only now that he had done something so outside of his normal routine, could he see how narrow his existence had become. He almost didn't want to go back, but he knew running away was not the answer and any peace he found would have to be within himself.

*       *       *

The following day, he retraced his steps back to Munich airport, slept through the flight and then took the train to Termini and the underground to San Giovanni. Emerging from the station, he saw the Aurelian Walls and the statues of the Apostles on the top of the church of San Giovanni in Laterano apparently peering over the top of them. It was not exactly like going home, but it was at least a sense of familiarity, which was somehow comforting.

He decided to make a stop at Il Buongustaio, and Anna greeted him like a long-lost son.

'What do you suggest today?' he asked her.

'Allora,' she said looking around the shop. 'Si, a salad but with my secret ingredient.'

As usual, she went around the shop gathering up the ingredients Francesco would need: fusilli pasta, peppers, olives, onions and cheese.

'Do you have basil?'

'No.'

'Oregano?'

'No.' Despite Anna's good nature, she seldom failed to make him feel like a student who had failed a simple test.

'Pars … no, never mind.'

She disappeared and returned with a bottle. 'This is my own personal salad dressing. Better that you take this than try to make it.' She looked at him over the top of her glasses.

'I think you might be right.'

'And a loaf of rosemary bread. I made it this morning.'

Its aroma filled the air and had already made Francesco feel ravenous.

She waved it at him. 'Make sure you eat all of it. You need to put on some weight.'

'I run a lot,' he offered by way of explanation, keen to reassure her that he was not ill.

'Hmm,' she said sounding doubtful about the wisdom of such vigorous exercise.

Francesco paid the bill and was touched when she refused payment for the oil. 'That's not for sale. It's a gift.'

As he walked back to his flat, he reflected on the last month. He had taken a few steps outside of the bubble of grief in which he had been imprisoned. Nothing would ever fix him or fill the emptiness. Nothing would ever quieten the nagging doubts in his head about the events leading up to Lauren's death, but he was starting to realise he had to learn to live with what loss, doubt and guilt had done to him; to accept that was the way his life would be from now on. He suddenly remembered Henry who, months ago, had spoken to him of how he had learned to live with the way he had been changed by his experiences.

He realised he had started to make a life of sorts, rather than living almost entirely through others' lives in order to avoid his own. He was still dogged by his doubts, and his life was not professionally fulfilling in the way his previous life had been; nor was it personally fulfilling with the woman he loved and the child they would both have doted on, but it seemed it was perhaps at least a life he could manage to tolerate and inhabit. That, he assumed, was progress of a kind.

# CHAPTER THIRTEEN

Francesco was on the train heading to the airport. The trains on that route were usually packed, which he did not like much, but, on the other hand, on the occasions when they were not, those were journeys when he often found it particularly easy to strike up a conversation with someone. People who were leaving the country somehow seemed to feel more able to speak freely.

He battled to the end of the busy train, dealing patiently with all the questions he had by then heard tens of times. Reaching the last carriage, he found that there the crowds had thinned out considerably. He checked the last remaining tickets and then feeling his duty was done, sat down at the far end of the carriage opposite a woman he took to be in her late forties or early fifties. Her black hair, shot through with threads of grey, was piled on top of her head and her skin was deeply tanned. She was dressed in faded blue jeans and a white shirt. On her lap was a canvas bag which had seen better days and beside her was a large slightly scuffed suitcase. Despite the seeming lack of attention to her clothes, she had an air of elegant self-possession.

She looked across at Francesco and smiled. 'Judging by the crowds I saw on the platform, it must be a busy day for you,' she said in an accent which he placed as coming from somewhere around Venice.

'September is always the same, well, on this route anyway. It's still holiday season.'

'I've never understood why everybody piles into the first few carriages instead of moving down the train.'

'Neither have I,' Francesco admitted. 'Where are you going?'

'Armenia, but it's not for a holiday. I'm going to work out there.'

'What type of work do you do?'

'I'm a doctor. I work for Medici Senza Frontiere.'

'What's it like working for them?'

'Actually this is my first assignment with them. Even after the recruitment process, I'm still not entirely sure what to expect.'

'Why did you choose Armenia?'

'I didn't. You don't get to choose your destination. To be honest, when they offered me this assignment, I almost turned it down. I couldn't imagine what possible use I'd be there, but then I thought I might not get another chance if I turned it down so I said yes. I'm glad because now I know a lot more about the situation there, I really think I'm going to be able to do something positive.'

'What's your assignment?'

'MSF is working to help people with MDR-TB. Oh, sorry that's …'

'Multidrug-resistant TB,' Francesco finished automatically without stopping to think about it.

'Yes,' she said, looking surprised. 'And XDR-TB as well.'

'Extensively drug-resistant TB.'

'That's right,' she said, looking at him with more curiousity.

Francesco could see she was about to start asking questions so he moved the conversation along before she had the chance. 'I didn't realise that was a problem in Armenia.'

'To my shame, neither did I. Apparently, though, it has one of the world's highest rates of the disease. The treatment is long and hard, and it has side effects which some patients can't tolerate so they drop out. I'm hoping I can help, not just with administering the drugs, but trying to help with the support system they are putting in place.'

'People tend to think TB is a thing of the past, I suppose.'

'Yes, they do, don't they? It doesn't get much attention either so I think people assume it's gone away, but that's really not the case. In fact, it's not just the disease and the problems with the drugs that's the issue. It's the stigma attached to the disease. Not that there should be a stigma attached to it, but there is.'

'As if having drug-resistant TB isn't challenging enough.'

'Well, quite. My friends have been very supportive although there have been some rather grim jokes about what might happen to me. I'm not worried about death, though. I mean I worry about suffering but not about dying. I've already nearly done that once.'

Francesco knew well enough by then that when someone threw a statement like that into a conversation, they usually wanted the person listening to ask what had happened but were testing the waters to see if the other person would pick up on it or let it go. 'What happened if I can ask?' he said, fairly certain he could ask but being polite.

"Yes, you can ask. Sepsis. I was in my thirties. Before that I'd always thought I'd be scared of death, but actually I felt very peaceful. Because of what happened to me, my fear went, and it was very liberating. The thing is, though, you think at the time that you will always remember exactly how you felt and how it put everything in perspective and that you will carry that with you for the rest of your life but, in my experience, you don't. Not automatically anyway. Life sucks you right back in, and you have to work hard to remember the lessons you learned and think about how to use them going forward.'

'How has it changed you?'

'It's helped me professionally. For example, when I have to talk to patients about death, and it helped me to decide to accept this assignment. It's helped me personally too.'

Francesco looked at her, waiting. She met his eyes, and the silence prompted her to continue.

'My marriage broke down and when it did, I was consumed by anger and grief. We associate grief with death, but it can be any type of loss. The loss, in any circumstances, of the person you thought you'd spend your life with is hard to come to terms with. It was the usual thing, or it was to start with, anyway. He had an affair. I confided in some of my friends, a selection of the single, married and divorced. I was surprised by how many of my married friends confessed they'd been through it. I got every type of advice you can imagine from "Leave the bastard." to "Ignore it, it's a fling. It'll pass." '

'So what did you do?'

'I had an affair too.'

Francesco was rarely surprised, but he was momentarily taken aback.

'Some of my friends looked at me like that when they found out and others took the "Go for it" attitude.'

'I'm sorry, I wasn't being disapproving. It just wasn't what I'd expected you to say.'

'Honestly, it wasn't what I'd expected me to do either, but being that badly hurt can make you do things you'd never have countenanced before. I found out for the first time that sex and love didn't necessarily have to go together. I compartmentalised things the way I suppose a lot of men do. I loved my husband, but I was so angry with him … so ground down by his rejection of me… that I tried to validate myself by having an affair with someone else.'

'Did he ever find out?'

'Oh yes. I was careless. Deliberately, I think. Perhaps I wanted him to find out. I think that subconsciously I thought that if he found out, he would realise how far he had pushed me, how badly he had hurt me, and then he would realise how much he still loved me and somehow, we'd put all the pieces back together again.'

'It didn't work out like that, I take it?'

'No, he was so angry. He found ten different ways to validate his behaviour but mine was inexcusable in his eyes.

I mean, I know what I did was wrong, but at least I could see that. He didn't seem to feel what he had done was wrong in any way. He didn't see how his affair had eaten away at me, how devastated it had left me. It almost destroyed me, but then I remembered the lessons I had learnt from my brush with death. It took a monumental effort and a long time, but I got through it in the end.'

'And you kept working as a doctor throughout?'

'Yes, my job was the one thing I always clung on to. I never missed a day. It kept me sane, but then I was the little kid who lined my toys up in my "waiting room"; diagnosed them; operated on them. I think doctors are born, not made. I always wanted to fix people, but when I grew up I realised you can't fix everything. However hard you try.'

Francesco thought of his inability to cling on to his work after Lauren's accident. 'Not everyone could keep going at work through something like that without missing a step,' he said. Before he could stop himself, he added quietly, 'I couldn't.'

'Your wife had an affair?'

'No, well, no I don't think so. I don't know. I'll never know. She … she passed in an accident.'

'I'm so sorry. It must be terrible to be left with questions on top of your loss.'

Francesco nodded but said nothing. He could feel the muscles in his jaw clenching painfully as he tried to remain in control of his emotions. He sensed the woman had noticed this as she moved to a more neutral topic. 'What did you do before then? I get the feeling it wasn't this.'

Francesco took a deep breath. 'Why do you say that?'

'I don't think I've met anyone outside of the medical profession who knows what MDR and XDR TB are.'

'I was a doctor. Before.'

She nodded. 'I wondered, but I couldn't make sense of it. This is quite a change.'

'I couldn't continue.' He examined his hands. 'She was brought into A&E. I was on duty, and I couldn't save her.'

'Oddio. Did you have counselling?'

'No. I shouldn't have needed counselling. I should have been able to get on with my life like everyone else. Like you did.'

'It wasn't easy for me to keep going. I was only drawing on that experience I had had, being able to see a bigger picture if you like, I think that's what made it possible. Without that, I don't know how I would have coped, if I would have coped. And the fact is that work is therapy for some people, but not for others. It doesn't make one person better than the other. Also, what happened to me wasn't anything like what you went through.'

Francesco shrugged.

'Don't you ever miss it?' she asked.

'Every day,' he confessed. 'I miss the camaraderie; the feeling we were all there for a reason. Now I'm just going through the motions. I have no sense of purpose, but it's too late to do anything about it.'

'No, it's not. Listen to me. You can't change the past, but you do have a certain amount of control over what happens from now on. If medicine is your passion, you must do whatever it takes to reconcile yourself to what has happened so that you can go back to it.'

'I think I might be beyond repair.'

'No, there are a few people who are beyond repair, and I've met some, and I don't believe you're one of them. You owe it to yourself and all those people you could potentially be helping to put yourself back together so you can fix them too.' The woman reached into her bag and pulled out a notepad and pen. She scribbled something on it, tore out the page and handed it to Francesco. It was her name, Silvia, and an email address.

'When you are ready and if you need any help finding a counsellor, contact me. But remember, we're all a bit broken anyway; it's part of the human condition, I'm afraid.'

'Thank you,' said Francesco, genuinely grateful for her offer of help.

He would have liked to continue the conversation further, finding a little something of his old self in talking to a fellow doctor, but the train was drawing into the airport. Silvia retrieved her case from the luggage rack and turned to Francesco. 'You only have one life. You know that more than most. Make sure you live it to the full. And help others so they can live it too.' With that, she was absorbed by the crowd before Francesco could respond.

He walked slowly up the platform, replaying the conversation with Silvia, barely conscious of the people around him. He shuttled back and forth between the airport and Rome on automatic pilot, thinking about what she had said until his last journey of the day to the airport. He was standing on the platform at Termini when he realised someone was speaking to him.

'Hello'

He recognised her immediately. It was the young woman who had been looking for her father, or the man she thought might be him. 'Hi.'

'Small world!'

'How are you?'

'Long story. What about you?'

'Same as ever,' he said although he wasn't entirely sure that was true. He had started allowing himself to open up to people, and he was finding that it was not as terrible as he had expected; that people did not judge him or blame him. 'Did you find out anything?'

She shook her head and bit her lip. 'No. So much for my theory that Italians keep houses in the family. I went to the address on the letters, but the people there had never heard of him. I even went all round the town asking in shops and bars if anybody knew him. By the second day, people were pointing me out in the street and talking about me. I did find someone who knew the family, but apparently his parents died, and he sold the house and moved. They couldn't remember where he went, but he's never been seen in the village since. So …'

'A dead end.' Francesco remembered his visit to his old family home and how he had left empty-handed. He knew only too well how she must have felt.

'Yes.'

'What are you going to do now?'

'I haven't the faintest idea. Every day I wake up and think "Today is the day when I'll decide what to do", but by the end of the day I've just thought myself to a standstill again. I feel stuck. It's like my brain has turned into cotton wool. You can't imagine how frustrating it is.'

Francesco reminded himself that she could have no idea that he knew exactly how frustrating it was; the sense of not knowing how to move forward and then the renewed frustration at the failure to achieve anything constructive. 'What are your options?'

'Forget all about it, but I don't know if I can. I worry that it will always be there eating away at me. Or, confront my parents and risk destroying my relationship with them forever. It doesn't seem like much of a choice, does it?'

'No, I suppose not. What about a DNA test?'

'I thought about that, but you need the person's permission, and I can hardly ask.'

'In that case, trying to let it go sounds like a better option than falling out with your parents. The lesser of two evils anyway.'

She looked at him intently. 'Do you really think it's possible to go through your whole life without knowing the truth about something so important?'

It was a question which Francesco had asked himself so many times. He thought again about how Lauren's actions still played on his mind every day to the extent that sometimes the not knowing even overshadowed the pain of her loss. In a sense it was easier for him than for her; he had exhausted all his options and had no choice, but she hadn't and could take it further. But he also knew what it was like to have no family, and it was a cold and lonely place.

'I understand the need to know the truth – more than you can imagine – but if I were you, I'd treasure my imperfect family. It's a tough world without anyone in your corner. I don't know if that helps.'

She nodded almost imperceptibly. 'When we first met, I was all for knowing the truth at any cost, wasn't I? But maybe you're right. The man I grew up thinking of as my father has been a great dad. How much would I hurt him and myself and us if I opened all this up? Perhaps all I can do is learn to live with not knowing. Perhaps my biological father would have been a disappointment and I'd have gone through all that, destroying so much, and for what?' She hesitated. 'I suppose nothing is ever clear cut, is it? Nobody is all good or all bad. Well, rarely anyway. My mum and dad may have deceived me, but equally they may have meant well. Perhaps they just found themselves in a situation where they did the best they could at the time.'

'Perhaps,' Francesco acknowledged and wondered if Lauren had also been trying to do the best she could in whatever situation she had got herself caught up in.

After he had finished his shift, he walked home, taking his time, trying to stall what was coming. He didn't even attempt to sleep but sat at his kitchen table and watched as the hands of the clock on the wall ticked round to midnight – the 27th of August, the anniversary of Lauren's death. She was moving further away from him all the time.

# Autumn 2019

# CHAPTER FOURTEEN

The first thing he noticed about her was that she had been crying. Only after that did he notice how young and lost she looked. She could be no more than sixteen or seventeen. As she passed him her ticket, he was unable to stop himself from asking her if he could help. He had been expecting a brief dismissal or an everything-is-fine type of reply. Instead he heard a quiet voice say, 'No, nobody can. Not now.' Her Florentine accent was immediately recognisable.

'Maybe things are not as bad as you think,' he ventured, considering it a dull response even as he uttered the words. He knew things could indeed be that bad.

She laughed bitterly and snapped back, 'And maybe they are.'

'I'm sorry that was thoughtless. It's one of those stupid things we come out with when we don't know what else to say, isn't it?'

She met his eyes for the first time, and it was clear to Francesco that she was reappraising him.

'I could listen if you would like me to,' he offered. 'I'm

better at that than I am at platitudes.' He shrugged and spread his arms wide, a gesture which seemed to embrace an open, honest offer and concede his shortcomings at the same time. He received only a small, sad smile in return, but he could see her defences were coming down. 'I'm Francesco.'

There was a moment's hesitation. He could sense her weighing up whether to respond and then, 'Valentina.'

As he had learned, the best way was often to say as little as possible. Most people found silence hard to deal with and would say almost anything rather than endure it. So they sat in silence for a while, and then she began. 'I hate my parents.' She looked at him, searching for a reaction.

Francesco knew what she was waiting for so he deliberately ensured his face gave nothing away.

'Aren't you supposed to tell me that I shouldn't, or that they be hurt if they heard me say that or, or something?'

'Am I? I don't know them or anything about them so I can't say.'

Valentina looked at him even more closely than before. Puzzled but somehow trusting him more. This was someone who didn't seem to want to pass judgement on her. 'They've ruined my life.'

'How?'

'They won't accept the man I love.'

The man, not the boy. Francesco wondered if that was why her parents had not been happy. He imagined the parents of a teenage girl might not be too happy about her having a boyfriend who was a lot older than her.

'His name is Étienne. He's twenty-two.' She seemed

animated for the first time in the way someone can only be when they talk about the person they love.

Twenty-two, thought Francesco; not so old then. 'Étienne. That's a French name, isn't it?'

'He's from Gabon,' Valentina said defensively.

'And?'

'And that is the problem. My parents are racists.'

'Ah.'

'Yes, "ah". They judged him from the moment I told them about him. I'm sure they were never prejudiced when I was younger but in the last few years, my father has changed. He keeps going on about his taxes going towards paying for illegal immigrants. But quite apart from anything else, Étienne isn't an illegal immigrant. They just assumed he must be. He's got a French passport, and he's living and working here totally legally. He went to university in France, and then he decided to settle in Italy because he said that after travelling around Europe, he thought some of the friendliest people he'd met were Italian. Except my parents. It had to be my parents, didn't it? They hadn't even met him properly, but they took against him immediately. Well, my father did, and my mother went along with him because that's what she always does. "Yes, dear. Whatever you say, dear." Cavolo, I hate it.'

'They said you couldn't see him again?' Francesco could almost imagine the scene playing out in front of him.

'And plenty more, most of it unrepeatable. I should just have continued to see him in secret until I could get a job and leave home but, oh no, I had to push it.' She shook her head as if trying to rid herself of some unwanted memory, and her corkscrew curls flew around her face.

'So?' Francesco asked softly.

'I decided I wasn't going to let him be my secret. It would have made everything seem sordid, and it wasn't. I thought that if my parents just met him, just gave him a chance and got to know him, they would see he's as human as they are and a good person.' She started to cry again. Francesco waited while she found a tissue and tried to compose herself.

'It was awful. I'd told my parents I'd be bringing a friend over for dinner. We arrived, and I let us in. Étienne was smiling at me and saying how wonderful the dinner smelled when my mother came out of the kitchen. Her smile just froze, and she looked frightened. I think that was because she knew how my father was going to react.'

'Not good, I take it?'

She was sobbing once more, twisting the tissue round and round in her fingers until it started to disintegrate. Tiny shards of paper started to scatter across her jeans. She looked at them with a puzzled expression as if wondering how they had got there. She found another tissue and wiped perspiration from her forehead and neck.

'It was worse than anything I could have anticipated. The things he said to him, to us, were horrible. I knew at that moment I would hate him for the rest of my life. But that's what hate does, doesn't it? It breeds more hate.'

'What did Étienne say?'

'That's the thing. He said absolutely nothing. He stood there, took it all and then, when my father finally seemed to have run out of insults, he just turned to me and said "Let's leave now." He was so dignified. He took my hand, but my father pulled me away. He physically restrained me. Time seemed to stop. It was like a standoff, and I think Étienne knew he couldn't win so he … he just said goodbye and left. He didn't even slam the door the way I would have done. He simply closed it behind him while I was screaming at my father to let me go.' Valentina looked at Francesco in complete bewilderment.

Francesco closed his eyes, his own memories of being restrained by people in the hospital who had thought they knew what was best for him starting to close in on him. No, not now. He summoned all the willpower he had in order to drag himself back into the present. Valentina was sobbing, and he was relieved that she appeared not to have noticed that he had momentarily become lost in his own memories. He studied her. She reminded him of Teddy, particularly of the last time he had seen her on that night when their family had been ripped apart. In his then seven-year-old's eyes she had seemed so grown up, so sure of herself and what she wanted and was determined to do. Now, from his perspective as a thirty-four year old, this young woman who was not so different, just a few years older than Teddy had been then, looked vulnerable, abandoned, hurt and defeated, anything but sure of herself.

She met his gaze. 'You're a nice person,' she said suddenly. 'You haven't judged me, and you were right. You are a good listener. I wish my dad was like you.'

Francesco had never before considered the fact that he

was old enough to have a daughter of Valentina's age. He suddenly felt extremely old.

'Have you got children?' she asked.

Francesco's mind taunted him with images of Lauren lying on a stretcher bleeding out. Then back further still to the moment she had told him she was pregnant. He made a monumental effort and pushed them away. 'No.'

'You'd be a good big brother too. I'm an only child.' She sighed and rubbed her abdomen as though trying to soothe some discomfort and took a few deep breaths.

Francesco sensed they were in danger of veering into territory he had no wish to enter. He needed to change the subject. 'What happened after Étienne left?'

'More shouting and screaming and finally I said I was going to bed. I think they were relieved as they'd had enough by then too. But I didn't go to bed. I packed a bag and later on, when I was sure they must have gone to sleep, I crept out.'

She paused and dabbed at her forehead and neck again and took another deep breath. 'Santo cielo, it's hot. I phoned Étienne, but his phone was switched off. Then I thought I'd go to his flat, but I'd forgotten it was the Festa della Rificolona. I got caught up in the procession, and it took me ages to get through the crowds. I never liked that festival. All those paper lanterns with faces. I used to find them so creepy when I was a child and last night, with all those people and the heat, I just wanted to get away from the whole thing as fast as possible. But when I finally got there he wasn't at home anyway.'

Francesco had no idea what the Festa della Rificolona was, but it was hardly the time to ask. He saw the anguish and indecision written across her face as though her first doubts had started to form about how serious Étienne had really been about her if he had simply disappeared.

'I knew I couldn't go back to my parents. I'll never go back. How could I? I have no respect for them. But I couldn't find Étienne either. It was too late to go to any of my friends' homes, and their parents would only have phoned mine so what was the point? I spent the night sitting outside the entrance to the block of flats where he lives. I was frightened, but I was sure he'd come back and then everything would be OK.'

Francesco could barely imagine what that night must have been like for her.

'The trouble is he didn't come back, and he's still not answering his phone. I waited until this morning, and then I went to the railway station and got a ticket.'

'Why are you going to Rome? What are you going to do? Do you have family there? Friends?'

'Rome?' She looked startled as if this was something new which had not occurred to her before. 'I don't know.' She slurred her words slightly.

Francesco noticed she suddenly looked very flushed, and she was sweating more profusely.

'Doesn't matter anyway. I've lost everyone.' Her voice was becoming drowsy.

Francesco took her wrist and felt her pulse. He thought about her rubbing her abdomen, taking deep breaths, complaining of feeling hot and sweating. 'What have you taken?' he said sharply, grabbing her by the shoulders. There was no time for niceties now.

'A few asp…. I had such a …. a head, headache.' Her head dropped forward onto her chest.

They were drawing into Orvieto now, and Francesco pulled the emergency lever and phoned for an ambulance. The training he had assumed he would never use again kicked in automatically. He manoeuvered Valentina down onto the floor and checked her pulse and breathing again. Her vital signs were weak, but they were there although now her eyes were starting to become puffy. He undid the top two buttons of her shirt and saw that her chest was covered in hives. Anaphylaxis. He was vaguely aware of passengers starting to gather around him trying to see what was going on, but Francesco ignored them. The driver appeared and seemed stunned by the scene unfolding in front of him.

'Get the first-aid kit,' Francesco said in a tone which commanded the man's attention. 'And the defibrillator.'

It worked, and the driver reappeared quickly with the items Francesco had requested. 'Do you know how to use this?' he asked dubiously, looking at the defibrillator.

Francesco gave him a look which made clear the stupidity of the question in his eyes. 'Hopefully, I won't need it.'

'What can I do?'

'Pass me the first-aid kit and get everyone out of here.' He glanced up and noticed people reaching for their phones, lifting them to take photos. 'What the hell are you doing? Put those bloody things away.' Turning to the driver, he said, 'Get them out of here now.' He turned away, disgusted that people would think of taking pictures in such a situation.

Something about the authority with which Francesco was dealing with the situation galvanised the driver, and he started shepherding people out of the carriage and onto the platform. In the carriage, Francesco was opening the first-aid kit. 'Please, please, please,' he muttered to himself. Then thanking everything and nothing in particular, he found the epinephrine auto injector he had hoped would be there in the kit. He cut her jeans and stabbed the pen into her thigh. He checked her pulse and breathing again; she was holding on. Then he heard the sirens of the approaching ambulance and, for reasons he didn't stop to question, he opened her bag, found her phone and identity card and slipped them into his pocket.

The paramedics boarded the train, and Francesco gave them a comprehensive summary of everything that had happened and what he had done. One of the paramedics looked at him, and raised an eyebrow. 'Not bad for a beginner.'

Francesco bit back a variety of replies and simply said, 'Where are you taking her?'

'Ospedale Santa Maria.'

'Where's that?'

'Ciconia. Do you know her name or anything about her?'

'No. Where's Ciconia?'

The paramedics were busy following their protocols and had lost interest in Francesco the moment it seemed he could provide no further information. Francesco watched them work, desperately wishing he were in their place, back at work.

'Where's Ciconia?' he asked again.

'It's a frazione of Orvieto. Look we have to leave.' Then to his colleague, 'Perhaps there's some ID in her bag.' He gestured at it with his chin. Valentina was on the stretcher by now. 'Let's go.'

Francesco watched them leave, a multitude of thoughts battling for supremacy, but the driver was back bombarding him with questions. Then passengers and local railway staff descended upon him as well, and he was swamped by their competing demands for attention.

When they finally got back underway and he had finished checking everyone's tickets, he went and sat down where had been before, opposite Valentina's now vacant seat. There was still plenty of time to go before they arrived in Rome. The remaining people in the carriage were a few seats away, and he was, to all intents and purposes, alone. He took out her Identity Card and her phone. Why had he taken them? What was he going to do now? As he thought about it, he realised he had taken them because he hadn't wanted the hospital staff to contact her parents. He could imagine they were the last people she would have wanted to see. Or maybe he was wrong. Perhaps he shouldn't have interfered and just let events take whatever course they would. He would never have had to see her again. Except … except for the fact that she had trusted him and confided in him. He couldn't just walk away. He had to try to do the right thing.

He tapped the screen of her phone and it came on. No password was requested. Twelve missed calls; seven from her mother and five from Étienne. There was nothing from her father. There were messages too, but Francesco couldn't bring himself to read or listen to those. It seemed far too intrusive. More intrusive than taking someone's phone and going through it, he thought to himself grimly. Perhaps he ought to contact someone. He started scrolling through the contacts on her phone and dismissed them one by one: Mamma - no, Papà – no. Numerous people he assumed were friends, but as he had no idea who they were or how close they were to her, he dismissed them as well. He scrolled back up again. Étienne. His finger hovered over his name. If only he knew who she would want him to contact, or even if she would want him to contact anyone at all.

He snapped the phone cover shut again and returned her possessions to his pocket. He rested his head against the seat back and stared at the ceiling. Would she make a full recovery? What should he do about contacting someone? And other issues started to gnaw away at the back of his mind. What was he going to do with her ID and phone? How would he explain how they had come into his possession or the lie to the paramedic that he didn't know her name or anything about her?

His shift ended when the train arrived in Rome, but instead of going home as soon as he could get away, he went to the staff area and bundled his cap, jacket, tie, ID badge and ticket reader into his locker. He swapped his shirt for a t-shirt and then caught the next train back to Orvieto. All he really wanted to know was that she was going to recover, and then she would be able to tell him what she wanted to do.

The gentle countryside with its rolling hills and grazing sheep usually made for a relaxing journey, but Francesco felt his anxiety building by the minute. He saw the city of Orvieto rising above the surrounding countryside, and then they pulled into the station. As he left, he realised he had no idea where the hospital was or how to get there. At Termini, there were always taxis queuing up, but Orvieto was a quiet sleepy station and there was not a single one in sight. Now he had got that far, he was impatient to get to the hospital.

He stared at the little fountain outside the station, remembering the sight and sound of water was supposed to be calming. Five minutes passed then ten and any idea he might have had about that theory faded away. A bus arrived to take passengers up to the city, and the driver told him that it was not the bus he needed. Another ten minutes crawled by, and then a taxi appeared and finally he was on his way.

They passed through the lower part of Orvieto and away from the old town in its dramatic location on the summit of a hill of volcanic rock rising from the countryside, a sight which he had seen so often from the train. Then they drove through the quiet outskirts, through tunnels and over the river.

He saw the old town again dominating the gentle Umbrian landscape and to the other side, a signpost indicating they were entering Ciconia. They headed further out into the countryside, and Francesco started to wonder where they were going. The road headed up, and Francesco saw the lower town spread out below him and the old town on its bluff. They rounded another bend, and finally Francesco saw the hospital loom up in front of them, the walls the colour of burnt cream in the warm sunlight of early autumn.

This was the first time he had been anywhere near a hospital since the day he had resigned. Between Lauren's death and his resignation, every time he had got to the door of the hospital where he had worked, the flashbacks and cold sweats had started but today there was no panic, there were no flashbacks and no cold sweats. He was focused on finding Valentina, and he was filled with a sense of purpose he hadn't felt in a very long time.

There was a reception area, but it was unattended and when he stopped a couple of staff passing through, nobody seemed able to offer him any advice as to how to find a patient. Eventually he decided to head straight for the A&E Department and see if she was there. He found he was able to walk straight in, and he started checking all the beds for her. After a fruitless search, he stopped at the end of the ward, a sense of despair settling over him and replacing his earlier sense of being on a mission.

'May I help you?'

Francesco turned round to find a nurse looking at him curiously. He was suddenly conscious of the fact that he probably looked somewhat dishevelled and realised the sight of him scanning all of the beds in the ward must have looked strange at the very least.

'I'm looking for someone.'

'And who is that?' She spoke to him as someone might

speak to a child they feared was on the edge of a tantrum and might be provoked by the slightest wrong word.

'Valentina.'

'Is she a relative?'

'Yes,' he said on impulse, knowing that no information would be given to him otherwise.

'And how is she related to you?'

Francesco felt himself beginning to sweat. He had started digging a hole for himself and now he had no choice but to keep going and hope he could bluff his way through the situation.

'She is my niece. I must see her. I know she's here as I received a phone call from someone to inform me of that. She was admitted to A&E earlier today. I came as quickly as I could.'

'Who phoned you? And why would they phone her uncle and not her mother or father?'

'Her parents are away. They're out of contact at the moment.'

'Who phoned you?' she persisted.

'I didn't catch the caller's name,' Francesco said, improvising as he went along. 'But how would I know she was here if I hadn't been advised? How would I know her name and why would I be looking for her?'

The nurse stood back and appeared to evaluate him. 'What's your name?'

'Francesco De … De Rosa' he said, almost saying De Luca and realising just in time that giving his real surname would be unwise. He could feel himself in danger of starting to get tied in knots, and if they knew his real name he might not be able to extricate himself from the situation. He was grateful he had left his uniform and ID in a locker.

Whatever the nurse had been weighing up, she seemed to have found him to be genuine. 'Come with me.'

They made their way back to the reception desk at A&E. 'Wait over there,' the nurse said, waving in the direction of a row of plastic chairs bolted to the floor.

Francesco obediently sat down and watched as the nurse spoke quietly to a colleague at the desk. They looked over in his direction a number of times. Heads shook and nodded and papers were reviewed. Time seemed to slow down, and Francesco wondered how he would ever talk his way out of this. He considered getting up and leaving, but he had to see Valentina, whose ID card and phone seemed to be burning a hole in the rucksack he had grabbed from his locker.

He got up and started pacing up and down. Saying he had been called had been a stupid lie; if they checked her belongings, they would find no phone and no phone meant they would have no contact details for her family.

The nurse who had stopped him earlier approached him. 'This is a very delicate situation for me. We have a young woman who was admitted this afternoon, but she had no identification on her.'

Francesco started to describe Valentina to the nurse, but she shook her head. 'I didn't see her.'

'Is this woman still here?'

She hesitated. 'Yes.'

'And is she OK?'

'Yes, but you must understand that this young woman might not be the person you are looking for, and I cannot give you any further information.'

'But you must understand that, as I said, her parents are away. Valentina, if this is her, is all alone, and she needs someone from her family to be with her.'

'Yes, yes, I do understand.' She debated what to do. 'There is someone else I can ask, but she won't be on duty for another two hours. Could you wait?'

'Of course.'

'Very well. I'll show you where you can get a coffee, and I'll come and find you there later. I'll warn you now, though that she might not be able to see you straight away. It could be a long wait.'

# CHAPTER FIFTEEN

After three cups of poor coffee from a vending machine, which almost made him miss Arturo's ristretto, and a two-and-a-half-hour wait, Francesco was even more on edge. He had tried to formulate a coherent story; one which would convince them he was indeed Valentina's uncle and that they should let him see her, but he just went round in ever more frustrating circles as he found holes in every version he came up with.

He looked at his watch again. Nobody was going to come. He felt that sense of helplessness and hopelessness that washed over him whenever he had to deal with anything involving the Italian authorities. He checked Valentina's phone again; another set of missed calls from her mother and Étienne. There were lots of notifications of messages as well, but he couldn't bring himself to look at them and, besides, if he did, it would show that Valentina had, apparently, read them but chosen not to respond. He shoved her phone back into his rucksack.

Another twenty minutes passed, and then the nurse he

had spoken to earlier appeared with another woman dressed in a tight black suit and high heels. The nurse indicated him to her colleague and said something he couldn't hear. He sat up straighter as she approached him.

'Signor De Rosa?' she said, making it sound more like a challenge than a polite social question.

'Yes,' he said, standing up. 'Signora...?' he said, extending a hand which was pointedly ignored.

'I understand you have been enquiring about a patient you believe is in this hospital?'

'Yes. Valentina, my niece. May I see her now?'

'Just a moment. As far as I know, we have not even established that the person you are looking for is here.'

'As I said, her name is Valentina. She is my niece, my sister's daughter. I received a call advising me she was here.'

'May I see your ID?'

'I don't have it with me.' Even as he said it, he realised how unlikely it sounded.

'Excuse me?' Her tone made it clear she found it equally implausible.

'I was in such a panic when I received the phone call from the hospital that I just left home straight away.'

'I see you managed to remember some things,' she said, nodding at the rucksack at his feet.

'Signora, what can I say? How can I convince you to let me see my niece?' Francesco asked, trying to appeal to the better nature he hoped she had hidden away somewhere.

'Tell me about her,' she said, the abrupt change of tack throwing him momentarily.

'You mean describe what she looks like?'

'For example.'

'Well, she's got dark, shoulder-length hair, very curly. Green eyes. And freckles. Lots of freckles. She's about 167 centimetres tall.'

'How old is she?'

'Eighteen.' Francesco knew from her identity card that she was not quite eighteen, but if she was an adult it eliminated the hospital's pressing need to contact a parent.

'This is highly irregular.' She looked around as if hoping someone who could solve her dilemma would materialise.

'I do understand about patient confidentiality, signora but, as I said to the nurse, she should have someone with her.'

'If it is her.'

Francesco could see they were getting nowhere. He decided to gamble. 'Tell her that her Uncle Francesco is here. Ask for her permission.' He paused. 'If she is able to give it.' The last sentence was clearly a question even if not phrased as one, but he did not receive an answer.

'Wait here.'

She walked off, radiating irritation, and Francesco returned to his seat. What had he done now? He was just digging an even deeper hole for himself.

He watched the hands of the plastic clock on the wall judder past, counting off every painful minute, which seemed to stretch out and become longer than the preceding one.

Another quarter of an hour passed, and the woman

reappeared. 'Come with me.'

Francesco got up, retrieved his bag and followed her. They walked to the lift and waited in silence. As the doors opened, the woman finally spoke again. 'I believe the patient we have here is Valentina,' she began reluctantly. 'She certainly matches your description. She seemed confused when I told her you were here, but she's still a little disoriented so some confusion is to be expected. My problem is that I have no idea who either of you are. I really don't like any of this, but she wants to see you so I suppose I'll allow it.'

Francesco felt himself start to relax for the first time since he had started this mission. The lift doors opened, and they stepped out into a corridor with a lino floor, yellow walls and a faint smell of bleach permeating the air.

They took a few turns, and then she stopped abruptly. 'Letting you see her is as far as I will go. I will not divulge any information about her condition or her treatment. Do you understand?'

'I do.'

'Please remember she's been through a lot, and she's sleepy and confused. Don't press her if she's not ready to talk.'

Francesco nodded.

'Before you go in, I'd like you to confirm that is Valentina.'

Francesco peered through the wire mesh glass panel in the door. 'That's her.'

'I'm still not happy about this.'

'As I said, her parents are away. It's surely better she has me with her than nobody.'

'I suppose so.' She gave him a look. 'I'll be waiting here until I'm sure she's comfortable with this.'

'Of course.'

Francesco entered the room quietly and took a seat on the far side of the bed so he could face the door and keep an eye on the woman whose name he had still not discovered.

Valentina's eyes were closed so he lightly rested his hand on hers. 'Valentina,' he said gently.

She opened her eyes and turned in his direction. It took her a moment to focus, and she blinked a few times.

'Valentina,' he repeated, looking at her, and then turning his eyes towards the door where the anonymous woman stood warily watching them. He could feel his heart racing as he wondered what she would say. Everything would turn on the next few moments.

The pause continued while Valentina struggled to slot all the pieces into a place. She turned with some effort to look at the woman and then back to Francesco. Then, a little more loudly than absolutely necessary she said, 'Uncle Francesco, I'm so glad you're here.'

Francesco shifted his angle slightly so his back was now to their observer. 'I came as soon as I could, Valentina. It was the least I could do with your parents being away.' He gave her a meaningful look which he hoped she would pick up on.

'What? Oh yes, always travelling.' The effort she had made had exhausted her, and she was becoming drowsy again. 'Will you stay with me?'

'If I'm allowed to.' He turned and looked at the woman in the suit who had by now ventured into the room.

'I suppose it wouldn't hurt, but we'll be back to check on both of you regularly. And you can fill in all this paperwork while you're here.'

'Paperwork?'

'Yes, with Valentina's details.'

'I might not know some of them.'

'I'm sure you'll know enough, being her uncle.'

Francesco wondered whether she has really emphasised those last three words or if it was simply his guilty conscience. 'I'll do what I can,' he said trying to sound amenable.

Time drifted past. Nurses came in to check on Valentina, and one took pity on Francesco and brought him a cup of coffee and some biscuits.

Francesco stared at the blank form. He could get most of the information he needed from her identity card and contact numbers from her phone, but the very reason he had taken them in the first place was to give her the choice as to what to do and whom to contact. He fiddled with the forms, folding the corners back and forth.

'Francesco?' Valentina had woken up.

'Yes, I'm here. How are you feeling?'

'Like I've been run over.' She focused on him. 'I think they think I was trying to kill myself, but I wasn't. I just wanted the headache to stop, and I hadn't slept all night so I got confused and couldn't remember how many tablets I had taken. I had no idea I was allergic to aspirin.'

'I can understand that. Do you know where you are?'

'Orvieto, I think they said. Is that right?'

'Yes, it is.'

'You must think I was so stupid getting on that train. I was just so stressed that I needed to go somewhere. Anywhere. I couldn't keep still.'

Francesco remembered what had led him to taking the job he had now. It didn't seem stupid at all, but there were other thing he needed to talk to her about. The timing was terrible, but he had no choice. 'Valentina, I took your ID card and phone when you were on the train so they couldn't phone your parents. After everything you told me, I thought I was doing the right thing. Now I think I just acted on impulse. Then I made up that stupid story about being your uncle so I could check on you and give you your things back.'

'You saved my life.'

'I did what anyone would have done.'

'No. Nobody else would have sat and listened to me. Anybody else would have been gone by the time, well, you know, and then it might have been too late.'

Francesco shrugged, feeling embarrassed.

'So I say you are my honorary uncle and big brother. I'll never be able to thank you enough for what you've done.'

Francesco squeezed her hand. 'You're welcome. But we have a problem.'

'What?' She looked alarmed.

'The hospital wants me to fill in all this paperwork. I told them you were eighteen, but if I give them your details, they'll realise you're a minor, and then they'll want to contact your parents.'

'No.' She looked horrified at the prospect.

'There are also lots of messages and missed calls on your phone.'

'Who are they from?' she asked, looking half hopeful and half fearful.

'The calls are from your mum and Étienne.'

'Étienne called?' She looked happy for the first time. 'Did he leave a message? What did he say?'

'I don't know. It wasn't my place to listen to or read your messages. I think I've already interfered more than I should have done.'

'Will you listen to them for me now?'

'Wouldn't you rather do that?'

'No, if it's bad news I want you to prepare me first.'

'Well OK, but, thinking about it, we don't want anyone to see your phone.'

'Take it to the bathroom.'

'Do you want me to read your messages too?'

'Yes, please.'

'I won't be long.'

True to his word, he was back in less than ten minutes.

'Well?' she said anxiously, propping herself up.

'Your mother has apologised over and over again and begged you to let her know you are safe.'

'And Étienne?'

'He apologised for leaving, but said he couldn't see what else to do. He also apologised for missing all your calls. And he loves you.'

'He does?'

'He does.' Francesco smiled. 'Here, take the phone and put it under the sheets. Read the messages at least. I'll keep a look out.'

He stood by the door as Valentina went through them.

'Francesco?'

He turned. 'Yes?'

'I've decided what to do. I'm going to send my mum a message to tell her I'm fine, and I'm staying with a friend for a few days.'

'And Étienne?'

'I'm not sure.'

'And I need you to help me get out of here before the hospital finds out who I am and contacts my parents.'

'I don't know what your medical situation is. And I'm pretty sure that as you overdosed, even unintentionally, you'll probably be required to have an evaluation before you can leave.'

Valentina looked at him curiously. 'How did you know what to do? Earlier, on the train, I mean? And how do you know this stuff?'

Francesco knew he had reached a crossroads. He could lie, which he had seemed to be doing rather more than he had felt comfortable with in the last few hours, or he could tell the truth, but where would that lead? Valentina had trusted him implicitly; she didn't deserve lies in return.

'I used to be a doctor.'

'But you're a ticket inspector,' she said incredulously.

Despite himself, Francesco laughed at the comment and

the absurdity of the situation. 'Yes, now I am, but I was a doctor.'

Valentina shifted up further in the bed, all thoughts of her own predicament temporarily abandoned. 'But why did you stop being a doctor? And why did you become a ticket inspector? Sorry, I mean there's nothing wrong with that, but it's not exactly a normal career move.'

'My wife was in an accident. She didn't make it, and I changed. Everything changed.'

Valentina gasped. 'I'm so sorry.'

Francesco took a deep breath. 'Thanks. Listen, I think we should get back to your situation,' he said trying to sound efficient. 'Send that message to your mum before your battery dies, and then we'll work out what to do next.' He resumed his position by the door while she composed her message.

'OK, done. I've told her I'm nearly out of battery, and I don't have my charger so that's bought us some time.'

Francesco took the phone and slipped it back into his bag. He felt better once it was out of sight.

'You know,' he said thoughtfully, 'doctors are renowned for their terrible handwriting.'

'Are they?' She was becoming sleepy again.

'When I complete the form some of the details might be … open to interpretation.'

He looked at her, hoping for confirmation that he could go ahead but she was asleep so Francesco filled in the form being as sparing as he could with the details. As if on cue, as he finished, the woman in the suit reappeared.

'Do you have those forms ready?' she asked brusquely.

Francesco handed them over without a word, suddenly tired of her constant hostility.

She flicked though them. 'They're barely legible.'

Francesco shrugged apologetically.

'And there are gaps.'

'As I said there would be, signora. I'm afraid that is all I can give you. The rest will have to wait until Valentina can complete them herself.'

'The contact numbers for her parents are missing. You must have those.'

'Actually I don't. Like almost everyone else, I put telephone numbers in my phone so I never need to memorise them.'

'And where is your phone?'

'It was stolen.' Francesco found he was almost enjoying frustrating this woman, given her objectionable manner.

'That's … unfortunate.'

'I thought so too,' he responded.

'Well, where is Valentina's phone? We apparently got your number from there so it must be here somewhere.'

'I expect so,' he said, more coolly than he felt.

She started going through Valentina's bag and the pockets of her clothes.

'It's not here.' She looked at him accusingly.

Francesco decided attack was the best form of defence. 'Then I suggest you find out which member of your staff has taken it, signora.'

'None of my staff would ever do such a thing.'

'No doubt you believe that as you are clearly an honest

person but, sadly, less virtuous people do exist, and they take advantage of others who cannot look out for themselves.'

She was eyeing him as if trying to decide whether he was being sarcastic or not, but Francesco was picking up momentum now. 'Valentina's father is very well-connected, but he can be a little "intemperate", shall we say. He would not be happy to hear that his daughter's phone had disappeared while she was in your care. I strongly suggest you make enquiries. Perhaps it has just been misplaced.'

'Misplaced, you say?' He could see she was considering the well-connected father, which could mean any manner of things, none of which were likely to be good from her point of view.

'It seems quite possible. It could be in the A&E department or even the ambulance.'

'I'll investigate.'

'An excellent idea. I would also add that as Valentina is an adult, you don't actually need to contact her parents.'

She gave him a look which seemed to encompass fear, suspicion and respect and then retreated, leaving the forms behind. Francesco slumped back down in his chair and glanced at his watch. He had missed the last train of the night back to Rome. He wasn't due at work until early afternoon on the following day so he could still get back in time, but he couldn't abandon Valentina now. He ran his hand over his stubble, remembered how he had left his uniform stuffed in a locker and considered how scruffy he would look unless he could get back to Rome early enough to go home, shower and get a change of clothes.

He slipped out of the room and went back to the bathroom. He took his phone out of his bag and noticed the battery was getting low. He had to make a decision. He phoned the contact number for staff reporting in sick. The person who took his call was pleasant enough, but he sensed she was now contemplating the difficulties involved in finding someone to cover his shift and the inevitable paperwork that would be involved.

He made his way back, noticing the hush that had fallen over the hospital now that night had arrived. It brought back memories so intense of so many nights on duty that it was like a physical blow, and he had to stop and wait for the impact to pass. As he entered Valentina's room, he found a nurse he had met earlier checking on Valentina. She smiled at him. 'I'm sorry, visiting hours are over.'

'I live in Rome, signora. I have missed the last train and I have nowhere to go.'

'There are plenty of hotels in Orvieto.'

'I left my ID card at home so that is not an option.' It was not true, but it was consistent with what he had said earlier. He must have looked as exhausted as he felt for she relented. 'I suppose you could sleep over there,' she said, pointing to an armchair in the corner.

'Thank you,' he said, truly grateful. 'How is she?'

'She's doing very well. She's lucky someone got her medical attention straight away. Her guardian angel was certainly looking out for her today. She's young and otherwise in good health so I'm optimistic. Now get some sleep.'

# CHAPTER SIXTEEN

Somehow he managed a couple of hours of sleep, but the trade-off was a stiff neck. He stretched and checked his watch; almost seven. He looked over at Valentina who was still sleeping and crept out of the room to go to the bathroom. He stripped to the waist and splashed cold water over himself. Glancing in the mirror, he realised that although he looked tired and dishevelled, something had changed. He felt better about himself, but in a way he could not quite define.

When he returned to the room, he found Valentina propped up on the pillow. A table had been pulled over her bed and a plastic tray placed on it with a glass of water and a plate of dry toast.

She looked astonished as he walked in. 'You're still here.'

'Of course. How's the breakfast? Looks appetising.'

'They won't let me have anything else,' she said glumly, picking up a piece of toast, examining it and dropping it back on the plate.

'You should try to eat it or at least drink the water. But slowly.'

'OK … uncle,' she said managing a grin.

'How much do you remember about our conversation yesterday?'

'Everything.'

'Really?'

"Yes, the messages from my mum and Étienne and the one I sent back to her. And the hospital forms. What happened about those?'

Francesco told her, and she laughed at the thought of her well-connected father.

'We'll just have to see what happens next,' he said.

'I can't believe you're still here,' she repeated. 'Why would you do that for me?'

'Because you needed someone on your side.'

'I don't think I deserve your kindness. I've made a terrible mess of everything. I was so careless.'

'We all do things we regret at times, but you can sort this out. First let's see what the doctor says.'

The doctor finally arrived, and Francesco was asked to leave so he took the opportunity to locate the hospital's café, where he finally had some reasonable and much needed coffee and a pastry. Their offerings didn't meet Matteo's standards, but they were welcome nonetheless.

After what he judged would be a sufficient amount of time, he returned to Valentina's room

'What did the doctor say?'

'Physically I'm fine, but they want me to see some sort of mental health specialist before they'll let me leave. The appointment's at 11.30,' she said apprehensively. 'I knew it.

They want to decide if I'm crazy.'

'It's not unusual in the circumstances.'

'Would you …? No, you've done enough,' she said, shaking her head.

'Would I what?'

'Would you just stay until I've seen him?'

'I was planning to stay all day.'

'But what about your job? I don't want you to get into trouble.'

'I've told them I'm sick. The trains will still run.'

Valentina smiled. 'OK. I'd really appreciate it if you stayed. Have I got any messages?'

'Hold on.' He reached into his bag and retrieved her phone. 'The battery's dead.'

'Oh,' she said and bit her lip.

'Try not to worry about that. Get some more sleep.'

Valentina didn't need much encouragement and dozed on and off for a few more hours. Francesco was then banished while she was given a bed bath and dressed. He came back to find her sitting in a wheelchair, ready to be taken for her evaluation. She looked at him nervously. 'They're not going to lock me up, are they?'

'They just want to check how you are and try to determine whether you actually meant to hurt yourself or whether it was purely accidental.'

'I truly didn't mean to harm myself. I only took about five or six, I think.'

'Just be honest. Tell the doctor everything; what happened at your parents' home and everything that happened afterwards. He will also have your records from your admission showing you had a severe allergic reaction. That will help to prove it was accidental as well.'

A nurse came in. 'Ready?'

'I suppose so.' She looked at Francesco. 'Wish me luck.'

After she had gone, Francesco went to explore the hospital. He found a small kiosk selling toiletries and was able to clean his teeth, shave and have a proper wash. By the time Valentina returned, he felt close to human again.

'Well?' he asked as she appeared.

Valentina was smiling broadly. 'I did exactly what you said. She was so kind and sympathetic. She reminded me of you.'

'And what was the outcome?'

'I can leave, but she'd like to see me again as an outpatient next week just to see how I'm feeling. Emotionally, not physically.'

'So you're free to leave?'

'Tomorrow, yes.'

'That's fantastic news and I have some good news too. Not as good as yours, but I managed to borrow a charger from one of the nurses. You should be able to check your messages.'

'You really are my guardian angel.'

Francesco laughed. 'Not much of an angel. I've told a lot of lies recently.'

'But with the best of intentions,' she said solemnly.

'Yes,' he conceded.

'I don't know what to tell Étienne. I don't want us to

have any secrets but suppose he thinks I'm crazy?'

'I don't know what to advise you to do, but I'd suggest you be honest with him. Secrets can do a lot of damage.' As he said it, thoughts of Lauren booking that hotel room danced across his vision. He felt the familiar unwelcome doubts coiling inside him.

'Yes, Dottoressa De Luca told me …'

'Sorry. Who?'

'Dottoressa De Luca, the doctor I've just seen.'

'De Luca?'

'Yes. Why?'

'Nothing.' It couldn't be. De Luca was not an unusual surname. But still. 'Valentina, how old would you say Dottoressa De Luca is?'

'Oh, quite old. Older than you. About 40? 45 maybe.' Despite everything, Francesco smiled inwardly at the youth and innocence her comment betrayed.

'Where is her office?'

Valentina gave him directions.

'Will you excuse me?'

'Sure,' she said, looking puzzled.

'I will come back. I promise.'

Francesco walked out into the corridor. Out of sight of Valentina's room, he stopped and tried to collect himself. 'Don't be ridiculous,' he muttered to himself. But perhaps, just perhaps, it wasn't so ridiculous. The right surname, the right age. What had Valentina said? 'She reminded me of you.'

He took some more deep breaths and set out to find the

office. At her door, his confidence failed him. What would be worse? Finding out it was her or finding out it was not? He raised his hand to knock and dropped it again. He stood there, tormented by his lack of courage and indecisiveness.

'May I help you?'

In the seconds as he turned, he wondered if this could be the moment he had dreamed of and feared in equal measure. He opened his eyes to find a tiny woman, much shorter than him, peering at him over a pair of delicate glasses. Not Teddy.

'Oh, I, er, I was looking for Dottoressa De Luca.'

'Let me see.' She consulted the tablet perched in the crook of her arm and tapped the screen a few times. 'Do you have an appointment?' she said, looking concerned.

'No, I don't, but I only need five minutes of her time.'

'Well, I'm sure she'll make time for you if she can. She does that for everyone,' she said warmly. 'Why don't you take a seat in her office?'

'Well, I don't know …'

'Go on. You'll be more comfortable. There are no state secrets scattered about,' she said, smiling at him.

'Thank you.'

Francesco slowly walked into the room. Although nobody was there, he was struck by the welcoming feel of the place. It was totally different to the clinical world just outside.

He closed the door and as he did so, he turned and saw the painting. It was a stunning rendition of a Tuscan farmhouse surrounded by poppy fields. From her desk,

Dottoressa De Luca would be able to see it almost directly opposite her.

His heart was pounding now. De Luca; about 40 or 45; *she reminded me of you*; the painting. He felt slightly dizzy and thought he should sit down, but he couldn't keep still. He paced up and down, trying to regulate his breathing.

He heard the movement of the door handle, and he turned to face the woman entering the room. His heart was pounding so hard that it hurt. And then he saw her. The teenager was now an adult, but there was not a trace of doubt.

'Teddy,' he said, his voice breaking.

She looked at him, stunned into silence. Then, with wonderment in her voice, 'Fran?'

There were tears in his eyes as he nodded. He waited for the rejection he was sure must be coming, wondering if he had enough resilience left to endure it.

'Fran.' She opened her arms, and he went to her without hesitation and they embraced each other, both openly crying.

They held each other as if they would never let go, but eventually they broke the embrace to look at each other.

'I can't believe it. You're here,' she said, reaching for his hand as if to reassure herself that he really was there in front of her.

He took her hand in his and nodded, unable to say anything.

'Let's sit down,' she said, trying to compose herself. They took the comfortable armchairs on the patient's side of the desk, still holding hands as though terrified that letting go would result in another separation.

A few minutes passed in silence as if neither was sure where to start, and then Teddy said, 'So Lauren finally told you where to find me, did she?'

'What?' Francesco looked at Teddy, totally dumbstruck.

'Lauren. She knows I work here. She must have eventually got round to telling you.' She sounded irritated by Lauren, but that made no sense; then again nothing she had just said made sense.

'Teddy, I don't understand this. How did you know Lauren? And if you knew her, you must know what happened.'

'Know what?'

'Lauren's, she's ….she's not with us…' He shook his head and looked at Teddy. His meaning was clear.

Teddy's face fell and the irritation vanished. 'What? I had no idea.' She paused, looking confused. 'But when?'

'Thirteen months ago.'

'I'm so sorry.' She hesitated. 'How?' she asked gently.

'A car accident.'

'Wait. Thirteen months ago? Last August. What date?'

'What date?' Francesco repeated.

'Yes, please. It's important.'

'The 27th of August.'

'It can't be surely.' She was speaking to herself now rather than him.

'What? Teddy, I don't understand.'

'Wait just a moment, please. I have to check something.' She got up and moved around to the other side of the desk, fished a key out of her pocket, unlocked a drawer and pulled out a large 2018 desk diary. She leafed through it, finally landing on the date he had given her.

'No, it can't be.'

'Teddy? Please talk to me.'

She pulled herself back to the present and moved back to sit beside him again.

'Lauren told me she'd been searching for me because she thought you would want to meet me again, and she wanted to find out if I felt the same way. She was very cautious, though. I think, as much as she wanted to reunite us, she was also afraid of bringing me back into your life. She was wary of me and how you'd react. She thought it might be like throwing a hand grenade into your life.

'She seemed to think it was for the best to take it slowly, not to reveal too much in case I wasn't the person she hoped I'd be. I think she was scared I might have turned out to be, oh, I don't know, a disappointment or a troublemaker. Who can say? Or perhaps she just didn't want to tell you and get your hopes up until she knew what I was like. She told me you hadn't tried to look for your family because of things mum had said to you. She wouldn't give anything away about you, or even much about herself for that matter, but there was something about her I liked. I could tell she adored you so that was a definite point in her favour.' Teddy smiled, but it was a slight, sad smile.

'I still don't understand why the date is relevant.'

'We talked several times, and we built up a certain rapport even though she was so cagey. We eventually agreed to meet. I said I'd fly over. She was anxious and said she needed to meet me first before deciding what to do next. I think she was terrified of you getting hurt. We agreed to meet at Manchester airport. She said she'd book me a room at a hotel; she didn't say which one. I didn't ask as I'd assumed she'd be at the airport to meet me. She said we could go there and talk properly in private.'

'And?' Francesco asked, although the pieces were starting to fall into place and some of the weight was lifting. Lauren had been at the hotel for the most innocent of reasons. She hadn't been betraying him; she had been trying to give him something back.

'And she never turned up.'

'So what did you do?'

'I phoned her over and over, but I couldn't get a reply. It just rang and rang. I waited at the airport all night. I didn't dare leave and book into a hotel in case she arrived and I missed her, but by the following morning, I was angry. Probably being so tired didn't help. I never did do well without sleep, did I?' Teddy smiled ruefully. 'So with nothing to go on, I booked a flight straight back home. It seemed like she'd led me on and yet that didn't seem to fit with what I knew of her, or thought I knew, which confused me. Then I thought she might have had second thoughts, or she may have spoken to you and you'd said you didn't want to see me. Whichever way you look at it, I was hurt. But the day I flew to England was …'

'The day that Lauren died.'

'So all those things I assumed were wrong.'

'The accident happened on a road not far from the airport. And she had booked a hotel room so she was going to meet you. That was Lauren, she always kept her word.'

'So if she hadn't been coming to meet me, she wouldn't have … she would still …'

Francesco shook his head. 'She was driving away from the airport. I don't know why, and I don't suppose I ever will, but it's not your fault. You have no reason to feel guilty.'

Teddy was silent, trying to process the horror of him losing his wife so suddenly. She was also unconvinced that she had played no part in what had happened, but saw no point in protesting. She could see how much it had cost her brother to tell her what had happened. Why should she expect him to salve her conscience on top of that? She decided to change tack. 'So how did you find me? The same way Lauren did, I suppose'

'No, Lauren was an investigative reporter. I wouldn't have a clue how to track anyone down.'

'But with social media these days…'

'I haven't got any social media accounts. Lauren used that stuff now and again,  but it's always been a mystery to me. I didn't really understand why she enjoyed it or what the point of it was. I'm not comfortable with all that sharing stuff on the Internet. Lauren respected that and never posted any information about me.'

Teddy nodded. 'But if not via the Internet?'

'I've been visiting a patient you saw earlier today. Valentina. She told me she had seen a Dottoressa De Luca, and I just had a feeling. I can't explain it.'

'How do you know her?'

Francesco explained the events which had led to him meeting Valentina and brought him to Orvieto.

'Wait a moment. You're living in Italy now?'

'I came back in January. After Lauren I needed … a change. I tried to find you. I went back to our old flat, but the woman living there now hadn't heard of you.'

'We moved years ago, but we can talk about that later.' She paused. 'And you're working as a ticket inspector?'

He nodded.

'Valentina didn't mention you by name, but she said the man who helped her on the train had medical knowledge. You know, without your intervention, she'd probably be dead.'

'I was a doctor in England.' She heard the wistfulness in his voice for a time now lost to him.

'Why did you give that up? '

Francesco told her about Lauren's arrival in the A&E Department, the loss of not just Lauren, but also their child and the aftermath. 'I just couldn't go on.'

'Oh Fran, she said, taking his hand again. 'You've been through so much. I wish I'd been there for you. What do you think now? Do you think it was the right decision to give up medicine? It sounds like you regret it.'

'At the time I didn't feel like I had any choice. I couldn't function properly. But yesterday, helping Valentina, watching the paramedics at work, I finally realised how desperately I miss helping people.'

'It's not too late to go back. If you had proper counselling to deal with what happened, I'm sure you could do it.'

'Do you really think so?'

'Of course. Fran, listen to me. There's absolutely nothing wrong with your job if you like it, but if what you actually want is to go back into medicine you have to do it. I know how much you have lost, but don't lose this too.'

'I just assumed it was over for me.'

'I don't believe that and needing help to move on with your life is nothing to be ashamed of.'

'I've felt so guilty about not coping better,' he said only fully realising it as he uttered the words.

'You need to work with a professional who can help you put the pieces back together again.'

'I need time to think about that. I'd convinced myself that part of my life was over and I'd never be able to practise again.'

'I understand. If you'd like me to, I can put you in touch with someone. No pressure, though, I promise.'

'Thank you. But what about you? What brought you to Orvieto?'

'It's a long story.'

Francesco spread his hands. 'Try me.'

'OK, I'll try to give you the short version for now. Dad and I stayed in Rome until I'd finished studying at the liceo. Not in our flat, though. As soon as it became clear that you and mum were never coming back, he sold it. I think the memories were too painful for him. After university, I decided I wanted to move somewhere a bit less frenetic.

Don't get me wrong, I still think Rome is wonderful but it's noisy, chaotic and expensive. I wanted to live close enough to be able to visit easily, but in a quieter environment. Orvieto seemed to fit the bill and it turned out to be the perfect choice for me. I…. no, it doesn't matter.'

'What?'

'Another time.'

He looked at her and registered the wedding ring for the first time. 'You're married.'

'Yes, I met my husband here, in Orvieto I mean, but it doesn't seem appropriate to talk about that now.'

Because of Lauren?'

She nodded.

'Teddy, whenever I thought about you – and I did a lot – I always hoped you were happy. You are, aren't you?' he said, searching her face.

'Yes, I am,' she said, looking almost ashamed. 'And there's something else I should tell you. You have two nieces.'

Francesco did not trust himself to speak. In less than an hour he had gone from feeling totally alone to finding his sister and discovering she had a family. He tried to process the mixture of emotions washing through him.

'What are their names?' he asked eventually.

'Gabriela and Lucia; they're six and four. My husband's name is Pietro. I really want you to meet them. If you want to, that is.'

'I'd love to. And dad?'

'He's still with us, but he's very different from the person you knew.'

Is he ill?'

'No, no, it's nothing like that although he's slowed down a bit with age. Fran, how much do you know about what happened that night?'

'The night they had that huge row and mum and I left? I remember it, but I never truly understand what started it all, and mum refused to speak of it ever again. All I got over the years were occasional comments which gave me the impression that neither you nor dad wanted anything more to do with us.'

'Do you want to know what it was all about?'

Francesco took a deep breath. Today seemed to be the day when many of the mysteries of his past would be swept away. 'I do.'

'It's not a very pleasant story. I only found out everything much later on. It took me a long time to put it all together. Dad had been having an affair. It wasn't the first. That's why mum and dad argued so much. I think that's also why she took us to Tuscany for all those weekends and little breaks in the summer. She couldn't put up with it day in and day out, and I think she wanted to get us away from it too. Anyway, usually they were flings which fizzled out, but that affair was different. Dad took her to a dinner at work so mum felt publically humiliated as well as privately hurt. She confronted him about it that night. Give her up, give all of them up for good or she'd leave.'

'And he refused?'

'Exactly. He was selfish. He wanted to play the family man and also be a womaniser when it suited him, but mum wouldn't go along with it. So in the heat of the moment he issued his own ultimatum - put up with it or leave. I honestly believe he regretted it as soon as he'd said it, but he was too proud and too obstinate to take it back.'

'So that's why we left. But why didn't you come with us? Surely mum didn't want to leave you behind?'

'I didn't know about all the affairs back then. If I had, perhaps it would have been different, but I was always a real daddy's girl. Do you remember? I could twist him round my little finger, which was useful as a teenager, but mum wouldn't let me get away with half the things he did. Besides, I didn't want to change schools in the middle of liceo or leave my friends. I seem to remember I had a crush on someone too. I just thought mum was being totally unreasonable so that's why I refused to go. I was very angry with her for a long time until I understood what had really been going on. It sounds like my experience with dad was very much like yours with mum. We rarely spoke of her or you, but the few comments dad made convinced me that you and mum wouldn't want to know me,' she said sadly. 'Where did you go when you went back to England?'

'We went to live with mum's dad. Do you remember grandpa?'

'Only just. I remember grandma dying when I was about ten and mum going back to England for the funeral, and then he came over to visit us a year or two after that. I think that was the last time I saw him.'

"We lived with him in his bungalow at first, but it was a bit cramped. I hated being in England. I missed you, even though I thought you hated me. I missed all my things, my friends and everything about Rome. I asked mum several times when we would be going home, and she just told me to stop asking, told me we were home and that was the end of the conversation. Anyway, after a while, mum got a job, and we moved into a flat nearby. It was pleasant enough, but it never felt like home.' Francesco thought back to something Teddy had said earlier about their father. 'You said he's different now?'

'Yes, he's more thoughtful, more reflective. As far as I can tell, he finished the affair immediately. He might have had others since, I honestly don't know, but I'm sure he's never had a long-term relationship. He's certainly never introduced me to anyone. You know, I believe that he's never stopped loving mum. I suppose that's why I was able to forgive him. He's punished himself more than I ever could, even if I wanted to. You know, seeing how dad behaved … I think that's when I understood how differently men and women tend to view love and sex.'

Francesco remembered Silvia saying much the same thing about how men could separate love and sex far more easily than women, although he thought he had not been very successful at that. Could that ability be described as successful? He also remembered the pain Silvia's husband's affair had caused her, and how she had acted out of character in reaction to it. For the first time, he felt he could understand what must have motivated his mother to act as she had, and he regretted the times when he had been angry with her; an anger born of ignorance of the facts.

'Fran?'

'What? Oh, sorry. Does he still live in Rome?'

'Yes, he has a lovely flat just north of the Borghese. He's retired now and spends a lot of his time reading and painting. We usually get down there to see him once a month. Occasionally he comes up here. He adores the girls. I think he sees them as a second chance.'

'Do you think he'd want to see me?' Even as he asked the question, he wondered if he wanted to see his father.

'I don't know about the old dad but, as he is now, yes, I believe he would. What about mum? Do you think she'd like to see me?'

Francesco's heart sank. Of course, she wouldn't know unless Lauren had told her, which she obviously hadn't. Now, at this extraordinary reunion, he had to tell her. 'I'm sorry, Teddy. She's no longer with us.' He wondered why he couldn't say the word "dead" and always had to wrap up what he meant, what he felt, in euphemisms.

'Oh.' Teddy's expectant expression turned into something unreadable, and Francesco could only guess at the emotions she must have been trying to process. Finally she asked, 'When? What happened?'

'The flu outbreak in 2009. You know mum had always suffered from asthma. She couldn't fight it.' He looked at her at a loss to know what else to say.

'It's strange, isn't it? I've been able to put her to the back of my mind. Lock her off from my everyday life. It was easy at first because I thought she'd abandoned me. Later, of course, I realised it hadn't been that simple, but I'd adapted by then. But now, I know I'll never get the chance to speak to her again, and I want to so much.' She fell silent for a moment. 'What was she like?'

'What do you mean?'

'I only ever knew her as a child. She was just mum. I never had the chance to get to know her as a person.'

Francesco tried to find the words to describe her. 'I'm not sure I knew her very well either. When we left, it was like a wall went up. She was kind and generous with her time but very guarded. I felt … I felt she didn't want anybody to be too close to her. Above all, she was sad. I always sensed a terrible sadness in her, but she never let me get close enough to her to talk about it. I'm sorry; I wish I could tell you more.'

'I was very headstrong as a teenager. I gave her a hard time. I wish I hadn't.'

'You weren't like that with me.'

'No and I wasn't with dad either, but mum and I … and now I'll always regret the fact that I can't say sorry; that she'll never get the chance to see that I've grown up.'

'I think she would have been immensely proud of you.'

'Thank you.' Teddy paused and then ventured, 'and grandpa?'

Francesco shook his head and looked at Teddy with concern. Her sadness was palpable, but she surprised him by saying, 'Fran, you've lost so much, but I want you to know you have a family here and I so much want you to be a part of it.'

He thought of the unbridgeable gulf between their

parents, a rift which could now never be healed. Then he marvelled at the fact that they could perhaps overcome it. He thought of all the years which had passed and the losses they had suffered. He nodded, but found himself unable to speak.

# CHAPTER SEVENTEEN

Francesco and Teddy had become so involved in their conversation that they had lost track of time. There was a knock at the door, and the woman Francesco had met earlier put her head around the door.

'What should I do about your next appointment, Dottoressa?'

'What's the time? Teddy said, looking at her watch. 'Oh, my next appointment is in ten minutes. I had no idea it was so late.'

"I'm sorry. I didn't like to interrupt,' she said, looking at Francesco curiously.

'No, it's fine. Thank you for letting me know. Could you just give us a few minutes, please?'

'Of course,' she said, withdrawing from the room.

'Francesco, promise me that you're not going to disappear again.'

'There's no chance of that. I'm going to go back to see how Valentina is, and I'll have to go back to Rome tonight so I can go to work tomorrow, but I'm not going to vanish.'

'Will you come and see me before you leave?'

'Of course.'

'Promise?'

'I promise.'

They kissed on both cheeks.

'I don't want you to go,' Teddy admitted.

'I don't want to go but you have patients, and I am definitely not going to disappear.'

They parted reluctantly, and Teddy tried to focus on preparing for her next patient.

Instead of returning directly to Valentina's room, Francesco went outside and started to walk down the hill away from the hospital. After so long indoors, the sunlight hurt his eyes, but he needed fresh air.

He stopped from time to time to look at the view unfolding on his left-hand side. The cluster of cypress trees, dark and elegant in the clear light; the Umbrian countryside with the first hint of autumn making itself felt in a few golden leaves and there, in the distance, the city of Orvieto rising majestically above the valley floor. He leant against the railings trying to process everything that had happened. A bus swept past, delivering and picking up passengers at the top of the road. He found a bench and sat down. The warmth of the afternoon sun made him drowsy and he woke to find a couple of hours had passed.

He forced himself to get up, returned to the hospital and went to Valentina's room. A young man was sitting on the edge of the bed and, by the look of absolute joy on Valentina's face, it could only be Étienne. He debated walking away again, but he wanted to check on Valentina before he left and he was running out of time. He knocked and opened the door. Valentina looked over, smiled delightedly at him and motioned for him to come in.

Étienne turned and smiled at him. 'You must be Francesco,' he said getting up and extending his hand to shake Francesco's.

'Étienne?' Francesco said shaking his hand, noting a warmth and kindness about the man that made him take to him immediately.

'Yes and I can't thank you enough for what you have done for Valentina. If you hadn't been there …'

Francesco wondered what Valentina had told him and was keenly aware he might say the wrong thing. 'It was nothing really,' he said, looking embarrassed.

'It was. I wouldn't have known what to do, and I doubt most other people would have either. I was just going to get us some drinks. Would you like one?'

'Coffee would be good, thanks, but anything will do if they don't have that.'

'Right, I won't be long.'

Francesco looked questioningly at Valentina as he drew the chair up to the side of the bed and sat down.

'It's fine. I've told him everything. As soon as I called him, he left to come here.'

'He must have an understanding boss.'

Valentina smiled. 'He's his own boss. He graduated last year and like so many people he couldn't find work so he decided to work for himself.'

'That's pretty impressive. What does he do?'

'He's a website designer and developer. It's really complicated. I've watched him working, but I haven't got a clue what he's doing. Then I see the finished product and it's amazing.'

'It can't be easy being self-employed, though.'

'No, but all through university he built up an incredible portfolio of work, and he worked for free for anyone who would take him on during his holidays. As well as Italian, he speaks French and English, so that helps as well.'

'I admire that sort of dedication.'

'So do I. That's another reason I got so angry with my parents. If they had only taken the time to get to know him. Once we were at the station waiting for a train. I went to get some drinks from the vending machine and I saw these police officers walking down the platform. The only person they stopped was Étienne. They made him get out his ID, and then they started making phone calls. I was furious. I grabbed the drinks and went over to see what was going on, but Étienne just told me everything was fine and not to get angry.

'They were checking him out; making sure his ID was legitimate. He was so calm throughout the whole thing. Eventually they realised his papers were genuine and went away, but I watched them and they didn't ask to see anyone else's ID. I don't think I could cope with being treated like that; singled out just because of the colour of my skin. I'd never thought about discrimination before I started going out with Étienne, but now I see things so differently.'

They sat in silence for a while and then Valentina said, 'You were gone for a long time. Was it something to do with Dottoressa De Luca?'

Yes, it was,' Francesco admitted, wondering where he would ever start.

'Do you want to tell me?'

'It's such a long story but, to keep it short, she's my sister. I hadn't seen her for twenty-seven years. In fact, I didn't even know where she was, but when you mentioned her name, I don't know … I just had this gut feeling.'

He looked at Valentina and saw tears in her eyes. 'What happened when you saw each other? Was it … I mean, how did she react?'

'I've often dreamed of finding her and wondered what it would be like. I've been through every variation of how it would turn out and then today, well, it couldn't have been better.'

'That's beautiful,' said Valentina, backhanding a stray tear away. 'Sorry, I'm a bit over emotional at the moment.'

'I'm not surprised. You've been through a traumatic experience.'

'Do you believe in karma or fate, whatever you want to call it?'

'I can't say I do,' Francesco admitted.

'I do, and these last few days have proved it to me. Look at what's happened. I could have caught any train, but it just happened that the Rome train was the next one that was leaving so I got on that one, and you were there. If it hadn't been for you, I would have died. Then you came here to make sure I was OK. You didn't have to do that; you could just have left me to it. Then, in turn, you met your sister. Karma.'

Francesco tilted his head in acknowledgement of what she had said. He was unconvinced about the concept of karma, but he couldn't argue with the sequence of events Valentina had presented. Perhaps karma existed or perhaps it didn't. He wouldn't argue the point. Instead he changed the subject and asked, 'Did you find out where Étienne was the other night?' As he said it, he wondered if he should have been more tactful.

'Yes. He left his phone at home because he thought he wouldn't need it while he was at my parents' house. After what happened, he went to see Marco, that's his best friend. He thought I wouldn't want to see him again, and he couldn't face going back to an empty flat.'

Francesco thought of all the countless times he had dreaded walking back into his flat, and felt immense sympathy for how Étienne must have felt that night.

'What about your parents?'

'I left my mother another message to say I'm still at my friend's house. I just can't face having to explain all of this to her, and I don't want them coming down here, making another scene and trying to drag me back home.'

'So what will you do?'

'We were discussing that just before you came in. I think we're going to move, together I mean. Milan or Rome. There'll be more opportunities for both of us in a big city, and we'll be away from my parents.'

'They won't like that.'

'At this point, what they like or don't like doesn't bother me. Sorry, I know that sounds harsh, but I'm going to have to work very hard to find it in me to forgive them. In any case, I'll be eighteen in a few weeks, and they won't be able to have any say over what I do.'

'I know it'll take time, but try to find it in you to forgive them. It's a terrible burden going through life feeling badly towards someone.'

Valentina nodded and looked as though she was about to ask him something when Étienne reappeared. 'Sorry I've been a while. It took me time to track down a vending machine that was actually working. I couldn't get you a coffee, I'm afraid. It's fizzy drinks all round.' He perched on the other side of the bed and handed out the drinks, placed his own on the table and gently took Valentina's hand.

'I've been telling Francesco about our plans to move.'

'I hear you're thinking of heading to Milan or Rome.'

'We can't decide which would be better.'

'Well, I'm biased,' said Francesco, smiling. 'I live in Rome and it has everything. I mean, Milan is a nice city, but it's expensive; more expensive than Rome. The winters up there are pretty cold and grey too.'

'Perhaps we could look at Rome first? What do you think Étienne?'

'I don't see why not. And we'd already have a friend there,' he said, smiling warmly at Francesco.

'You certainly would. Anything I can do. You know how Italy is - it's who you know.' And, Francesco reflected, he had spoken like a true Italian for the first time.

Francesco left Valentina and Étienne, having exchanged contact details with them and agreed to meet up in Rome, and then returned to see Teddy. She was between appointments, and they did not have as long to talk as either of them would have wished.

'I am going to see you again, aren't I?' she asked, as they exchanged phone numbers and addresses.

'Of course. I'm not going to disappear again now. There is just one thing. The young woman you saw earlier, Valentina. I think there might be a few problems with the paperwork.' He quickly explained what had happened with the woman from the administration department.

Teddy laughed. 'Ah yes, I know who you mean. Don't worry; I'll take care of it. If you see her again, tell her to come and talk to me. You'd never believe it, but she actually does care about the patients, and she seems to think doctors can do no wrong. It's just the rest of the world she doesn't care for. Now, that's enough about her. I'd like you to come over to our house for dinner. When can you make it?'

Francesco ran through his schedule in his mind. 'Next Tuesday?'

'I can pick you up at Orvieto station at 6.30. Does that sound OK?'

'Yes, I'll be there,' he said and with that they hugged each other again before Teddy's secretary reappeared to announce the arrival of her next patient.

He walked down the corridor and pressed the button for the lift. As the door opened, the woman from administration stepped out.

'Are you still here?'

'It would appear that way, signora,' said Francesco smiling as sweetly as he could.

'Have you got the rest of the information I asked for? I'm still waiting for it so I can complete the forms you gave me.'

'Everything has been dealt with. If you have any problems, just speak to Dottoressa De Luca. She's familiar with the case and you.'

'Dottoressa De Luca knows who I am?' She looked marginally less glacial, almost flattered.

'Indeed she does. You have quite a reputation, signora.'

She looked at him, unsure how to take that, but he continued to beam at her.

'I'll talk to Dottoressa De Luca then.'

'You do that. Now I really must be leaving. Goodbye.'

Francesco walked out of the hospital. He suddenly felt hungry, unkempt and, above all, shattered. He got on the bus and as it trundled down the hill back towards Orvieto station, he had to fight to stay awake. The events of the last few days had truly caught up with him.

He made the journey back to Rome and to his flat on automatic pilot, managed to remember to set his alarm and then collapsed onto his bed, still fully clothed.

His final thoughts before falling asleep were of Lauren. She hadn't been cheating on him; she hadn't been planning to leave him. There were things he still didn't know, but he knew that much at least. 'I'm sorry,' he said softly to her memory.

He remembered nothing else until he awoke to the sound

of his alarm, aware of how dirty and dishevelled he still was, but then he realised he had slept for a whole night. It had been a whole night without hours spent lying in the darkness replaying his past; a whole night without nightmares.

*   *   *

Francesco opened the wardrobe door and looked at the modest selection of clothes hanging up in front of him. Never having been particularly bothered about clothes, he surveyed the assortment of jeans, trousers, t-shirts, shirts and his one suit. What, he wondered, was someone supposed to wear for a first dinner with his sister, her husband and two young daughters?

He got the suit out but decided it was too formal. The jeans were similarly disregarded for being too casual. He had been in Italy now for long enough to know that appearance mattered. He eventually settled on the suit trousers and a shirt. He picked up the presents he had carefully selected and wrapped, and then he set off on the journey to Orvieto.

Teddy picked him up at the station. They had phoned each other every day since their meeting at the hospital as if both were afraid the other might vanish again if too much time passed before their next meeting.

'Ciao Fran!' Teddy was a bundle of nervous energy, and Francesco suddenly realised she must have been anticipating this meeting as much as he had been and was probably almost as keen as him for it to go well.

'Ciao. How are you?'

'I'm well and so happy that you are going to meet everyone. And you?'

'Terrified.'

Teddy laughed. 'They will love you although I will admit two very little girls can be daunting. Even I find them slightly terrifying sometimes.'

'I brought a few things with me for all of you.'

'You didn't have to do that but it's a very kind thought. Thank you.' She looked at him. 'I still can't believe you're really here.'

They pulled away from the station and, unlike on his previous visit, they headed away from the river and towards the centre of the old city of Orvieto. As they climbed higher, he glimpsed beautiful views of the Umbrian countryside lit by the warm rich light of late afternoon. The countryside must have been parched after a punishingly hot summer, but it still seemed surprisingly green, and he imagined how beautiful it would look in spring. His mind drifted back to the summers he and Teddy had spent in the countryside with their mother. Much as he had come to love Rome, he appreciated the space and peace of the countryside.

Teddy expertly manoeuvered her small car around the winding streets, and then they pulled up outside a centuries-old stone house.

Teddy turned to him. 'Are you ready?'

Francesco nodded. 'I think so.' In reality, he was as nervous as he had ever been; so much depended on this meeting going well.

Pietro was by the door waiting to greet them. 'Francesco,'

he said, extending his hand and smiling broadly. 'I am so glad to finally meet you.'

'Likewise,' said Francesco feeling less anxious immediately.

There was a sudden whirlwind of noise and activity, and two small girls materialised in front of him.

'Hello,' said Francesco.

Gabriela walked straight up to him and solemnly put her hand out. 'Hello. I'm Gabriela. I'm six,' she declared, making it clear by her tone that this was highly important information.

'Six? You're very grown up.'

She nodded vigorously and smiled, clearly pleased that he had realised this. She looked round, saw Lucia clinging on to Pietro's leg, chewing her fingers uncertainly and turned back to Francesco. 'She's only four,' she said and rolled her eyes. Francesco held back the desire to laugh and nodded seriously.

'Hello Lucia,' he said.

In return, Lucia dropped her hand and gave him a shy smile and a barely audible hello.

'Well, let's not stand here. Come on, time for you to see what we're going to eat tonight,' said Teddy. 'Have you been keeping an eye on dinner?' she asked Pietro.

'I've been doing my best,' said Pietro amiably, putting an arm around his wife's shoulders.

'We should be fine then,' said Teddy, reciprocating and putting her arm around his waist. Fran saw the warmth between them and remembered how he and Lauren had been just the same. 'Fran, what would you like to drink?

Red?' she said holding up a bottle of Montesecondo.

'Yes, thank you,' he said coming back to the present and suddenly feeling a tug at his trouser leg. He turned and found Lucia staring up at him, apparently having got over her initial shyness now she had seen her mother's ease in this strange man's company. She beckoned to him, and he crouched down to hear what she had to say.

'I've got toys,' she whispered conspiratorially.

'I've got presents,' Francesco whispered back, and her eyes lit up. With that, Francesco was led away where he joined Lucia and Gabriela in a world which was completely new to him; an alien land of dolls' houses, Lego, teddy bears and glittery stickers.

He finally emerged when Teddy announced that dinner was ready, slightly bemused and yet more happy than he could express that his nieces had accepted him so readily.

Teddy picked some glitter out of his hair and gave him a reassuring pat on the back.

'Let's tuck in,' said Pietro, and they took their seats around the dining room table.

Teddy brought in two large plates of bruschetta with olive oil. 'These have garlic but those don't,' she explained, indicating the plates in turn. 'The girls aren't sure about garlic yet.'

Francesco opted for garlic and bit into the delicious crisp bread dripping with what proved to be a very high quality olive oil. 'It's delicious,' he said.

'I'm glad you like it,' said Pietro. 'We weren't sure what to make.' He paused. 'Teddy tells me you're a ticket inspector. I bet you meet some interesting characters.'

Francesco thought back over the months since he had started the job. 'You could definitely say that. There seems to be something about the anonymity, the transience of the situation, which makes people confide all sorts of things. What do you do?'

'I'm a lawyer so I spend most of my time in an office. Honestly, I'd like a job where I could get out more.'

'I can imagine.'

They talked more about the pitfalls and merits of their respective jobs, and then Teddy interrupted them. 'Come on you two,' she said with a smile. 'That's enough shop talk for now.' She turned to Francesco 'We never talk about work. We can't really, given what we do.' She picked up the plates. 'Pietro, let's bring the next course in.'

As they left the room, there was a silence as Gabriele and Lucia regarded their new uncle. Gabriela hopped down from her seat and went to get a teddy bear. She came back to the table and gave it to Francesco. 'You can look after him for me this evening.' Her huge dark eyes peered up at him earnestly.

'Thank you, Gabriela.'

'Well, here we are. Umbrichelli with amatriciana sauce,' said Teddy as they returned from the kitchen. 'I hope you like it, Fran. It's a little spicy.'

'I'm sure I will. It looks wonderful.'

Teddy and Pietro dished up, and as she sat down, she surveyed the faces around the table. Finally almost all the people she loved most were there. 'Mangia, mangia, eat, eat,' she said.

Dinner proceeded at a leisurely pace and more courses came out: baked chicken in a tomato sauce with a variety of vegetables presented in individual dishes; cheese; fruit; panna cotta and then a shot of espresso.

'That was so good,' said Francesco at the end, 'I don't think I'll ever be able to eat again.'

'We don't always eat like this,' said Teddy 'but we wanted to do something special tonight.'

'Would you like a drink?' asked Pietro.

'Yes, but not centerba if you don't mind,' replied Francesco, remembering his experience with Arturo's homemade brew.

'You've tried that, have you?' said Pietro laughing. 'I can't take to it either. Come and see what you'd like.' He led Francesco over to a cabinet where they chose Sambuca and then went out onto the terrace.

'It's very kind of you to invite me over. It must be a bit of a surprise having Teddy's long lost brother, a total stranger to you, suddenly turn up.'

'You've never been a stranger, Francesco.'

Francesco looked at him, failing to understand.

'Teddy has always talked about you from when we first met so I feel in a way that I do know you, at least a little. I have always known how much she missed you, and I know how delighted she is that you're here now. If she's happy, I'm happy.'

'Thank you. It means more than I can say to be here.'

'I know you've been through a hard time.' He shook his

head. 'I'm pleased you've found us.'

Before Francesco could reply, Teddy appeared. 'There you are. I have two girls in here who want to play with both of you, and I don't think they're going to take no for an answer. I'll get no peace until you two come in.'

*     *     *

'You can stay over, Francesco,' Pietro said, later that evening

'I'd really like to, but I have to work tomorrow.'

'I'll run you back to the station then,' said Teddy reluctantly.

Pietro waved them off, an exhausted Lucia in his arms and Gabriela standing beside him. As they were about to leave, Gabriela ran up to him and gave him a big hug.

'Good night, Uncle Francesco.'

'Good night, Gabriela,' he said, hugging her back. He thought of his own child, the daughter he would never get to cuddle and hoped the darkness was sufficient to mask the tears he was unable to suppress. How precious and fragile life was and how it could turn on the whims of fate.

'Come back soon,' said Pietro.

Teddy waited until the door had closed and then turned to Francesco. 'Are you OK?'

Francesco nodded, unsure for a moment if he could speak. 'More than OK. I can't thank you enough for tonight; for welcoming me into your family.'

'Fran, you are my family as well, and they love you already. It's just as well you like them because you're going to be seeing a lot more of all of us, I'm afraid.' She paused.

'Have you thought about visiting Papà?'

'Yes, I have. I'm not sure how I feel about it, but I suppose I can't put it off forever.'

'Let's not worry about it for now.' She glanced down as something caught her eye. 'What are those on your arm?'

'Lucia was putting stickers on me after dinner. She said they would make me look pretty.'

Teddy bit her lip as she looked at Francesco's hairy arms. 'They're going to be hell to get off.' And they both started laughing, overjoyed at being reunited and the evening having gone even better than either of them could have hoped.

# CHAPTER EIGHTEEN

Francesco fumbled around for the phone. 'Pronto?'

'Francesco? It's Pietro. I'm at my office in Rome so I thought we could meet for a coffee.'

He forced himself to wake up and squinted at the clock. It was only 7.30. 'Sure. I'm not working until later.'

'Excellent. At 10.00?'

'Yes, that's fine.'

Pietro gave him the address of his office and hung up, leaving Fran looking at the phone as if it would provide him with answers.

Francesco arrived at the elegant building on the outskirts of Rome which housed Pietro's office and felt shabby in its shadow. He hadn't given any thought as to what to wear and had thrown on a pair of jeans and a t-shirt. Suddenly it seemed like a poor choice, but he could hardly turn back now. His fears were confirmed when the receptionist fixed him with an expression which suggested she would like to set security on him.

'What do you want?' Suspicion permeated her voice.

'I'm here to see Pietro, signora.'

'Pietro.' Only one word, but she had managed to load it with both sarcasm and scepticism.

'Yes.' It occurred to him he had no idea what Pietro's last name was.

'Pietro who?'

As Francesco debated what to say, he heard Pietro. 'Grazie, signora. I will take care of our visitor.' He turned to Fran, 'Thanks for coming over.'

Pietro lead him down the hallway with Francesco acutely aware of the receptionist's eyes boring into his back. The journey in the lift was curiously strained. The ease of the night before in Orvieto seemed to have evaporated. Without the presence of Teddy and their daughters plus a few drinks added to the mix, Francesco couldn't think of much to say, and Pietro didn't seem inclined to engage in small talk either. Francesco was relieved when the lift doors opened.

Pietro led him down another hallway and into a vast corner office. The building spoke of discreet wealth, and Francesco was fairly sure the suit Pietro was wearing cost more than he earned in a month.

'That's quite a view,' Francesco commented.

'Yes, not bad.' Pietro paused to survey the scene and seemed to drift into a reverie. Then, as quickly as he had slipped into his thoughts, he was back. 'Where are my manners? Please take a seat. Coffee?'

Francesco nodded, and Pietro picked up the phone and requested their drinks.

'You're probably wondering why I suggested this meeting.'

'I suppose I am.'

'I thought it would be a good opportunity to get to know you better.'

Francesco nodded for want of a better response. He had assumed they would get to know each other over family get-togethers rather than in Pietro's office. This felt more like an interview to judge his suitability for a job. Something in Pietro's demeanour seemed off too. He was the same confident, pleasant man he had met the night before, but there was something different about him. Something indefinable which made Francesco uneasy.

Francesco realised Pietro had asked him a question. 'Sorry?'

'Are you planning to stay in Italy?'

Francesco was temporarily saved by the arrival of the coffee. After it had been delivered and they were alone again, Francesco said, 'I came here after Lauren died in the hope I might find my family. By some miracle I have. There was a time when I would have said I will never leave, and I can't imagine that I will, but I've learned that life makes its own plans.' To fill the silence which followed, he added 'Why?'

'Teddy and the girls are my priority. I don't want them to get attached to you and then get hurt.'

'I would never hurt them. Even if, and that's a big if, I decided to leave, I would always stay in touch with them. With all of you.'

'That's good to know. What happened to your wife, to Lauren, was terribly sad.'

Francesco nodded. He felt his throat start to tighten; a reflex beyond his control.

'Would you like to talk about it?'

'There's not much to say. As you know, Lauren was going to meet Teddy, but then for some reason, she got into her car and started driving in the opposite direction.'

'You never found out why?'

'No. The police closed the case, and that was the end of it.'

'I see.'

'She must have lost control of the car. It's strange because the weather was fine, but there was no CCTV to look at because the cameras were out. Never there when you need them, are they?' he said, aiming for a conversational tone.

'A tragic accident.'

Francesco caught the rising tone of an unasked question, turning a summary of the situation into something else. He was aware that some type of response was required, but he was back in the hospital in Manchester when he had been told Lauren and their daughter had died, time contracting and expanding, everything shifting, nothing making sense. Then the police had come to his flat, with their questions. There was something flickering in the corners of his mind and taunting him, something that still didn't make sense, but he couldn't grasp it. A canyon of silence opened up, ready to engulf them.

'Francesco?'

He forced himself to look at Pietro but saw nothing other than genuine concern. 'I'm sorry. I shouldn't have started this conversation.'

Francesco tried to collect himself. The Pietro he had met

last night was back. 'Please don't apologise. It's just still … raw even now.' Raw. It was so inadequate.

He thought he saw Pietro relax but dismissed it. The silence resumed, and then they both started to speak at the same time.

'After you,' Fran offered.

'I really am very sorry. You know we Italians like to find out everything about everyone. Sometimes we forget boundaries.'

'I'm Italian too,' he said feeling vaguely irked. He wondered why he was always considered English when he was in Italy and Italian when he was in England. Would it ever change?

'Yes, yes, of course. But you lived in England for a long time. You have English sensibilities. Anyway, I hope you will accept my apologies.'

'Really, there's no need.'

Francesco sipped his coffee and tried to think of something to say. 'What sort of law do you practise?'

'Company law, mainly. It's usually extremely dull, but it pays the bills.'

'And you work here and in Orvieto?'

'Yes, although I try to spend most of my time in Orvieto so I can be home in time for dinner. Speaking of which, would you like to come over for dinner next weekend?'

Francesco realised the subject was swiftly being changed. For some reason, Pietro's work was not a subject he wished to be drawn on. Perhaps it was simply as tedious as he had said.

Pietro interrupted his thoughts. 'So are you free for dinner next weekend?'

Francesco thought of Teddy, Gabriela and Lucia and said, 'Yes, of course.'

'Excellent.'

They drank the rest of the coffee, and then Pietro accompanied Francesco back to the station, even though he would have preferred to be alone with his thoughts.

They said goodbye, but as Francesco was about to walk into the station, he paused and turned back. Pietro was making a phone call, gesticulating generously. At that distance and slightly angled away from him, it was impossible to read his mood.

Francesco caught himself. What was he thinking? He couldn't even form it into something coherent. Pietro had shown him nothing but hospitality and kindness and now he was … what? Stop looking for problems, he told himself. Allow yourself to be happy.

# CHAPTER NINETEEN

As he had promised, Francesco had kept in touch with Valentina and Étienne. He had discovered that Étienne shared his passion for running and so on the 22nd of September, he lined up for city's half marathon alongside both Matteo and Étienne.

He remembered waiting at the starting line for the fun run in August; how he had stood there watching groups of friends chatting and how lonely he had been in that happy crowd of people. His life had changed so much in a month. He felt the change not only in his circumstances but within himself as well.

Valentina, who seemed to share Arturo's point of view that nothing good could come of running, happily saw them off, waving a huge chocolate croissant at them.

The route initially took them along the banks of the Tiber and towards the Circus Maximus, the area where Francesco had grown up, but unlike his first visit there in January, when he had tried without success to find Teddy and his father, there were no ghosts from the past.

From there, they went past the Colosseum, turned and headed through the streets of the old city. Francesco found his thoughts turning to Ellie and the night of Ferragosto but forced himself to stop. He was determined to start living in the present rather than the past. They ran along the banks of the Tiber, where he had so often run alone and then headed back towards the finish line and found Valentina, who was waiting for them.

One of his most prized possessions was now the photos of the three of them at the finish line, tired but happy, arms around each other's shoulders, beaming widely as Valentina snapped the moment for posterity.

*     *     *

As autumn progressed, Francesco followed the familiar rhythm of his life. He continued with his job, his trips to the gym and his regular runs by the Tiber, sometimes accompanied by Matteo and at other times by the music of Alessandro's band and the music collection he was beginning to amass.

He saw his family as regularly as his hours allowed and often dropped in to see Arturo who remained as curmudgeonly as ever towards his guests, yet always pleased, or as close as Arturo ever got to being pleased, to see Francesco.

More than once, he found himself in Anna's kitchen at the back of Il Buongustaio being alternately affectionately berated or praised for his culinary efforts while her husband chuckled in the background. Encouraged by Teddy, he also started attending counselling sessions regularly and despite his initial scepticism, found they helped him far more than he had anticipated.

As he started to emerge back into the real world, living rather than simply going through the motions of existing, he found this brought him a whole new set of decisions to make. Finally he had decided that he wanted to become a counsellor himself, to be at the patient end rather than the clinical end. He had also assumed that door back to being a doctor was closed anyway.

In the process of trying to piece his life back together he had needed to get copies of his qualifications and references. That was when an unexpected offer had come up; the chance to work back in England. He replayed the conversation in his mind.

'I was really so disappointed when you decided to resign, Francesco. I understood, of course, given the circumstances, but it's time to look at getting back to work.'

'I will be getting back to work but in a different capacity and in Rome.'

'But it was Britain which educated you and the NHS which trained you. I would have thought you would have wanted to make a contribution to the country and health service which enabled you to become a doctor.'

Francesco had felt the guilt starting to seep into him but pressed on regardless. 'I contributed to Britain and the NHS for many years. And I will still be caring for people. Surely you would agree that everyone who is in need deserves help regardless of nationality?'

'I'm sure they have counsellors in Italy, but that's not the point. You are a doctor Francesco.'

'We will have to agree to differ on my career path, I'm afraid. I'm really only trying to sort out some documentation.' He had replied as levelly as he could but, too late, he had heard the tone he had been unable to keep out of his voice.

The other man had clearly picked up on it as he decided on a more conciliatory approach. 'Look Francesco, we seem to have got distracted from the main point here. You are a fine doctor, and the NHS needs talented and dedicated doctors like you. Counsellors are very important, of course, but I am confident that you will have a better professional life working as a doctor here rather than as a counsellor there – or anywhere for that matter.'

Francesco had wavered.

'Do you remember Dr. Greenfield and Mr. Martin?'

'Yes, I do.' Francesco remembered his former colleagues who had been amongst those he had most respected and enjoyed working alongside.

'I'm sure you'd welcome the chance to work with them again.'

Francesco had sworn silently to himself. The man certainly knew all the buttons to press. 'I need time to think about it.'

'Yes, I understand, but I'd like you to be on board fairly early next year, and it's not going to be entirely straightforward. There are a lot of steps we'll have to go through before we can get to that point. Think very carefully. I know you, and I am sure you will be much happier with what we can offer you here.'

'I will certainly consider it.'

'Good. We'll talk again soon.'

The conversation had played on his mind ever since, and he had started to wonder if he had debts of time and work still to pay. Would he be happier as a doctor? He had dismissed it as he had assumed it would be never be possible. It was tempting, but then he thought about his desire to help people in a different way, and he also thought his family and the life he had started to build in Rome, which made the thought of leaving seem impossible.

As late October approached, autumn truly began to make its presence felt in Rome. It was still warm in the day, but the intense heat of high summer had bowed out. There was a chill in the air early in the morning and after sunset and the leaves which had turned russet were starting to carpet the pavements.

Autumn was a time of year he had never loved, and its intrusion into his life was unwelcome and could no longer be ignored. As he walked back to Flaminio underground station after his run, the leaves crunched underfoot. Autumn – his second autumn without Lauren.

In some ways, the second seemed worse than the first. The first year had simply been a blur of grief, punctuated with constant wondering about what Lauren had been doing. Now the worst of his doubts had been swept away and the grief, although still acutely painful, was slightly less raw as long as he didn't scratch at the surface. Sometimes not scratching was easier than at other times.

What made it worse for him was that time was steadily taking him further and further away from her, making her a little more distant with every passing day, week and month. There would come a point not so far in the future, when more time would have passed since her death, than they had spent together. And then what? He did not want to contemplate it.

He forced himself to stop and to think about the two paths his life could take now. He asked himself yet again what he was going to do, but no answer was forthcoming. He returned to his flat, showered and then headed for the underground to go to the other side of the city.

*    *    *

After some further debate over the relative merits of Milan and Rome, Valentina and Étienne, who had been staying with friends, had decided to move permanently to Rome. They had found a studio on the side of Trastevere furthest from the city centre, but, despite the fact that it was tiny, they were thrilled with it, and Francesco had offered to help them move in. Once they had got the last of their possessions in, Étienne offered to go out to get some food.

'I can go,' said Valentina.

'No, you stay here. You know where you want all these things to go. I haven't got a clue.'

Valentina and Francesco organised boxes and cases, moving one into the bathroom and others into the kitchen. The suitcases containing their clothes got pushed in the general direction of the wardrobe and they finally fashioned a path through all of it and slumped down on the sofa.

'Thank you so much for helping us.'

'You're more than welcome,' said Francesco who had come to like both of them immensely. 'How are things with your parents?'

'Mum starts every conversation with apologies. One to me for the way things have turned out and one on behalf of my father for being a stubborn idiot. Those are her words, by the way, not mine.'

'I imagine you might use stronger words. In fact if I recall correctly, you did the first time we met.'

'Yes, I believe I did, but I've calmed down a lot since then. I've started to accept that my father and I are never going to see eye to eye. I find his views repugnant, and he finds my choices equally unacceptable so what more is there to say? I doubt we'll ever speak again at this stage so we all just have to muddle on as best we can.'

Francesco regarded her and thought how much she had matured in the short time they had known each other. The trauma she had been through and the rupture with her father had changed her. She seemed older than her years now whereas before she had seemed younger.

'We haven't had a proper chance to talk for a while. How are things going with you?' asked Valentina.

'I'm doing well. Better than when we first met, that's for sure.'

'So much has happened in the last few months.'

'That's true enough. When do you start work?' he asked, referring to the job she had found working in a hotel as a receptionist.

'Next Wednesday. I was so lucky to get that job. And I'm going to look at studying part time as well. I got good marks at school so I'd like to get a degree if I can, even though it will take me longer than most people. What about you?'

'Me?'

'Yes. You're a doctor. Don't you think you'll ever go back to medicine?'

'I've been thinking about it,' Francesco admitted. 'But I've got a lot of decisions to make first.'

Valentina started to say something but, at that moment, Étienne reappeared with a huge portion of supplì, soft balls of fried rice filled with mozzarella and tomato sauce, and an assortment of drinks.

The conversation somehow drifted away from his future plans, and for that he was grateful. He had no idea what he was going to do. He had not even spoken to Teddy yet. Old habits were hard to break, and he still preferred to listen to other people rather than talk about himself.

*     *     *

'Fran, we're going to the chestnut festival in Pietro's village on Sunday. Can you come with us?'

'Yes, sure. Where is it?'

'A little town called Bolsena. It's on Lake Bolsena. We'll pick you up from Orvieto station. Can you be there at about eleven?'

'I'll make sure I am.'

Teddy arrived in the car with Pietro, Gabriela and Lucia. Francesco squeezed in, and they set off. They drove through the Umbrian countryside dotted with tiny villages much like the two-street village Ellie had described her home town as being, although without the imposing mountains of the Abruzzo as a backdrop.

Francesco wondered how she was, and if she was finding her new life as suffocating as she had feared. His guilt about that night had passed, but despite his promise to himself not to live in the past anymore, he still wished he could go back in time and explain to her why he had acted as he had.

They arrived in Bolsena and were greeted by Pietro's parents and his sister and her family. There were so many introductions and so much activity that Francesco and Teddy did not get a chance to speak to each other properly for some time.

They headed into the centre of the town and wandered from stall to stall, trying the various chestnut dishes and talking to the vendors. While everyone was discussing the recipes and merits of the various dishes, Teddy drew Francesco to one side.

'I would really like to tell Papà that you're here now. I don't think we can keep it from him much longer.' They had decided some time ago that Teddy should be the one to break the news.

'I know, we can't put it off any longer,' said Francesco. He wondered what his father would be like and what he would find to say to him now that he knew what he had done to their mother.

'I will never forget what he did to mum and the impact it's had on all of us, but I truly believe he's suffered too and learned from what happened. Will you give him a chance?'

Francesco reflected on his own shortcomings as a husband. His willingness to take the easy option when Lauren had so obviously been preoccupied, paled next to his father's infidelity, but it reminded him that nobody was perfect. If he had had the chance to go back and do it again, he would have done better, or at least he hoped that would have been the case. Perhaps his father felt the same. 'Yes, I will, but it might not go very well.'

'I know. Just try.'

'I will,' he promised and then, thinking of Lauren, he remembered the question he had been meaning to ask Teddy for so long. Every time they got together, there was so much going on that it either slipped his mind or there was not a suitable moment. 'Teddy, the day you flew to England to meet Lauren…'

'Yes?'

'Did you speak to each other that day? On the phone, I mean?'

Teddy thought back. 'No, we didn't. We had spoken a number of times before but not that day. Why?'

'It's nothing really. It's just that sometimes I go over things even now.' For some reason, he didn't want to tell her about the phone call the receptionist at the hotel had overheard.

Before Teddy could respond, Pietro appeared. 'What are you two chatting about?' he asked. 'There's some wonderful chestnut soup you have to try. Let's join the others.'

They went back and were soon busy sampling the various

delights of the chestnut festival again. The smell of wood smoke filled the air – the scent of autumn out in the country. He chatted happily with Teddy, Pietro and his family as they walked down to the lakeside and watched the children chasing each other along the promenade shaded by trees whose leaves were turning to gold. For the first time, he felt the start of a sense of belonging, something which had always eluded him.

Teddy smiled at him and linked arms with him. 'You told me one day that you didn't feel Italian or English, but you are more Italian than you realise. We need what is familiar to us, particularly when we are sad. It's a source of comfort, and I can see that in you.'

'I've been offered a place on a counselling course, Teddy.'

'What? Where?'

'In Rome.'

'So you'll definitely be staying around? That's wonderful news.'

She beamed up at him and looked so happy that Francesco, who had been building up to mentioning the possibility of a job in England, found he could not bring himself to do so. He had no desire to spoil their day.

*　　*　　*

Francesco's phone rang. 'Ciao, Teddy.'

'Ciao. Fran, I saw Papà at the weekend and he's suggested meeting you next Saturday at seven o'clock at the Neptune Fountain in the Piazza del Popolo. He seems to think meeting on neutral ground would be a good idea.'

'You've told him about mum?'

'Yes.'

'How did he take it?'

'He didn't say anything at first. He just excused himself and went off to his bedroom. Then he came back and all he said was "I see".'

'"I see." You tell him mum is dead, and he says "I see"? What sort of response is that?'

'I know, I know, but Fran there's something else.'

'What?'

'When he came back I was pretty sure he'd been crying, and I've never seen him cry. Ever. So I suppose what I'm saying is try not to judge him too harshly. I know I have at times over the years particularly when I first found out everything he had done, but just give him a chance. Then if you decide you can't forgive him, I will understand.'

'I'll try but I can't make any promises.'

As Francesco hung up, he thought seriously about the prospect of meeting his father for the first time in twenty-seven years. He had had no preparation for meeting Teddy and meeting her family had been so important to him, but it hadn't been loaded with potential recriminations. Now it had come to it, he wasn't sure how he felt about meeting his father or how much it mattered. Perhaps it only mattered because it mattered to Teddy.

He calculated that his father must be seventy-three. He tried to imagine his father at that age and what changes the intervening years would have wrought. And what would his father think of him?

In the week before they were due to meet, Francesco thought of many reasons not to go and creative excuses he could make, but in his heart he knew he would go; that he would have to go. Teddy, being ever practical, had sent both her father and Francesco photos so they could identify each other.

Francesco arrived in the Piazza del Popolo ahead of time. He gazed up at the lookout on the Pincian Hill over on the far side of the square, bathed in the light of late afternoon, and crowded with tourists waiting for the sunset. He took some deep breaths, trying to ready himself, but in reality there could be no preparation for a meeting like this. He almost turned around and left a couple of times, but then he saw his father coming into view. Moments before he had been unable to keep still, but now he felt frozen to the spot.

He tried to compose himself and hoped he looked calmer and more collected than he felt. He couldn't take his eyes off him. If he hadn't seen the photo, he might have passed him in the street, a total stranger, and yet there was something so familiar about him as well.

He was aware this wasn't going to be the happy meeting he had had with Teddy's family. What was he even supposed to say to this man?

Carlo stopped in front of him, and they took the measure of each other.

'Hello Francesco,' he said finally and extended his hand.

'Dad,' he said, but almost choked on the word. He shook his father's hand, not because he wanted to, but because to have rejected it would have been too much.

'I, er, I've booked a table at a little place nearby. I suggest we go now.'

'Sure.'

They walked to the restaurant in silence and were shown to their seats. Francesco had thought the silence out on the busy streets was bad enough, but here in the quiet, refined restaurant, staring at each other over a table with no distractions, it seemed infinitely worse.

The waiter brought menus and made recommendations. His father asked the man various questions while Francesco silently screamed inside. *I haven't seen you for twenty-seven years and you're asking the waiter about the intricacies of the wine list.* He clenched his fists under the table and looked out of the window.

'Francesco?'

'Hmm?'

'Are you ready to order?'

'I'll have whatever you're having.'

'Don't you want to choose?'

'It's fine.' He heard the edge to his voice, and seemingly his father did too for he did not press the point.

The waiter withdrew, and they were left staring at each other once again.

'Teddy told me you came back to Italy in January.'

'Yes, that's right.'

'And how are you finding it here? It's somewhat of a change to living in England, I imagine."

'You could say that. It's not the first time I've had to make that sort of adjustment, though.'

Carlo picked up his fork, examined it and put it down again. He moved his plate a fraction to the right.

'And you found Teddy quite by chance?'

'Yes.'

They lapsed into silence again. Francesco wondered what he had expected; what he wanted from this man. An emotional embrace for the long-lost son? A long apology and tortuous justifications for his behaviour towards their mother? He clearly wasn't going to get either of those so was he supposed to make small talk with someone who was effectively a complete stranger for the next few hours as if nothing had ever happened between them? He wanted to walk out, but he had promised Teddy he would give him a chance so he remained seated, enduring the excruciating silence.

His father tried again. 'Teddy said you're working as a ticket inspector.'

Francesco thought he sensed an air of disappointment in his father's voice, which irritated him. 'I enjoy it,' he said defensively although his father had not asked him whether he did or not.

The waiter brought drinks, and they waited until he had gone again.

Francesco cast around for something to say. 'How's retirement?'

'It has its pros and cons. I miss the thrill of the deal sometimes, but I like not having to answer to anyone. I've taken up painting.'

'What do you paint?' asked Francesco, relieved that they

seemed to have found a safe topic to discuss.

'Landscapes mostly. You've been to Teddy's office, haven't you?'

'Yes,' said Francesco, confused by the sudden change of direction.

'I painted that picture she has in there. The one with the poppies.'

For some reason this grated on Francesco. Tuscany was where he and Teddy had gone with their mother to escape from him. He felt his father had no right to encroach upon that territory, and even as he had the thought, he realised it was absurd.

'Teddy told me some of her fondest childhood memories were of Tuscany so I thought I'd try to give her a reminder she could look at every day.'

'You never came with us.' Francesco tried to make it sound light, but he could hear the accusation running through the words.

'No, I didn't. I was always so … busy.'

Busy with other women, thought Francesco bitterly. 'With what?' he asked.

'Excuse me?'

'What were you so busy doing?'

'Working mainly, to make sure I could provide a good home for all of you.'

There was a trace of indignation in Carlo's voice, but Francesco thought he sensed regret as well. He found himself thinking about Ellie, and how she had regretted putting work before everything else. At least she had not been serially unfaithful to her boyfriend in the process.

The waiter reappeared, and Francesco silently welcomed his intervention.

Carlo made an attempt at resuming the conversation after he had gone again. 'Where did you go when you left Rome?'

'To England. We stayed with grandpa until mum got a job. Then we got our own place.'

'Oh yes, I remember him. I don't think he ever liked me very much.'

Francesco felt he was supposed to deny that, but instead he said, 'I wouldn't know. I was very young at the time, and I had other things to worry about.'

His father studied him. 'Yes, I expect you did.'

This time Francesco heard the unspoken regret and felt his anger start to dissipate.

'Will you stay here? In Italy, I mean.'

'I don't know what the future holds.' That was only partly true, but he would not share his dilemma with his father before he had spoken to Teddy. 'I've learned not to make too many plans. Things seldom turn out the way you think they will.'

His father hesitated. 'Teddy told me you came back because your wife passed away.'

Francesco nodded slightly but did not trust himself to speak until he knew where his father was going.

'I was very sorry to hear that.' His father sighed and sat back in his chair. 'You're far too young to have had to experience that.'

Francesco looked at his father in surprise. Whatever he had expected, it had not been that. He wondered if Teddy had been right. Perhaps his father was not the villain he had built him up to be in his mind. Or perhaps he was just like almost every other person, a complex mix of light and shade, impossible to put into a neat box marked good or bad.

'Thank you. I appreciate that.'

The meal continued and although the conversation did not flow, it was less awkward than it had been at the start. They parted outside the restaurant with another formal handshake, and Francesco watched as his father walked away. He was thinner than he remembered, but the frailty of later years had not yet set in. His apparent inability to go beyond stiff courtesy hurt Francesco, and yet anything else would have been out of character.

His father disappeared around a corner without looking back. The chill of the autumn night bit, and Francesco pulled his jacket tightly around him, turned in the opposite direction and headed back to the underground.

# Winter 2019/2020

# CHAPTER TWENTY

Francesco boarded the train, aware that this stage of his life was now drawing to a close. The thought made him feel almost nostalgic. He caught fragments of conversations, sometimes banal, sometimes tantalising; from worlds he would never know or be a part of. Now that he knew it would not last much longer, he made an effort to remember what this was like while he could.

After making his way up and down the train after every stop, he finally sat down for the last leg of the journey. There were no further stops now.

The man opposite him swore under his breath, and Francesco looked up and met his eyes. In uniform, he felt obliged to say something. 'Is there a problem?'

'I bloody hate this country.' He flicked his fingers contemptuously at the page of the newspaper he was reading. 'It's my country, but I hate it. It's impossible to live like this. Six hundred strikes a year.'

Francesco had no idea how many strikes there had been that year. Six hundred seemed unlikely, but he had no facts with which to contradict the man. On the other hand, he felt as though he had experienced more strikes in the past year than in all of his years in England so perhaps he had a point.

He continued. 'The country doesn't function. It's chaos. You have to struggle whether you're in a queue at the post office or trying to get from one place to another. If you take public transport, you have to deal with the strikes. If you take your car, you get stuck in a traffic jam, and then you can't park. It's just one damn thing after another.'

'It can be very frustrating.'

'Frustrating doesn't even come close. Our default mode is chaos. We create it, then we complain about it and throw our hands in the air, and after that we moan about people who are complaining. Then we do the same thing all over again. We just shrug and say "This is Italy." And "So what's new?" as though that explains it and makes it OK. Our country is broken, but we hide behind a veneer of cheerful acceptance. I sometimes think that one hard shove, and that veneer would shatter.'

'It's not really that bad, is it?' Francesco was not sure whether he was defending Italy or hoping for reassurance.

'Without a doubt it is. And it's not just the strikes, it's the bureaucracy. Listen, I run, or at least I'm trying to run, a business. In any normal country I'd get support. I'd be seen as someone trying to create wealth, perhaps provide employment for other people once I'd got established but not here. They're not happy unless they're tying me up in red tape.'

This was a theme Francesco could identify with more than the strikes. 'It is terrible. I don't know what can be done about it, though.'

'There's no appetite for change. All I know is that I'm tired of fighting this faceless bureaucracy which demands so much from me and gives me nothing but stress and sleepless nights in return.'

'Don't you think there any positive aspects to life here?'

'I suppose it makes us resourceful because we have to fight the system every day. The system that feeds itself until it's so bloated from its greed and sloth it should explode, yet somehow never does. It just expands ever further making our everyday lives more and more painful. We help each other, but do we do that because we are better than other people? Perhaps we do it because we know our institutions – the very people in whom we should be able to place our trust – won't help us.'

Francesco looked at the man and the crumpled newspaper. For once this was a conversation he did not want to have. Particularly not now that he was so close to committing himself to a life in Italy. But perhaps he shouldn't ignore the less pleasant realities either.

'People joke about the Italians not paying their taxes, about avoiding them being an art form here. Why do you think that is? Is it because they are inherently less honest than other people? I don't think so. I believe it's because we get nothing for them. Look at the Scandinavian countries. They pay lots of tax, and I don't think they have significant problems with tax evasion. Why's that? Because they see some return for all that money they pay in. What do we see here? Next to nothing. It gets sucked into a black hole of corruption and we, the little people, get nothing.'

Francesco looked at him earnestly, truly curious to know the answer to his next question. 'If you find it so frustrating here, why don't you consider running your business in another country? With technology and the EU, it's easier to work from a different location. Depending on what you do, of course.'

The man looked at him with astonishment. 'Because it's my country. I'm allowed to moan about it, but I could never abandon it. You wouldn't would you?'

And Francesco found he had no answer for the man.

By the time he got off the train, he felt tired and dispirited. The man's rant had not been what he had needed to hear. He was already torn between two countries and two futures. Now, in the starkest terms, he had been confronted with some of the harsh truths about life in Italy, which he had tried to avoid thinking about. Yet, even for the man he had just met, the idea of abandoning the country was unthinkable.

He took the underground to San Giovanni, and as he walked to the exit, he noticed for the first time the missing ceiling panels, the trailing cables, the air of neglect; the general sensation that it was just too difficult to get anything done; that muddling through was the only option.

He decided he would do what he often did when he needed a quick pick me up and headed for Il Buongustaio.

'Oh, ciao Francesco.' Anna looked genuinely pleased to see him.

'Ciao. How are you?'

'Cervicale,' she said, rubbing at her neck. 'I always get it at this time of year. It's the cold that does it. And you?' She paused and frowned at him. 'You're not wearing a scarf.'

'No.'

She tutted. 'You've got to keep the draughts out. If you don't, you'll get sick.'

'Right, thanks, I'll remember that.'

'Make sure you do or you'll end up with a neck like mine and you don't want that, I can promise you.'

'Have you seen a doctor?'

Anna flapped a hand in the air. 'Doctors, what do they know?'

Francesco let that pass. 'I'm looking for a recipe. What do you recommend?'

'Well, it's got to be something to keep you warm. Let me see. She picked up a bag and walked through the shop, looking for ingredients, picking up various items and discarding others.

She placed the bag on the counter and Francesco peered inside. 'What am I going to make?'

'Pumpkin gnocchi.'

'Is it difficult?'

'Not if you follow this recipe,' she said writing it down. 'And I have a little something extra for you. I made some chocolate biscotti today. She reached under the counter and produced a beautifully wrapped package. 'No charge.'

'Thank you, Anna. Good night.'

'Good night Francesco. And don't forget to wear a scarf.'

Back at his flat, Francesco set the ingredients out, and followed Anna's meticulous instructions. Less than an hour later, he dished up something he would not have been embarrassed to serve to guests. He resisted the temptation to allow his thoughts to wander to other matters. There would be time enough for that later; he had learned that good food was to be savoured.

*　　*　　*

Francesco finally finished work in early December. He had expected to feel happy and free, and to an extent he did, but those feelings had been mixed with a sense of regret. That had not been unexpected as he knew himself well enough to understand how he resisted change. He had finished his final shift, and then he had walked out of Termini realising that, once again, his life was about to take another major turn and soon the job which had kept him going over the last year would be another before to add to the list: the before he had been forced to move to England; the before he had lost Lauren.

The freedom gave him more time to run, to spend time with the friends he had made in Rome and, above all, with his family. More than once he had ended up at Arturo's kitchen table, knocking back the ristretto to which he seemed to have developed immunity.

'Have you made a decision?'

'No. I've thought myself to a standstill.' Francesco said at which point Arturo responded by reaching for a bottle of Centerba.

Francesco had long ago learnt his lesson where that was concerned and limited himself to one glass before making his excuses and heading back to his flat.

His phone rang as he got into the lift. It was Alessandro.

'Hi.'

'Hey Francesco. How are you?'

'Getting by. And you?'

'I've got some good news. We've been signed by the new label.'

'That's fantastic. Congratulations.'

'Thanks. This is the start of a whole new stage for us. We'll be back over in Europe next summer for the festivals. We might even get to stay in hotels rather than a scuzzy van. You gonna catch some concerts?'

'I'll be there,' Francesco promised, remembering vividly the last time he had seen them play. He wondered where he would be travelling from to see them play by the following summer.

'What's happening with you?'

'I have two options. Training to be a counsellor here or possibly going back into medicine in the UK.'

'That's cool. Except you don't sound too happy about either option.'

'I was set on counselling, but then the possibility of returning to medicine came up, which I really didn't expect.'

'But that means leaving Italy, and now you've found your family.'

'Exactly. I loved being a doctor, but that was back then. In some ways, I feel I still owe the British health service for training me, and it sounds like I might be able to start working and earning decent money fairly quickly. That sounds mercenary, but I need to think about it.'

'Everyone has to make the rent.'

'Yes. Whereas if I go for the counselling course, I'll have to work part time, and it will be hard financially. But I think it might be more rewarding, and here I'm close to my family and, well, you know.' He had told Alessandro about how he had lost touch with his family and found them again in a previous phone call and what that had meant to him.

'That's a really tough call. What are you going to do?'

And, as he had said to Arturo earlier that evening, Francesco had to admit he had no idea.

'Remember you still have an open invitation to come to Boston. Maybe a change of scene would help. You know, get away from everything. Distance can help you get perspective.'

'Perhaps, but even if I don't come over now, I'll get there at some point.'

'You'd better. My mom is waiting to fatten you up.'

They said goodbye, and Francesco returned to his contemplation. The complete neutrality of Boston seemed immensely appealing, but it wasn't the time. He slept fitfully and then the next morning did what he always did when he was trying to make a decision and went for a long walk through the city.

What Alessandro had said about getting away had given him pause for thought, and he eventually came to the realisation that there was only one way he would be able to make the decision.

# CHAPTER TWENTY-ONE

By the beginning of the second week in December, Rome sparkled under the glow of thousands of Christmas lights reflected back in the cobbled streets, burnished to perfection by the footsteps of all those who had passed through the city over countless years. The whole city was bathed in a golden light, which helped to offset the night time chill. The heat of summer was now no more than a distant dream.

Christmas trees appeared by the Colosseum, Piazza Venezia and in St Peter's Square, and the Christmas markets started to open. Francesco enjoyed wandering around them, stopping at the little huts, sampling the food and drink and looking for gifts. He noticed that he was starting to take an interest in what was happening around him rather than drifting along, oblivious to almost everything, simply waiting for the days to pass.

He tried ice skating for the first time at the temporary rink by the Castel Sant'Angelo and reflected that, a year ago, he would probably have been unable even to drag himself out of bed. The ice was painfully bright and sharp in the winter sun and dotted with brightly wrapped children and adults displaying varying degrees of skill. He went with Valentina, Étienne and Matteo, who all seemed to have some idea how to stay upright. As he stumbled towards the barrier, he turned to see them smiling at him, encouraging him, giving him the thumbs up and felt the sense of contentment that came with friendship.

Although the trauma of losing Lauren was still very real, a vivid scar running through the fabric of his life, he felt he had started to absorb the loss and accept it as a part of him. Even the still unanswered question about where she had been going that day was something he was learning to live with. She was always there, and she always would be, but he didn't feel quite as guilty when he found himself enjoying something.

There was, however, still the problem of work to solve, but Francesco put it to one side as Christmas came ever closer. He had time, and he would focus on it again after Christmas. For now, he wanted to appreciate spending time with his family and friends.

It had been decided that they would spend Christmas at his father's home in Rome. The news of Jenny's death seemed to have slowed Carlo down, and it was felt it would be better to take Christmas to him. His apartment, north of the Villa Borghese gardens in a tree-lined street, which exuded quiet wealth and an air of tranquillity, was somewhat different from the area where Francesco lived.

Francesco tried to time his arrival on Christmas Eve so that Teddy would already be there. He was still not entirely comfortable around his father even though he had met him a few more times since that first strained encounter. He was unsure how his father felt about him and, much as he tried, he still felt angry about what he had done to their mother and the consequences of that, which had deprived him of his family for so long. He was happy to find that Teddy, Pietro, Gabriela and Lucia were already there, busily unpacking huge bags of shopping. Teddy appeared to have brought enough food to feed a not particularly small army.

'I'm going for my walk,' his father announced, carefully folding his newspaper and putting it to one side before easing himself out of his chair.

'Alright Papà, see you later,' Teddy said.

Francesco looked questioningly at Teddy, surprised their father was not staying to take part in the build up to the Christmas Eve dinner.

She shrugged. 'He goes every day. Whatever the weather, whatever is happening, he goes for that walk. I've said I'll go with him sometimes, but he won't let me. Last time, he actually said he didn't want me to go.' She shook her head. 'I think he's getting a bit set in his ways, but it's good for him to get out.'

As the unpacking progressed, Teddy drew Francesco to one side. 'I have all the girls' presents from Father Christmas in the boot of the car. If I keep them busy, can you get them and put them away somewhere where they won't find them?'

'Sure,' said Francesco taking the car keys. 'Does La Befana bring them presents too?' he asked, referring to the friendly witch who delivered presents to Italian children on the 6th of January.

'Yes, we celebrate both,' said Teddy, looking slightly guilty as if she had been caught committing a minor crime. 'They don't get twice the number of presents, though. We just split them between the two days. I always loved the excitement of Father Christmas coming, and I wanted the girls to have those memories too. Anyway,' she said looking over her shoulder, 'could you go while they're distracted?'

'OK, I won't be long.'

Francesco retrieved the presents and cautiously went back into the flat. He could hear the girls excitedly chattering away to their parents. They had just discovered some chocolate torrone and were pleading to be allowed to open it.

He considered a suitable hiding place. The bedroom the girls were sharing was out. Teddy and Pietro's room was the obvious place, but that meant walking right past the open kitchen door. The only place he could think of was his father's bedroom. He quietly shut the front door and went to his father's room. He had never been in there before and felt a little uneasy about walking in there without his permission, but he had no choice now. Rather that, he decided, than risk spoiling the girls' Christmas. He opened the door, slipped in and closed it behind him.

The room was, as with the rest of the flat, elegantly and expensively furnished. He slid the bags under the far side of the bed where they would not be seen even if the girls opened the door. As he knelt back up, his eye level was almost exactly at that of his father's bedside table. He hadn't noticed it before in his hurry to hide the presents, but now he stopped, and what he saw made him stop to draw breath. On the table were several framed photos of his mother. They included a shot of her and his father on their wedding day and the happiness they radiated filled him with an extraordinary sadness when he thought of all that had followed. All that love and hope extinguished; thrown away for what? There were also photos of her on a bridge spanning the Tiber; on a beach and in front of a small, white farmhouse surrounded by poppies in a landscape which surely had to be Tuscany.

The last photo was one of her with Teddy and him. His mother's expression was unreadable. It could be interpreted as sadness or almost a look of accusation, but he couldn't see it objectively, not knowing everything he did now. In the photo, he could only have been about six or seven and Teddy fourteen or fifteen. Looking at his younger self staring shyly back at him from across the decades, so innocent, so unaware, was unsettling. As he stood up, his father walked in.

Neither of them moved or said a word. The acute silence was interrupted only by the steady ticking of the clock on the wall, which became louder as the silence stretched out, measuring each painful second until Francesco found something to say.

'I'm sorry.' He felt he had intruded on a very private part of his father's life.

'What are you doing?' His father's face was impassive and his tone flat; impossible to interpret.

'Teddy asked me to hide the girls' presents. It was the only place I could think of.'

His father nodded slightly, but another uncomfortable

silence followed. The ticking resumed and seemed to pound inside Francesco's head. He wished his father would say something; anything.

'I'll go back and join them then,' Francesco said awkwardly.

'You were looking at the photos.' It was almost a question; almost but not quite.

'I noticed them, yes.'

'Do you think I didn't love your mother?'

The bluntness of the question stunned Francesco and left him unable to formulate an immediate reply. Then the thought which had been worming away at him since Teddy mentioned his walks, decided to make its presence felt, and Francesco heard himself saying, 'Where do you go on your walks? Who do you meet?' He imagined his father meeting another woman he had kept hidden from his family.

Carlo sighed. 'Sit down, son,' he said, crossing the room and sitting on the side of the bed facing the photos.

Francesco sat down beside him. He couldn't recall his father calling him "son" at any point in time.

'I made a lot of mistakes. I don't find it easy to say that, and I doubt you'll ever hear me admit to it again but, there, I've said it. I was selfish. I wanted to acquire everything. Money, a nice home, expensive possessions, a beautiful wife, a family, but I forgot that people are not possessions. They must be tended to; you can't put them aside on a whim just because you take it into your head that you feel like doing something else.'

Francesco said nothing. Teddy had already told him

everything he wanted to know about his father's affairs. He had no desire to know anything else about them.

'I don't intend to go into all the details, but I think I owe it to you to tell you this. I had affairs, and I wasn't a good husband or father, but after your mother left I missed her every single day. I was just too proud to do anything about it.' He got up slowly and placed a hand on his son's shoulder. 'I don't go out to meet anyone. I go to Ponte Milvio. It's the first place I ever saw your mother. I go there to remember her, and that's why I like to go alone.' He rubbed a hand over his face. 'I missed you too. More than you can imagine. Pride is a terrible thing. You should never let it get in the way of what – or who - really matters.'

With that, he got up and he walked out, leaving Francesco sitting on the bed, his mother's wistful expression gazing back at him. He sat there, looking at her and thinking of all the conversations he wished he could have had with her, all the things he wished he had known while she was still alive. 'I love you, mum,' he said softly. He sat there for a while longer, immersed in memories and regrets and finally willed himself to get up and join the others.

The happy chaos of the sitting room was the perfect antidote to the still reflection of his father's room. Gabriela was dressing Lucia up in a butterfly costume which did not seem very seasonal, but Francesco had quickly learnt not to question such things. It made perfect sense to the girls, and that was enough.

In the kitchen, Teddy and Pietro were busy cooking, and Francesco now felt proficient enough to lend them a hand.

That night they ate a traditional Christmas Eve meal of olives, fried artichokes and broccoli, followed by vermicelli with mussels. With all of them there, the conversation was more relaxed and the girls' exuberance rubbed off on all of them.

After dinner, Pietro and Francesco cleared up while Teddy tried to settle the girls in bed. 'They are so excited,' she said, as she came into the kitchen. 'I don't know where they find the energy, and we've somehow got to stay awake until the early hours of the morning so we can deliver the presents.'

Later that night, Francesco made up his bed on the sofa. He settled down and stared up at the ceiling, wondering for a moment what was missing – the traffic that was it. From his flat the hum of traffic was a constant, but in his father's flat, it was so quiet.

He tried to recall what he had been doing last Christmas Eve, but found he could remember nothing about it at all. Like so much of the time following Lauren's death, it was a blur. He could never have imagined that a year later he would have been reunited with his family. His mind fast forwarded over the intervening year and all that happened, and he felt a wave of exhaustion overcome him. The sofa was a little too short for him, but he curled up and slept peacefully.

The serenity of early morning was brought to an abrupt end by the excited shrieking of Gabriela and Lucia as they discovered that Father Christmas had paid them a visit. Everyone was pulled into their room to watch them rummage through their stockings to see what had been left for them.

The day unwound more peacefully after that. His father went out and then returned to read his book, and Gabriella and Lucia played with their new toys. Francesco looked around the room at the now-familiar faces. Teddy was at the very heart of the festivities, organising everything and everyone while Pietro was conjuring something up in the kitchen.

He and Teddy had spent many hours talking since their reunion, filling in gaps and helping each other to understand more about two lives which had started together, veered dramatically apart and then come together again in the most unexpected of ways.

In the months since he had walked into Teddy's office and subsequently into their lives, his family had made him feel alive for the first time since the period of his life which he had shared with Lauren. He wondered at the fact that his family could help him heal and yet simultaneously remind his so acutely of his loss. He had also got past his doubts about Pietro, which had followed their meeting at his office. He was clearly devoted to Teddy and their daughters, and it was natural for him to want to protect them.

As he surveyed the room, his eyes came to rest on his father. He considered him closely. He thought he would never find it in his heart to forgive him completely, but he was still his father and what had passed between them the previous day had taken away the bitterness he had previously felt towards him. He had to live with regrets and consequences which clearly caused him pain. Francesco had noticed how, although he often seemed to be totally preoccupied with his newspaper or book, he would occasionally peer over the top of it and smile at some episode or other involving the antics of his grandchildren.

Francesco imagined what it would have been like if his mother and Lauren were still alive. They would have loved this, and their daughter would have been fussed over by her cousins. His thoughts were interrupted by the sound of the intercom buzzer. He went to the front door to pick up the intercom and release the door and then waited in the hallway for the lift door to open.

He had asked Teddy and his father if he could invite someone over. Carlo had simply nodded and Teddy had said, 'Natale con i tuoi, Pasqua con i vuoi.', referring to the Italian saying that people spent Christmas with their family and Easter with the people they chose, 'but as far as I'm concerned tuoi and vuoi are the same. Of course, you can.'

Arturo had had a shave and was wearing a suit and tie. Francesco had never seen him so smartly dressed. He was also carrying a couple of bottles of wine.

'I wasn't sure what everyone would prefer so I've brought white and red,' he said by way of explanation.

'I'm sure we'll get through both of them sooner or later,' Francesco said. 'Come in and meet everyone.'

Francesco made the introductions, and Arturo thanked everyone for inviting him.

'You're very welcome,' said Pietro. 'Any friend of Francesco's … but if you'll excuse me, I had better get back to the kitchen.'

'Would you like a hand?' asked Arturo.

'Yes, why not?'

With that, the two of them disappeared. Francesco stared after him in amazement. It was the closest Arturo had ever come to being affable. He and Teddy exchanged glances. 'He's not much of a one for conversation, but he's a good cook,' offered Francesco.

Pietro, with some help from Arturo, produced a Christmas lunch to remember. First came the antipasti of anchovies and cured meats, followed by tortellini in chicken broth and then turkey with side dishes of vegetables. After that, the pangiallo, Rome's very own Christmas cake, and the torrone made an appearance. Finally, they sat around the table drinking espresso unable to contemplate another mouthful while the girls finally ran out of energy and had a nap.

After the feeling of fullness had subsided, Carlo decided it was time for everyone to get some exercise. They walked through the Borghese, past the lake and continued on until they reached the terrace overlooking the expanse of the Piazza del Popolo, with the dome of St Peter's just visible on the skyline on the other bank of the Tiber. The magic of Rome and the power of family were distilled down into a single moment in time, which Francesco knew would stay with him forever and help to sustain him, whatever he did or wherever he went.

*　　*　　*

After Christmas, Francesco had returned to mulling over the future, frustrated with his inability to make a decision. He had finally found a moment to tell Teddy about the job offer in Manchester, at which she had gone quiet and said very little.

For now though, he put all that aside for New Year's Eve as they stood on the balcony of Teddy and Pietro's home in Orvieto, watching the fireworks welcoming in the New Year. Teddy slipped away looking lost in thought and, after a moment's hesitation, Francesco followed her.

'It's freezing out there,' he commented, hugging himself and then massaging his face in an attempt to get some feeling back.

'Sorry?'

'I was saying it's cold.'

'Oh, yes.'

'Are you OK?'

'Yes, I've just never liked New Year's Eve. Everybody celebrates it, but to me it's always been more of a time for reflection than celebration. It was always the time I particularly used to think about you and mum, wondering where you were and what you were doing; if the next year might be the year I'd see you again, all the while knowing that in reality it probably wouldn't be.'

Francesco poured two glasses of Prosecco and passed one to Teddy. 'I never used to like it much either but, I don't know, this year feels different. I feel … hopeful.'

'That's good. The last few months have been extraordinary. Sometimes I still can't believe everything that's happened.'

'Neither can I. The counselling helped. I'm glad you

talked me into going. I've realised what I was going through wasn't so unusual, that I wasn't weak or a failure. And I've accepted now that nobody could have saved Lauren. Her injuries were catastrophic.' They both fell silent as they reflected on that for a while.

'Solving the mystery of why she had booked that hotel room changed everything. It didn't stop the grief, but it stopped the worst of the doubts which always ate away at me. I still wonder sometimes why she left the hotel… I don't know, but I'm learning to stop going over it. Being able to sleep has made a huge difference too.'

'I can imagine. What shall we drink to?' As Teddy spoke, she silently hoped he would suggest drinking to starting his course in Rome.

'To remembering those we have lost, but also looking to the future?'

'I'll definitely drink to that.' Teddy said, fixing a smile on her face. She took a sip, examined the glass of Prosecco and looked up at him. 'When will you go?' She looked sad as she said it.

'Not until after La Befana.'

'Good. Gabriela and Lucia would be upset if you weren't around for that.'

At that moment, the rest of the family came back in from the balcony.

'Mamma, you missed the last of the fireworks,' said Gabriela.

'Uncle Francesco and I were just talking about next year, well this year now, darling.'

'Will you read us a bedtime story, Uncle Francesco?' Lucia asked him.

'Of course,' he said and found two small pairs of hands tugging at him.

Francesco finished the book with the classic words, 'And they all lived happily ever after,' and closed the book.

'Just like us,' said Gabriela sleepily.

'Yes, just like us,' said Francesco, straightening her blanket and bending over to kiss her forehead. He tucked Lucia in as well and closed the door behind him.

He leaned against the cool stone wall. Happily ever after; a sweet storybook construct but not the real world.

In the sitting room, Pietro put his arms around Teddy. 'You're really worried, aren't you?'

She nodded. 'We've only just found him and I'm scared he's going to go and not come back. I can't say anything, though. It's got be his decision, but I don't want him to go. More than that, I don't understand why he has to go.'

'If he was a patient, I don't think you'd say that. You'd probably say that getting away to gain a bit of perspective was a good idea.'

'Perhaps if he was going somewhere neutral, but he's going back there.' She made it sound like enemy territory, threatening to reclaim the brother she had only just found. 'But I'm going to miss him so much if he decides not to come back.'

'I know, sweetheart. We'd all miss him, but I think he'll come back.'

'You do?' she said, stepping back from him to search his

face for signs he was just saying what she wanted to hear.

'Yes. I really do. Come here,' he said and pulled her back into his arms which was the only place she felt she didn't have to be professional, strong, organised or competent and could just be.

# CHAPTER TWENTY-TWO

In the days following New Year, Francesco deliberately avoided going anywhere beyond quick trips to Caffè Lazio or Il Buongustaio. He had been given a very clear choice to make, and he spent a lot of time trying to work out which path he should take. The endless lists of pros and cons only seemed to muddy the waters. Frustrated, he renewed his commitment to running, which had slipped over the holidays. When he started running, he was able to stop thinking, which proved to be a relief as thinking seemed to get him nowhere

On the 6th of January, Francesco and his family congregated in the Piazza Navona. Gabriela and Lucia had already received some presents from their parents and now La Befana, the friendly witch, was handing more out. Valentina and Étienne had agreed to join them there too, and Francesco was happy that he had the chance to introduce them to his family. Valentina and Teddy were clearly pleased to see each other again. While Pietro and Carlo kept the girls occupied, Teddy beckoned for Francesco to join her on a bench.

'What time's your flight?'

'11.30 tomorrow morning.'

Teddy nodded, screwed her eyes up and scanned the square. She wanted to ask him to stay so much, but she couldn't. In fact, she couldn't get any words out at all.

'It's not forever. Whatever happens.'

Teddy nodded, feeling the muscles in her jaw stinging as they contracted. She couldn't bear it. She stood up and managed to say, 'There'll be no big goodbye scenes then.'

'Exactly.'

And so the goodbyes, when they came, were kept light and inconsequential with Teddy and Pietro acting as though they would see him again in a few days. He received big hugs from Gabriela and Lucia, who were too excited and too young to pick up on the underlying tension, something for which they were all grateful.

He went to shake his father's hand and was drawn into an unexpected embrace. His father murmured 'Don't make the same mistakes I did, Francesco,' and released him.

He looked at his father and saw fully for the first time the weight that bore down on him: a love for his wife which could never be reignited; apologies which could never be offered; forgiveness which could never be received and wrongs which could never be made right. For the first time, he felt a sense of affection for his father of which he had not thought himself capable.

Then Francesco watched his family walk past the Fountain of Neptune and disappear round the corner. Saying goodbye when the next meeting was uncertain was always sad, but that goodbye had hurt more than most.

Francesco stayed on for a while with Valentina and Étienne. They drank hot chocolate and talked about Étienne's latest project and Valentina's job and studies. They tried to draw him on his plans, but he seemed more subdued than they had ever seen him before, and they sensed this was not the time to push the subject.

Valentina nudged Étienne who looked dubious. 'There's something we'd like to tell you, Francesco,' she said.

'I'm not sure this is the time,' said Étienne.

'There might not be another chance,' Valentina responded.

Étienne nodded, acknowledging the truth of that statement.

She turned to Francesco. 'We're getting married.'

'That's wonderful,' said Francesco. With almost any other couple, he would have worried that they were too young, but he had a feeling they would last the distance. 'When?'

'We haven't set a date yet,' Étienne replied, 'but we're thinking about late spring.'

'And the thing is, the reason I had to tell you now is that we want you to be there. I'd like you to walk me down the aisle." Valentina looked at him with hope in her eyes.

Francesco felt himself choking up. 'I would be honoured.'

'But if you decide to stay in Britain ...' she began.

'If I do, I will come back for that.'

'You'd do that?'

'I wouldn't miss it for anything.'

'You've never let me down,' said Valentina, looking at him with wonder, just as she had when he had appeared in the hospital the morning after she had been admitted.

'Thank you Francesco,' said Étienne. 'It means a lot to both of us. I'm sorry about the timing when you've got so many other things on your mind.'

'Don't worry. I really am very happy for you, and I meant it when I said it would be an honour.'

The cold started to bite, and they decided to head for home. With the thought of his flight in mind, Francesco declined their invitation to have dinner at their flat, but walked back as far as the Ponte Umberto I with them.

Valentina reached up on tiptoe to give him a kiss on the cheek. 'Whatever happens, please keep in touch with us,' she said and he saw the sadness in her face. She squeezed his hand. 'And thank you again for everything.'

He shook hands with Étienne and they patted each other on the back. 'Don't be a stranger,' Étienne said. 'Whatever you decide to do.'

'I'll be in touch. I promise.'

He watched them cross the bridge hand in hand. Étienne's navy winter coat and Valentina's scarlet one outlined against the railings of the bridge, the colour of alabaster in the cool winter light. He thought of Lauren and was acutely aware of the empty space beside him. The leaves on the plane trees had fallen now, and their bare branches were etched against the pale sky. The city had shown itself to him in all its moods, and he loved it more with each new revelation.

He gazed at the Tiber, a sombre green-grey, and beyond it at the imposing building housing the Supreme Court. He thought about how often his mother would have crossed that bridge on her way to work and about the sadness which must have consumed her. Eventually he turned away and continued his walk by the river.

He thought about his father's parting words. *Don't make the same mistakes I made.* He wondered at first what he had meant. As he walked, it occurred to him that perhaps his father meant he should get his priorities right; family before work. Perhaps it had been his veiled or clumsy attempt to advise him to stay in Italy.

He turned onto Via di Panico and wandered through the cobbled streets of the old town. The lights started to flicker on, bathing the city in its characteristic golden glow. He had no particular destination in mind, but just to walk through the area was a pleasure.

At one time, he would have done that simply to avoid the dreaded moment when he would have to go back to his flat, turn the key and walk into the silence, but he found that he no longer feared going home. His use of that word brought him up sharply. He had thought of his flat as home for the first time.

He realised he had found a sense of belonging which was due in large part to reconnecting with his family but went beyond that. He would always be grateful for what England had given him, but now he was beginning to think that perhaps this was where he was meant to be. But then, there was the chance of becoming a doctor again – and so the cycle of indecision started up once more.

Rome was, by turns, a beautiful, frustrating, crazy, maddening and passionate city, a microcosm of the country it represented. Could he leave it again? He remembered what Dorothy had said to him all those months ago; love is loving someone or somewhere despite the imperfections.

He thought of her and of the other people he had met over the past months, people who had shared something of their lives with him. He thought about the friends he had made and the people his life had intersected with, but whom he would never meet again. Mentally he raised a toast to them, wherever in the world they all might be at that moment and wished them well.

As he arrived in the Campo de' Fiori, a family approached him. The father asked him in halting Italian if he could speak English and then for directions to the Pantheon. Francesco explained the route.

'Thank you so much. By the way, your English is really good. Where are you from?'

'Rome,' he said, before he had even really considered the question on an intellectual level, which was something he had always been inclined to do in the past. His response was spontaneous and purely emotional and took him by surprise.

'You're so lucky.'

Francesco looked around, taking in the timeless beauty of the city, thinking of his family and friends. Then he thought of the circumstances which had brought him there and of all he had endured to get to that point. How much we assume yet how little we really know about the lives of others. He had the grace to smile. 'Enjoy your time here,' he said. 'It's a wonderful city.'

*     *     *

'Why do I always leave these things to the last minute?' Francesco pulled clothes and cases out of cupboards. 'And now I'm talking to myself.'

He found the case he was looking for and opened it. He took a breath. He had forgotten he had left some of Lauren's possessions inside. He took them out one by one, holding them, letting the memories wash over him. Photographs; a soft toy she had won at a fun fair; her wedding ring; a wallet. He realised he had never looked in it before. He went to open it and hesitated. Even now it seemed like an invasion of privacy, but something prompted him to continue. There was nothing unexpected in it: a £5 note, a supermarket loyalty card and her National Union of Journalists press card.

He was about to put it away when he noticed a piece of paper, folded into a small square and tucked behind the £5 note. It would have been easy to miss. He smoothed it out and saw a phone number, starting with +39. The dialling code for Italy, but it wasn't Teddy's number.

Who else had Lauren known in Italy? He remembered his conversation with the receptionist at the hotel when he had gone to settle Lauren's unpaid hotel bill. What had she said about the phone call she had overheard? 'I did catch the word "si." '

He picked up his phone and was tempted to call the

number. He hesitated, looking at the time on the screen and became aware of how late it was getting. It wasn't the time to phone anyone, and he also had to start packing. He placed the wallet in his hand luggage. He would deal with it later.

*　　*　　*

The next day he stopped at Caffè Lazio and had coffee with Matteo.

'How long are you going to stay in England?'

I don't really know, Matteo.'

'That's a shame. Don't forget I need to know soon if you want the job here. It would fit in perfectly with your course. I was hoping we could continue training together too. And I want to introduce you to my cousin. She's coming to Rome next month. She's very pretty.'

Francesco smiled. 'I'll let you know as soon as I can.'

He got up and picked up his bags. He felt as though he was saying goodbye forever and wondered why he was even going through with something which made him feel so sad. What sort of masochistic tendency was driving him? Then he reminded himself that he had realised this would be the only way for him to finally reach a decision.

'Come back soon,' Matteo said, and Francesco turned and waved in acknowledgement.

His next stop was at Arturo's and they sat in his kitchen, his case by the door. They had been here before, almost one year to the day. They did not say a lot, but it was not necessary.

'Good luck,' said Arturo and patted him on the back.

'Thank you.'

'Ci vediamo dopo.' See you later.

'Si, dopo.' Later; whenever later would be.

# CHAPTER TWENTY-THREE

'Good morning ladies and gentleman. Welcome on board your flight back home to Manchester this morning. Our route today will take us …'

Francesco didn't hear the rest. Back home. It didn't feel like going home to him, and as the plane took off and made its way out over the coast, he felt a sense of separation he had not expected. He had not felt it when he had left England to go to Rome even after all the years he had spent there.

The plane descended through thick clouds and landed in the gloom of an English winter's day. It matched his mood, and he felt cold just looking out of the window.

The bus journey to his hotel took him through a world which had once been his; his world with Lauren. He felt closer to her being back in England, even though the logical part of his mind told him that made no sense. After he had checked in at his hotel, he went for a walk and visited the park, cafe and bookstore he had visited so often with Lauren. He felt her with him in a way he had not experienced during the past year. It comforted him and unsettled him at the same time.

That night, in his hotel, he flicked through the television channels, strangely happy to come across all the programmes he had watched so often in the past with Lauren. An image of Teddy came to his mind. He saw her standing on the lakeside promenade by Lake Bolsena in the clear autumn sunshine. It was the day they had been to the chestnut festival. She was smiling at him and saying how Italian he was; how he was drawn to the familiar; how he found it comforting. He had no idea where he belonged. He continued listlessly flicking through the channels and settled on a satirical panel show, in which the contestants mercilessly tore into politicians and celebrities. He appreciated their irreverent take on current affairs and realised how much he had missed that type of humour.

All the competing demands and desires started to crowd in on him. He wanted to be near to Teddy and the rest of his family, but he also had an illogical desire to feel close to Lauren and the places they had known as a couple. He thought of his love for certain aspects of Italy and his love for particular things about England. Then there was the course in Italy, compared to the possible job in England. Francesco experienced the feeling he used to have in the months after Lauren's death; a sense that he could not breathe and find a way through the fog he felt lost in. There is a solution he told himself over and over again, breathing deeply, until he almost began to believe it, as long as he did not examine too closely what that solution might be.

*       *       *

He woke up the following morning to the sound of his phone ringing. It was from a number in Italy he did not recognise.

'Buongiorno. Dottore De Luca? I'm calling about the counselling course.'

'Yes, good morning.' He was still half asleep.

'We haven't heard from you, and I would like you to come in and sign all the final paperwork. We do have other people interested in the course so if you've changed your mind, we do need to know.'

'I understand,' Francesco said. He was awake now.

'When can you come in?' She sounded pained.

'I'm in England at the moment to sort out some family matters. My business here shouldn't take more than a few days. I'll call you by the end of the week to let you know the situation.'

'Thank you.'

Francesco hung up and the phone rang again, an English number this time.

'Hello?'

'Good morning.'

His old boss. Francesco wished he had let the call go to voicemail.

'Francesco?'

'Yes, I'm here. Good morning.'

'I'd like you to come in and see me tomorrow. We need to start looking at the process for getting you back to work. The sooner we get started, the better.'

'I have a few appointments tomorrow,' Francesco said,

trying to stall him. 'I'll phone you the day after tomorrow.'

"Tomorrow would be better.'

'Yes, I understand, but unfortunately I can't cancel these appointments. I'll be in touch.'

'The day after tomorrow then.'

'Yes, goodbye.'

Francesco rolled onto his back. The time to decide could not be put off much longer, and yet he felt no further forward. He heard the rain hitting the windows and the wind howling, and buried his head under the covers.

When he finally managed to get up, he decided to pay a visit to his old local, a traditional country pub of the sort that he had never found in Italy. On one side it looked out onto farmland, bleak and lifeless in the middle of winter. On the other was the main road running into town.

The warmth hit him as he walked in, and sensation started to return to his numbed face. The memories of long country walks with Lauren, followed by a stop there for lunch, hit him even harder than the warmth had. He was once more transported back into the world he had inhabited with her, and it was as though no time had passed; he could almost believe that if he turned, he would find her standing beside him.

Francesco went up to the bar, taking in his surroundings, which were strangely familiar and yet alien to him at the same time: the thick carpet underfoot, the walls covered with paintings, the old wooden pillars lined with horse brasses. It was somehow all so comforting. The barman asked him what he wanted and then did a double take.

'Blimey, Frank! It's been a while. How are you?' Francesco saw Jim mentally kick himself as he realised what he had said.

'Not so bad. How about you?'

'Same old, same old,' Jim replied, clearly relieved to be able to change the subject. 'The country's going to the dogs, but what can you do? Politicians, big companies, none of them are interested in us little people. Well, only in what they can screw out of us, of course.'

'That sounds about right,' Francesco replied. It seemed to him that since he had woken up after what felt like a very long sleep, he had found himself in a world more ill at ease with itself than he ever remembered it being before. Or perhaps he was simply seeing it through different eyes. He recalled the complaints of the man on the train in Italy. Was Britain any better than Italy? Or was Italy any better than Britain? Nowhere was perfect, and if that was what he was looking for, he would have a long and fruitless search.

He took his pint, which had appeared in a traditional dimpled glass tankard, and settled down on a bench covered in red velvet upholstery, positioned between a window and the open fire, where a stack of logs was piled up ready to be added.

The sky darkened again, and the rain hit the panes with renewed strength. The drops started their inexorable downwards roll. He watched, almost hypnotised and became lost in thoughts which roamed in no particular direction over the training the National Health Service had given him, the idea of becoming a counsellor in Italy, the job with familiar colleagues in England, his family and Lauren.

How would he reconcile belonging to two different worlds? How could he reconcile the desire to be close to the memories of Lauren and the need to be close to his family? He remembered Alessandro identifying the conundrum that he probably never felt more Italian than when in England and vice versa. And he imagined Arturo questioning whether it even really mattered.

'Doctor De Luca? Francesco?'

Francesco looked up and saw a woman staring at him. He recognised her immediately as a fellow doctor from A&E. He searched for her name.

'Gina, it's good to see you.'

'And you.' She hesitated. 'Do you mind if I join you?'

'No, please do.'

'I haven't seen you around here for a long time. The last I heard was that you'd decided to leave after … well, after everything.'

'Yes, I've been in Italy for the last year. Catching up with family. Taking a bit of time out.'

'That sounds nice. I seem to be working longer and longer hours. The NHS is creaking at the seams. I looked into getting a job in a private hospital, and I was so tempted, but then I realised I couldn't abandon the NHS. I still believe in it and everything it stands for. So I'm stuck with the long hours by the looks of it, but that's life. You can't have everything, can you?'

'No, that's very true,' said Francesco.

'Are you back here permanently?'

'I really don't know.'

'I hope so. We need all the good doctors we can get, and you were a very good doctor.'

'That's kind of you.'

'It's nothing of the sort. You know me. I always speak my mind. You were a damn good doctor.'

'Thanks.' He sipped the beer and found it was flat.

Gina's phone started ringing.

'Excuse me,' she said, answering it. There was a pause. 'You've done what?' she asked, sounding exasperated. 'What? Yes, yes. I'll be home in ten minutes.'

'Problems?'

'Yes, it's Paul, my son. He's locked himself out again. I'd better go.' She picked up her coat and gulped down the rest of her drink. 'I'm sorry I can't stay, but I can't leave him hanging around in this weather.' She paused. 'I hope you decide to come back.' With that she was gone.

Francesco slowly worked his way through his pint. The rain had stopped by the time he had finished so he took the road into town and went for a walk through the park. So many memories had come back to him since he had been back there, memories he had thought were lost to him. He was surprised to find that despite his resistance to returning to England, he had missed being there, and yet he missed his family and Italy so much as well. He thought about what Gina had said in the pub and realised she was right; it was not possible to have everything.

He had one more stop to make before he made his decision; a stop that he had been considering since he had found that piece of paper in Lauren's wallet. He took the bus into the city centre and walked from the bus stop to Lauren's old offices. Within five minutes, he was sitting in the newsroom where Lauren had worked with her colleague Max.

'It's been a while, Francesco.'

'Your Christmas Party in 2017.'

'What a night that was.'

They fell silent remembering the night, remembering Lauren up on the dance floor, getting everyone to have a go at the salsa.

'What can I do for you?' Max asked.

'I was wondering what Lauren had been working on before the accident.'

Max puffed up his cheeks and exhaled. 'We're going back a bit, and Lauren was never very forthcoming about the stories she was working on. She liked to get all her ducks lined up, as she used to say, before she'd talk about a story.'

'So there's nothing you remember? Nothing specific that stands out?'

Max laced his hands behind his head, tilted his chair back and looked up at the ceiling as though he thought the answers might appear there. 'I do remember she was really consumed by a story around that time. I don't know what it was, though. As I said, she wasn't one to go into details until she was ready. But …' He trailed off, trying to recall what she had said. 'She said she was on to something and if she was right, it would be big.'

'And you have absolutely no idea what it was?'

'No, but as I said, she seemed consumed by it. It's the only word for it. And she was anxious as well, which wasn't like her. You must have noticed it?'

Francesco nodded, silently cursing himself once more.

He had failed her. 'Is there any way you could find out more about what she was doing?'

'No, not after all this time, sorry.' Max had been tapping his pen on the desk but suddenly stopped. 'Hold on, there is one thing I remember now I come to think of it.'

'What's that?'

'She made a joke about getting a trip to Italy out of it on expenses.'

'Italy? What else did she say?'

Max resumed the tapping. 'No,' he said eventually, shaking his head. 'I can't remember her saying anything else about it, and that comment about Italy was just an aside. I don't know if she was even really being serious.'

Francesco slumped back into his chair.

'What's all this about?' Max asked.

'I wish I knew. If you think of anything else, would you contact me?'

'Sure.'

Francesco gave Max his number and walked out into the dank chill of early afternoon. Some secrets, it seemed were destined to stay in the past, and perhaps that was the best place for them. He was no longer sure.

He walked until long after darkness had fallen and by that time, he had decided what to do. And once he had made the decision, he understood that there had never really been any other choice. The following day, he would make all the necessary phone calls.

*　　*　　*

'So that's what I've decided to do.' He had just finished recapping the events of the past year. 'I'm ready, and I think it's going to be good.'

There was no reply, of course, just as there would never be any reply, but he found solace just by being there, as close to her as he could ever be now.

He told her more about Teddy and the family. 'I'm sorry I couldn't come back before. I had to fix myself first. I just wasn't ready before. And I'm even sorrier that I let you down and that I ever doubted you. I just wish I could see you, hold you, and tell you that. I hope that somehow you know.' He gently brushed the last faint traces of frost from the top of the headstone. 'And I also want you to know that you'll always be with me every step of the way; both of you will be.'

Francesco carefully arranged the flowers. 'I wish I could have brought bluebells, but it's too early in the year. I know how much you always loved those. You said they represented hope and new life and anticipation of the summer to come. I'll bring them in the spring.' He sighed and got up off the damp grass. As he stood, a sudden gust of wind bit deeply into him. He wrapped his coat around him more tightly and pulled the scarf up around his ears. He had become unaccustomed to the cold.

He looked across at the graves of his mother and grandparents, where he had already laid flowers, on the other side of the gravel path, a dark, slate grey colour in the low flat light, and then back at the inscription on Lauren's headstone.

*To my beloved wife Lauren and our daughter Grace. Loved in life and beyond.*

'I'll come and visit again,' he promised and bent to kiss the stone.

He walked back down to the entrance to the graveyard, unlocked his rental car and got in. He sat there unable to face talking to anybody for a while. Eventually, he phoned Teddy and told her his decision. He heard her crying, and he was not ashamed of the fact that he felt as emotional as she sounded.

Then he phoned Matteo, Valentina and Arturo. After the phone calls, he continued to sit there thinking about what was ahead before starting the ignition and pulling out of the car park. The traffic was light, and he made good time. He handed the car keys back and went into the airport where he checked the departure board. The flight to Rome was showing up as on time.

He could feel that he was leaving a part of himself behind, and he experienced another pull to stay, to be close to all the places he associated with Lauren, which was almost physical in its intensity. And then he thought of Teddy and her family. They were his family too. And Lauren would have wanted him to be surrounded by his family.

He thought of the friends he had made in Rome. He missed Arturo's grumpy company; Anna's recipes; the runs with Matteo and the companionable meals with Valentina and Étienne. He remembered Teddy telling him he had to live the life Lauren would have wanted for him and that was the best tribute he could give her. He would try to do it, no, he corrected himself, he wouldn't try, he would do it, and he would do it for her.

Even so, his heart was still heavy as he boarded the plane and took his seat. Was he really doing the right thing? Travelling had its usual effect on him, and he managed to doze for a while. Woken up by the crew serving drinks, he decided to listen to some music and opened his bag to get out his headphones. As he reached around in the bag between his feet, his hand settled on Lauren's wallet, and he pulled it out, opened it and took the carefully folded piece of paper out again. He looked at the number of an unknown phone in Italy, written in Lauren's neat script.

Max had said she was working on something big, and that she had mentioned Italy. Was the number anything to do with that? Was the owner of that number the same person Lauren had been speaking to in the hotel? The receptionist had said she had been speaking a foreign language, which could have been Spanish. He had thought then that it must have been Italian. Lauren hadn't been able to speak Spanish. Was that phone call the reason she had left the hotel instead of going to meet Teddy? It was perhaps the final piece of the puzzle. Or the start of a whole new one. He wasn't sure it was a door he wanted to open, but he wasn't sure it was one he could leave closed.

He suddenly had a vivid memory of his seven-year-old self, standing in his grandfather's bungalow, asking his mother why they were there and when they would be going home. He had pushed and pushed until she had snapped. What had she said? *Stop looking for answers. Stop picking at things – it only leads to more unhappiness.* Had she been right?

He tucked the piece of paper carefully back inside the wallet and put it back in his bag. He thought that one day he might call that number, or perhaps he would push all thoughts of it into the darkest recesses of his mind, until he had convinced himself it had never even existed. He knew Lauren had loved him and wondered if that should be enough now. It seemed that whatever she had been working on had died with her.

The plane started to cross the Alps, and his spirits lifted at the sight of the snow-covered mountains, dazzling in the crisp winter sunlight. The view reminded him of the same journey he had made the previous January. He remembered how he had felt on that day and how much had changed, how much he had changed, since then.

His last lingering doubts about returning to Italy finally lifted. Whatever else the future held, he knew he wanted to be at home, and with a clarity and certainty beyond anything he had felt before, he realised that being at home meant being in Rome. Everything else would have to wait.

# About the Author

Alex Milan was born in England but has spent the last twenty years living and working in other countries. Italy, which the writer called home for a number of years, is the inspiration and setting for this novel. It is also a country with which Alex has had a lifelong love affair.